PRAISE FOR LESLIE CAINE'S DOMESTIC BLISS MYSTERY SERIES

false premises

"*False Premises* is a pleasant mystery that readers caught up in the current redecorating craze will not want to miss." —*Mystery Reader*

"Replete with interior decorating, antique furnishings, not to mention floor plan and clothing critiques." —Iloveamysterynewsletter.com

"Humor is never in short supply in this fun, engaging mystery, which is certain to delight fans of cozies." —*Romantic Times*

death by inferior design

"[An] appealing heroine and warm, genuinely winning voice." —*Publishers Weekly*

"Caine has created a cozy with an edge, and its twists ... keep the reader guessing until the end."
—*Romantic Times*, 3 stars

"For killer decorating tips, pick up *Death by Inferior Design*, a murder mystery by decorator Leslie Caine. ... rival

"What a delight! A mystery within a mystery, a winning heroine, a yummy love interest, some laugh-out-loud lines... and as if that weren't enough, some terrifically useful decorating tips."
—Cynthia Baxter, author of *Dead Canaries Don't Sing*

"Leslie Caine deftly merges hate-fueled homicide with household hints in her 'how-to/whodunit' mystery."
—Mary Daheim

"Witty and smart, with home decorating tips to die for!"
—Sarah Graves

"Leslie Caine's *Death by Inferior Design* sparkles with charm, design lore, and a sleuth with a great mantra. Cozy fans will embrace the Domestic Bliss series."
—Carolyn G. Hart; Agatha, Anthony, and Macavity Awards winner

"*Trading Spaces* meets *Murder She Wrote*! Talk about extreme makeovers! Dueling designers Gilbert and Sullivan might want to kill each other, but no one expected anyone to try it. Who will hang the trendiest curtains? Who will choose the poshest paint? Who will come out alive? I'm not tellin'." —Parnell Hall

manor of death

"A blueprint for murder." —*Mystery Scene*

"Caine delivers another top-notch Domestic Bliss whodunit.... Everyone in Maple Hills has something to hide, and the 'something' has to do with the decades-old death of Abby, the young girl who is rumored to haunt the Victorian mansion next door to interior designer Erin Gilbert. Can Erin unravel the truth before she becomes the next victim? Nifty decorating tips complete the package."

—*Publishers Weekly*

"The chemistry between rivals Gilbert and Sullivan has the appeal as the whodunit."

—*Booknews* from The Poisoned Pen

"Caine weaves an entertaining story filled with unique characters and humorous dialogue . . . keeps reader guessing right to the end. Fast-paced and suspenseful, this mystery will keep you turning pages."

—*Romantic Times*

"*Manor of Death* by Leslie Caine is a blueprint for murder as the third Domestic Bliss mystery unfolds. . . . Tips abound in this delightful package."

—*MLB News*

Also by LESLIE CAINE

Death by Inferior Design
Manor of Death
False Premises
Killed by Clutter

And coming soon from Dell

Poisoned by Gilt

a domestic bliss mystery

FATAL FENG SHUI

Leslie Caine

A DELL BOOK

FATAL FENG SHUI
A Dell Book / November 2007

Published by
Bantam Dell
A Division of Random House, Inc.
New York, New York

ISBN 978-0-440-33599-3

Printed in the United States of America
Published simultaneously in Canada

www.bantamdell.com

OPM 10 9 8 7 6 5 4 3 2 1

To Sheila Hanley King
in appreciation for thirty years of friendship
(Fortunately, we met as infants.)

acknowledgments

I owe an enormous debt to Pam and Paul for allowing me to turn their calamity into my subplot. Now that I've made this public admission, I can't give their last names for fear that readers might make incorrect assumptions, but I'm tremendously grateful, nevertheless. During my research, many experts—especially the wonderful subcontractors hired by Odom Construction Service to work on my house—tirelessly answered questions for me. I wish I'd been more careful with my notes so that I could list them by name, but undergoing a major house remodel during the writing of this book proved to be my organizational undoing. Thanks to Sheila, Dan, and Gus for providing me with an office during the aforementioned remodel. My network of author friends provides me with a fabulous and absolutely indispensable support system, and I'd be negligent not to mention Francine Mathews, Diane Mott Davidson, Kay Bergstrom, Christine Jorgensen, Kenn Amdahl, and the supremely talented and generous writers in my Boulder critique group. Thanks to Nancy Yost, agent extraordinaire. Thanks to Mike, Carol, Andrew, and Taffy for everything. Last but far from least, I would like to thank my brilliant editor, Kate Miciak, and all the talented and hardworking folks at Random House.

FATAL FENG SHUI

chapter 1

"Confidence and optimism," *I muttered as I made* my way along the curving concrete walkway toward Shannon Dupree Young's front door.

"Pardon?" Steve Sullivan said.

"Nothing." My cheeks warmed; I hadn't realized I'd spoken aloud. Steve and I had merged our interior design companies less than two months ago, and I'd have preferred not to have him discover my idiosyncrasies quite so soon. "Just the mantra I use whenever I get nervous."

"You're nervous about this job, Erin?"

I scanned his handsome features, surprised by the lack of the wry grin, which would indicate he was being sarcastic. Things had grown steadily worse here in the six weeks since Shannon had signed on as our very first client. "A little. Aren't you?"

"Nah. What's there to worry about? Just a feud raging between neighbors, and our client on the verge of a nervous breakdown. That's par for the course for us."

Steve was being gracious in not pointing fingers. In the past year, my one-woman company, Designs by Gilbert, had experienced such bizarre problems with a few of its clients that I qualified for hazardous-duty pay. And, despite what at the time had been a fierce professional rivalry, Sullivan Designs had somehow gotten dragged into the fray—*my* fray—more than once.

On the south side of Shannon's original entranceway, the construction of her addition was finally starting to take shape. We were about to enter the fun phase of remodeling. Normally, I'd have to hold myself back from racing to the door. My head would be filled with one magical, delectable possibility after another—rainbows of colors, astonishing materials, and splendid furnishings. For me, designing a space is nothing less than being able to make my clients' dreams come true, and every step of the way is a joyous journey.

This particular client's "dream" was turning out to be a nightmare, however. Thanks to the proverbial Neighbor from Hell—Pate Hamlin.

I turned and eyed his house. Last night, Shannon had called us in hysterics about Pate's sprawling, fortresslike structure looming directly across the street. The protruding peak of the roof over its new porch was indeed pointing straight at this home—a feng shui no-no. "It's just that Shannon seemed so nice and rational at first," I explained to Sullivan now. "I never imagined she'd wind up so paranoid... thinking her neighbor's architecture was putting her in physical danger."

Although neither Sullivan nor I was an expert in the

art of feng shui, we weren't neophytes either. We had a healthy respect for its ancient principles, which after six thousand years have more than stood the test of time. Feng shui was among the first schools of design—a beautiful philosophy of harmonizing one's home with its surroundings. Yet during our phone conversation last night, Shannon had declared that this was "now officially a no-holds-barred feng shui war." And then she'd asked us to launch a counteroffensive against her neighbor's designer. That notion made me a little queasy. Granted, Sullivan and I had waged many a battle against each other, but I'd naively thought those days were behind me, now that we'd joined forces.

"Everybody was feng shui fighting..." Sullivan sang to the tune of "Kung Foo Fighting" as we headed up the walk.

"Not funny," I said, resisting a smile.

"Why is Pate Hamlin so determined to buy this place?"

"Shannon says it's because she's got a better view of the Rockies than he does. Plus more land... eight acres."

We climbed the steps to Shannon's front porch, which would soon be removed. In its place, we had a fabulous design for a cedar wraparound deck. Its rich wood and gorgeous geometric patterns would embrace both the new and the original entrances of this sixty-year-old home. *Our* additions emphasized and augmented the home's best elements. Unlike her *neighbor's* slap-happy add-ons, which the architect had apparently drawn up while bouncing around in an old pickup truck. (My refusal to engage in a feng shui war did not, alas, morph me into the Mother Teresa of interior designers.)

"Aw, jeez," Sullivan said. I followed his gaze. Shannon had recently painted a red dragon on the center panel of her front door. While I was studying her intricate handiwork, Sullivan suddenly staggered forward, clutching at the center of his back. "Ow! Help me, Gilbert! I think I just got hit by a feng shui arrow!"

"Keep your voice down!" I pressed the doorbell. "If Shannon hears us making cracks about this, our first official job as Gilbert and Sullivan Designs will end today."

"You *mean*—" he paused as Shannon threw open the door "—*Sullivan* and *Gilbert*," he continued with a smile, deftly turning his correction of me into a greeting.

"I remember who you are," Shannon snapped. "Hurry up and get in here." She all but yanked us inside and banged the heavy door behind us. She seemed quite certain we'd *literally* be shot if we lingered on her porch.

Shannon had always struck me as being wound far too tight, but now the thin, attractive, fortyish woman appeared to teeter on the edge of snapping. Her eyes were bloodshot, and she puffed fiendishly on a cigarette. Her strawberry blond hair was an unruly mess—a Bride of Frankenstein look. She wore a navy blue artist's smock over a plum-colored jogging suit. Her feet were clad in mismatched sandals and white socks.

"Well?" She looked at us expectantly. "What are you two going to *do* about this? You can see for yourself what that awful man is trying to pull!"

"With his front porch, you mean?" I was dying to open a window. The air reeked of stale smoke.

"The eave of the roof over it!" she shrieked, trembling with fury. "It's a triangle! And not just *any* triangle. This one's a *jutting* triangle! Pate Hamlin is deliberately *aiming* that sharp point through my window! I haven't been able to work with that... that *vile* weapon aimed straight at me!"

"We sympathize," Sullivan said. "But anything Mr. Hamlin can do to you with his exterior design, we can undo with yours."

Shannon put a hand on one hip and looked up at him in disgust. " 'Anything you can do, I can do better?' " she mocked. "This is all just fun and games to you too, isn't it! You design a new entranceway to my house, he aims his roof right at the windows of my studio."

Calmly trying again, Sullivan began: "One possible solution would be—"

"My studio is where my creative yin forces are the strongest," she interrupted. "I can't work anyplace else! What am I supposed to do? Build a fence out of funhouse mirrors? How the hell will I get any work done with something like that *uglifying* my environment?"

I gazed into her studio, which was adjacent to the stark foyer where we now stood. Unlike this whitewashed, forlorn space, that room was warm and spacious. Its walls and beamed ceilings were rough-hewn wood, its windows and skylights flooded with buttery light, the red terra-cotta tile floor...

"Haven't you people ever worked for an artist before? Don't you know anything at all about creative inspiration? Artistic vision?"

The harsh words snapped me out of my reverie. "Of course we do, Shannon." My tone, I was proud to admit, sounded both soothing and professional. "Steve's and my occupation also hinges on creative inspiration. *And* on our artistic vision," I couldn't resist adding.

Behind the outside wall of the current living room, two or three carpenters suddenly struck up quite a racket as they worked to finish the addition. It occurred to me all that noise wasn't helping Shannon's mood. Or her "artistic vision."

She took a drag on her cigarette and lifted her chin as she blew out a cloud of smoke. "You're right... you're right. I'm so rattled, I don't even know what I'm saying. Artist's temperament. Forgive me."

"That's totally understandable, Shannon," Sullivan said gently.

Seemingly oblivious to his charm, she said nothing. Instead, she corkscrewed an already tangled lock of hair around her index finger and glared at the checkerboard linoleum floor at her sandaled feet. We'd soon be replacing the vinyl with yummy wide-plank maple.

Although high-strung, Shannon was undeniably talented and extremely successful. Her haunting paintings with their bright primary colors and vibrant shadings had struck a chord with art collectors all over the world. She'd recently been profiled in several magazines, and more than one enthusiastic reviewer had stated that Shannon Dupree—she signed her work with her maiden name—was doing for Crestview, Colorado, what Georgia O'Keeffe had done for Santa Fe. She was also a relatively recent feng shui devotee, with all the boundless zeal of a new convert to a worthy cause.

"Our use of mirrors can be subtle, as we reflect the negative energy lines right back at him, Shannon," Sullivan soothed. "We should be able to install one-way glass in your windows. You'll be able to see out as though they were clear glass, but on the other side, they're silver or gold mirrors."

Puffing on her cigarette, she nodded. "Erin already mentioned that idea last night, over the phone."

I decided to pose the obvious question. "Have you tried talking to your neighbor about his porch roof?"

"*Talk*? To *Pate*?" She chuckled. "Puh-lease. You've obviously never met the man. Trust me. *I'm* not a glutton for punishment."

"How about having your husband talk to him, then?" I persisted. "Pate might be the macho type. Maybe he does better with man-to-man conversations."

Shannon's husband, Michael Young, was a talented

chef whom my dear friend and landlady, Audrey Munroe, hosted periodically on her television show. Lately Michael had dropped a few hints to me that he was increasingly concerned that his wife was slipping over the edge. Perhaps with good reason.

"Man-to-man conversations!" Shannon snorted. "Oh, that wouldn't do any good. Michael doesn't understand why I love this place so. He doesn't have all that shared family history. I inherited this house from my parents, long before he and I met. I told you about all this when I first hired you, remember? And about how Pate is trying to force me to sell to him?" She cast a disparaging glance out her front window as she stubbed out her cigarette in a striking—if oversized and overflowing—ceramic ashtray, undoubtedly yet another of her amazing creations. "You know, Pate isn't really even a feng shui practitioner. The pompous phony just wants to use my beliefs against me. He's trying to drive me so nuts that I'll sell just to get away from him. As if all those big, octagonal caps on his fence posts weren't bad enough! Now I've got a *knifepoint* aimed straight at my studio window! At least it's out of line with my new entrance... and the storefront."

"*Storefront?*" Sullivan and I echoed simultaneously, bewildered.

"You wanted that space to be your new living room, didn't you?" Sullivan asked.

"Things have changed. Ang Chung says I'll be able to double my profits by setting up a gallery here."

Sullivan and I exchanged glances. In a New Age college town like Crestview, we had several feng shui experts. Ang Chung, however, had failed to impress either of us. We'd been extremely disappointed to learn last month that Shannon had already hired him to work in tandem with us.

"Ang's advising you to sell your work here, in your home?" Sullivan asked her.

"Absolutely. I can't control the feng shui environment of the galleries downtown, like I can here. Some of them are just...all *wrong*. Those people are cutting *chis* as if energy lines were sandwich meat! So as soon as the remodel is finished, I'm pulling all my pieces from all the other galleries. I'll market them myself. Ang says he can tell me exactly where to place each painting here in my house so it'll fetch the highest price. He's charting out the most profitable alignment for my new showroom. He guarantees this'll be a regular financial windfall." She frowned. "Just so long as the forces haven't been thrown off-kilter by outside energy fields. And now, thanks to Pate Hamlin, that's *exactly* what's happening!"

"But you're fifteen miles from downtown Crestview here," Sullivan pointed out, a moment before I could raise the same objection. "You'll lose all the exposure of having your paintings in gallery windows along the pedestrian mall."

She shrugged. "That's what I was worried about, too. But Ang swears his plan will prove to be far more profitable for me this way."

"Have you gotten any second opinions on his readings, Shannon?" I asked. "There are lots of highly qualified feng shui consultants in Crestview—"

She narrowed her eyes at me as though I was spouting blasphemy. "That's part of what I'm paying you two to do. So far, the three of you are in perfect harmony. Ang *also* says a good start would be for us to install mirrored windows. In every window in the house that faces Pate's... *monstrosity*." She spat the final word, reaching for a fresh cigarette as she did so.

"That's what we'll do, then." Sullivan forced a smile. "We'll make it work."

"We can also do some creative things with your landscaping to ward off negative energy fields," I added.

"Ang told me the same thing. In fact, he's outside with the contractor right now, showing him how to build the gazebo we want. Ang's also a certified landscape artist, you know."

He must have gotten his certification out of the same Cracker Jack box that held his feng shui credentials, I thought, but for once kept my mouth shut.

Shannon whirled, went into the studio, cranked open a window, and leaned outside. "David? Can you come in here, please?"

Sullivan and I migrated into the studio behind her. "We'll turn your living room design into an art gallery, if you're sure that's what you want," I told her.

"It *is.*" Shannon fired up the new cigarette.

David Lewis, her contractor, gingerly entered the room. He had been hired from Sullivan's list of subcontractors instead of from my own. David was a tall, angular man with sandy-colored hair that seemed to be perpetually flecked with sawdust. At the moment, he had the beleaguered look of someone who'd taken a few too many directives from our hard-to-please homeowner. His eyes looked glazed and deeply unhappy.

"Just like Ang and I predicted yesterday," Shannon declared firmly, "Gilbert and Sullivan here want me to use one-way glass. You'll install it in every window with the slightest view of Jerk Face's monstrosity."

David shook his head miserably. "We can't do that, Shannon. I already checked with the building inspectors." Confused, Sullivan and I exchanged glances; we'd also done some preliminary checking and had been told differently. David continued, "Crestview County doesn't allow one-way glass to be installed in private residences.

They feel the sun reflecting on a mirrored surface doesn't... look good."

"But this *isn't* just a private residence!" Shannon snarled. "Some of the windows will be in the portion of my house that's used to create the source of my income!"

"Doesn't matter," David said. "Mirrored glass is banned in residential neighborhoods, Shannon."

As though she was speaking to a simpleton, Shannon spread her arms and commanded, "Then make them *change* the rules, David! *Make it happen!*"

"I'll... see what I can do. But there's going to be layers upon layers of red tape.... And it'll take several months to push a thing like that through."

She sneered at him. "You've certainly got quite a no-can-do attitude, there, David. Maybe I should get a contractor with more clout—"

"Clout's got nothing to do with it. It's the building code—"

"Oh, please! You think Jerk Face Hamlin didn't pay off city officials so they'd approve of all his ridiculous-looking additions? Don't be *naive!* This has *everything* to do with clout! But just because Pate Hamlin is some kind of hotshot multimillionaire doesn't give him the right to destroy my *home!* We're waging a counterattack," she announced. "And you're either capable of going toe to toe with that bastard, or I'm replacing you with someone who can!"

"I'll look into this matter, too." Sullivan intervened with extra vehemence—another obvious attempt to diffuse the tension. "A city official I spoke with earlier this morning said the ban extended only to the city limits. Maybe the building inspector David consulted with didn't realize your house is outside Crestview limits."

She took a noisy drag on her cigarette and narrowed her eyes at poor David. "Speaking of exceeding one's limits, have you talked to that foreman of yours yet? There's *no* way I'm going to allow you people to fraternize with the enemy, you know."

"Yeah, I did. You're sure it was *Duncan* you saw with Pate Hamlin?" David asked.

"I'm positive! The two of them were over here yesterday, sharing a beer and a laugh at my expense."

"Duncan swears he doesn't touch the stuff, Shannon. And I believe him. He's a recovering alcoholic."

"So maybe he was drinking soda, but Pate was guzzling beer. That's not the point! I'm certain he took Pate on a guided tour of my home while I was out." She looked at Sullivan and me and cried, "I could *smell* that vile man's cologne throughout my entire house!"

Frankly, it was hard to believe a chain smoker's sense of smell could be all that keen. (Considering Shannon's current mood, however, that was another observation best kept to myself.)

David said, "My foreman swears he's never taken anyone inside your house—"

"He's lying." She waved her lit cigarette inches from David's nose. "A habit of falsification which he probably gets from you. *You* told me the front construction would be complete by mid-October, and it's already November. Meanwhile, your work here is so shoddy, it's like you're getting paid to *sabotage* the construction."

It was true that the construction was behind schedule, but that wasn't uncommon, especially when the homeowner kept changing her mind about what she wanted. An ugly flush crept up David's neck at her accusation, and he balled his fists.

"Before we order the one-way glass, Shannon," I interjected hastily, "Steve and I will talk with Mr. Hamlin and his designer. Maybe we can call some sort of truce."

She rolled her eyes. "Suit yourself, but you'll be

wasting your breath, Erin. Rebecca Berringer knows precisely what she's doing. She's a lot feng-shui-ier a designer than you two are. In fact, Rebecca was my first choice, until I learned she was working for Pate. No offense. It was *Michael* who wanted us to hire you."

I was taken aback by this news but managed to murmur, "That was nice of him."

"Oh, well, he was just trying to suck up to Audrey Munroe." She took another anxious drag on her cigarette. She looked remarkably like the fire-breathing dragon she'd painted on her front door. "My husband knows how close you and your landlady are. He wants more money for his appearances on her show. Though I've gotten to be friends with Audrey myself lately. We share an interest in preserving Crestview's character. Did she tell you about our committee?"

I shook my head, struggling to focus on this abrupt turn in the conversation; David was still red-faced and tense. He glared at her with raw fury. "Hey," Sullivan said, laying a hand on the contractor's shoulder, "let's take a look at your plans and see how things are coming along."

"Yeah," he growled. "Sounds like a good idea."

"We'll be back soon, Shannon," I said, seizing the opportunity to escape with them. Quietly closing the door behind us, I took some greedy breaths of the sweet crisp autumn air.

My "confidence and optimism" mantra would be getting quite the workout. Now that we'd finished some short-term jobs, we had more time to devote to Shannon's home. That, unfortunately, meant we'd spend more time with feng shui designer Ang Chung, who we both suspected was either a flake or a con man. Meanwhile, Steve's contractor, David Lewis, had missed one completion deadline after another. The brilliant client we'd been so ecstatic to land was swiftly turning into a whiny shrew before our eyes. I didn't even want to *think* about the personal ramifications of having to persuade designer Rebecca Berringer, of all people, to cooperate with us; no ethical feng shui practitioner would have designed a porch roof like that in the first place.

As we rounded the house, Sullivan said quietly to David, "Shannon's something of a . . . crab at the moment. But she does have a point. The front's finally coming along, but you haven't even started on the back. What's the holdup?"

"Problem's with the new foreman I hired last week. Thought he'd work out better than he has so far. You'll see what I mean when you meet him."

Despite Shannon's mention of Ang Chung's having been outside with David, there was only the one person behind the house. My jaw dropped when I spotted the huge lumberjack of a man bent over the table saw with his back to us. The guy had the exact same build and brown hair of my half brother. It couldn't actually *be* my half brother, of course. Taylor Duncan was only halfway through a one-year sentence in the county jail. The man turned.

"Taylor!" I cried.

He shut off his saw and removed his safety goggles. "Hey, sis," he said.

chapter 2

Y*ou look less than thrilled to see me,*" Taylor teased. He'd gone from baby-faced to ruggedly handsome in the three or four months since I'd last visited him in jail. His hair was now closely shorn, and his brown eyes seemed to be sadder, his gaze more penetrating.

"I'm just surprised, that's all," I replied. "When David mentioned his new foreman, I assumed Duncan was his first name, not his last."

"Erin Gilbert is your *sister*?" David asked in surprise. Sullivan, meanwhile, was watching me with obvious concern; he and I had worked with my half-brother once before, and the experience had been miserable for both of us.

Taylor ignored David's question. Instead, he said to me, "Guess Mom didn't tell you I got an early release. Right?"

"No, she didn't." Which was both astonishing and discouraging. I'd had lunch with our mother only ten days ago, and we were trying hard to build a relationship. We had a lot of ground to cover. She'd put me up for adoption when I was a toddler—a source of tremendous pain for both of us. We'd located each other only last year. Until then, I hadn't even known my half brother existed. Taylor was nineteen—ten years younger than me—and our personalities were complete opposites. "How's everything going, Taylor?"

"Not bad. Boring as all get-out, but not bad."

Does that mean you're going to start using drugs again to liven things up?

"Don't give me the evil eye, sis," he said, as if he'd read my mind. "I got time off for good behavior, and that's how I want things to stay." He gave David a sheepish smile. "Like I said, Boss—I'm off the stuff for good now."

"Let's keep it that way," David replied.

Taylor smirked at Steve. "You're Sullivan, right? We worked together on my stepfather's house."

"I remember." Sullivan held out his hand. "Hi, Taylor."

Neither man feigned any pleasure at seeing the other again, but at least they shook hands grudgingly.

Just then, a fit-looking fifty-something man with a full head of snow-white hair came jogging through the brushy, hardscrabble portion of Shannon's property. Though I'd seen him only once before and at a distance, I recognized him immediately. Pate Hamlin, Shannon's viciously despised neighbor. We watched in silence as he continued toward us, trotting carelessly through Shannon's dormant flower bed in the process. "'Scuse me," he said with a smile. "Needed to take a shortcut." He winked at Taylor. My half brother gave him a thumbs-up.

"What was *that*?" Sullivan asked Taylor when Pate vanished around the corner of the house.

"What was *what?*"

"You just exchanged friendly greetings," David piped in.

"With Hamlin? Why not? I like him. He's kinda cool... for an old guy."

"Shannon Young thinks he's trying to make her life miserable," I explained. "It's not wise for you to make friends with him while you're working for *her*."

"No sweat. I'll quit talking to him. Ain't like he's my best buddy or anything." Taylor chuckled. "Told me he changed his first name from Pete to Pate, just to be more unique. You gotta like a guy who's willing to make up a name just to be different, you know?" He grinned at me. "We should do that, too, sis. What would you think about me changing my name to Toylor Duncan? And you could be... Urin Gilbert."

"If either of us is going to be called 'Urine,' I'd much rather it be you."

He laughed heartily at that. His rich chuckle was infectious and I couldn't help but chuckle as well. David Lewis interposed firmly, "Like Erin said, Hamlin is feuding with the homeowner you and I are working for, Duncan. At a time when she's accusing our construction crew of sabotaging this job! That makes *me* look bad!"

Taylor shrugged. "Not my problem."

"It *is* your problem if it's true," David fired back.

"Hey! I already said I'd quit talking to the guy! What more do you want me to do? Shoot him?"

David's cell phone was ringing. He snarled a gruff, "Just don't let me catch you fraternizing with him again," in Taylor's direction, then snapped, "Yeah?" into his phone as he stalked away. Sullivan gave me a quick glance then followed David, probably to have a private word.

I wished Taylor wouldn't be so confrontational with his boss, but held my tongue. I was about to ask him where he was living now when he stepped closer and said quietly, "Erin. Something's . . . not cool. About this job, I mean."

"There are a lot of 'not cool' things going on here. The work's behind schedule. The neighbor you've been palling around with is trying to force Shannon into selling. We're running a feng shui war to send poison arrows back and forth between the two houses." *Not to mention that the homeowner would have preferred to hire the neighbor's designer.*

Taylor snorted. "You left out how your ex-con half brother is the foreman on the job."

"That too," I replied with a smile.

"Plus Pate Hamlin's designer has the hots for me."

"Rebecca Berringer!?"

He lifted his palms and gave me a crooked grin. "Hey, what can I say? Some chicks really go for the rugged cowboy type."

He could be telling the truth. From what my landlady had told me, Rebecca Berringer flirted with every guy in Colorado. Audrey had little regard for Rebecca for other reasons, however; Rebecca had started a TV show, one copying Audrey's, on a rival station. And Audrey was taking a beating from her "younger and hipper" counterpart. "Taylor, Rebecca's probably just trying to cozy up to you to keep tabs on our progress. She's supercompetitive and wants to prove to everyone that she's a better designer than Gilbert and Sullivan."

"Whatever," he agreed, sounding disinterested. "In any case, I think someone's playing for keeps. You know?"

"What do you mean . . . 'playing for keeps'?"

He hesitated. Then he said: "Mom's worried."

"What does this job have to do with Emily?" I wasn't comfortable calling her "Mom"; we'd agreed upon my calling her by her first name.

"Mom heard about that ratings war between your landlady and Rebecca. She figures you and your landlady are such close buddies, you're going to let that mess up your own career."

"How could Audrey's and Rebecca's conflicts interfere with *my* work?"

"Mom says that Rebecca talked on her show about the battle between Pate's and Shannon's houses. That Shannon started using ancient Chinese . . . fungy shoe stuff to tick off Pate."

"It's pronounced *fung shway*, Taylor. And Shannon says *Pate* was the instigator."

"Whatever. Mom figured you and me should stick together and watch out for one another."

I was more than a little skeptical of that. Taylor was not the most trustworthy of sources. Besides, if Emily had told my brother that he and I should "watch out" for each other, she would have told me the same thing. Yet she hadn't even seen fit to mention that Taylor was working on the construction site of the very same job I was overseeing. Maybe he was trying to tell me, without bruising his male ego, that *he* was worried.

He went on, "According to what Mom said, Shannon and Pate are using their houses like two businesses in China did, ten or twenty years back. They were, like, sending out these negative funk sway vibes to hurt the competitor's business and get more customers for themselves."

"Well, I guess if it's good enough for businesses in China, it's good enough for two houses in Crestview, Colorado."

"Yeah. But I'll bet nobody was making death threats back in China."

"Death threats?" I cried.

He shrugged. "Not literally. But everyone around this joint sure seems mad enough to kill me. David says: 'Make it eight feet.' Then what's-his-name, Chang Chunk . . . that crazy Italian guy who thinks he's Chinese, comes along and says: 'Make it nine feet.' Then Shannon yells: 'Why isn't this seven feet?' These clowns all think they're top dog."

"Things will calm down soon. Sullivan and I will get everyone on the same page. We just finished another job. Now we can spend more time here."

"Well, I'm just saying, Erin, you'd better hurry. Chang Chunk and my boss are doing their best to make me the fall guy while *they* screw up."

"His name is *Ang Chung,* Taylor. If you want to get along with him better, you should learn the man's name."

"Yeah, sure. Blame it all on me," he grumbled. "That's what everyone *else* always does." The back door creaked open. Taylor stared past my shoulder and muttered, "Speak of the devil."

Ang Chung was striding toward us. Although his brow was creased in anger, his every movement was characteristically self-aware. It was as if the man envisioned himself in a never-ending tai chi session. I hoped a swarm of bees would swoop toward him one of these days. My hunch was he'd drop that phony measured glide of his and run as awkwardly as an overweight businessman trying to chase down a bus.

Ang seemed to own just two outfits. Today it was his white karate *gi* underneath his unbuttoned camel hair wool coat. On warmer days he would wear black satin pants and a matching robe with a red dragon embroidered on the back. In spite of his name, Ang did indeed have the olive complexion, dark brown eyes, and the dark curly hair of someone with Italian ancestry, as Taylor had noted.

At the edge of Shannon's rock garden, Ang gave us a slight bow. With his typical careful diction, he said, "Please come with me, Mr. Duncan and Miss Gilbert."

I headed toward him. "Is something— "

"What's your problem *now*?" Taylor interrupted, staying put.

"I would say it is more your problem than mine, Mr. Duncan," Ang replied.

"Come on, Taylor," I said with a sigh. "Let's get this handled."

Taylor waited a beat, but then lumbered after me.

"I've been taking readings of our surroundings with my geomancer's compass for the past hour." Ang's jaw was tight, and his eyes flashed in anger. "There are no two ways around it. The addition was built in the wrong place."

"What?!" Taylor and I cried in unison.

"Come along and I'll show you."

Muffled tones emanated within the house, and I recognized Michael Young's deep, consolatory voice. He must have returned home just now; the attached garage was on the opposite side of the house, where we wouldn't have seen or heard his arrival. The back door banged open and Shannon rushed toward us. "Well, Erin? Has Ang told you what's happened now? Are we going to have to rip everything down and start over from scratch?"

"No," I answered, just as Ang was saying: "Probably."

Michael followed his wife onto their worn-out redwood deck and put his arm around her. "Let's give the professionals a couple of minutes to discuss this, shall we, dear? Okay? *Then* we can scream at them to our hearts' content." He winked at me, then ushered his wife back inside. As the door closed behind them, I saw him nodding at her continued protests about what a potential catastrophe loomed before us.

Steve Sullivan was in the front yard, holding what appeared to be a hand-drawn map. He mustered a smile as we approached and waggled his thumb over his shoulder. "Hamlin says his porch roof stays, and Shannon can move if she doesn't like it. David had to leave to—"

"Who authorized this framework in the first place?" Ang snarled at Taylor.

"*You* did!" Taylor fired back.

"I did no such thing! The cornerstone of this room is off by *six inches* from where I wanted it! This structure is still directly in front of hostile energy lines!"

"You know, Ang," Steve said, still eyeing the map, "I've worked with geomantric charts before, but this one—"

"I use my own notations. To simplify." He snatched the sheet of paper from Sullivan's hands. "Look. You see this triangle? That's the symbol for a dragon. Dragons are good. They protect the house." He pointed at the Rockies' Front Range, rising in the distance behind the house. "*There's* the dragon. We want to chase the dragon, yes?"

"Uh, yeah, we do, but—"

"Ideally, for the best protection, you want your dragon to be the high ground found to the left, and your white tiger to the right."

Sullivan and I both looked to the right, where Shannon's extensive property included a small marshy area. "Well, the milkweed gets white and furry this time of year," I offered.

Ang arched his brow. "Are you mocking me, Miss Gilbert?"

"No, I'm not, Mr. Chung."

"Good. Because the key to building a structure the feng shui way is to let the land invite you to interact and participate in its secrets."

Hadn't I read that recently in a book? "It's just that we went through all this before with you when you first started working for Shannon, and you approved our architectural plans at that time."

"Not this front corner, I didn't," Ang declared. "You've cut right through a dragon vein! That's the path of concentrated earth energy from that mountain, right there!" He stabbed his finger at one particular mountain, shimmering some fifty miles in the distance. "Do I really have to *tell* you people that forcing a vein to end is sudden death? It's absolutely disastrous for the occupants of any structure located at this point!"

Sullivan stifled a groan. "I take it, then, that the low brick fence we're going to have built out here to act as our red raven won't... *deflect the vein*? So that the vein misses being lopped off by the corner of the house?"

"Of course not! A red raven is never half as strong as a dragon!"

"Well, sure, but you'd think even a *bird* would be able to tackle a dragon's vein that's already fifty miles long," I said.

Listening in, Taylor guffawed. Ang crossed his arms and glared at him, then at me.

I added, "Sorry, Mr. Chung, but I find it hard to believe that this particular chi line hasn't already been cut more than once by the numerous homes in downtown Crestview."

"I assure you, Miss Gilbert, if you look with your heart and your mind and not just your eyes, you can see the severed vein for yourself."

Taylor chortled. "Dude! Are you listening to yourself? This is, like, *nuts*!"

"Taylor, let us handle this, please. All right?"

He gaped at me. "Aw, come on, Erin! Next he's going to be telling us that we're all gonna croak because we stuck the Porta Potti on the dragon's toes!"

The front door opened—thankfully after and not before Taylor's wisecrack—and Michael emerged, closely followed by Shannon. As they headed toward us, I urged my brother, "Please, just go back to what you were doing. We'll tell you what changes need to be made later."

"Fine. No problemo." With a cocky grin on his face, he nodded at Michael before turning and sauntering away.

Michael paused, and once again put his arm around his wife's shoulders. The energy and exuberance that he always had on camera, which had made him such a hit with Audrey's audience, was now held in check. That seemed to be the typical dynamic between him and his wife, which was probably fortunate. Shannon had been so emotional lately that if they'd both responded with equal fervor, we might have been tempted to install thick padding on all their walls.

"So, how's it going, folks?" he asked with a smile.

"Not well, my friend," Ang replied. "The addition is all wrong, I'm sorry to say. It's got to be rebuilt from scratch."

"Oh, my God!" Shannon shrieked. "We've wasted all this time and money!"

Michael groaned and turned to his wife. "We've got to stop this remodel right now! It's going to cost a fortune to redo everything!"

"And *then* what will we do?" Shannon demanded. "Leave it half built? Tear it down to the foundation? We'd be stuck with a big hole in the ground."

"True," he replied. "And that's going to be a lot more dangerous than any feng shui poison arrows that you keep insisting Pate Hamlin's house is flinging our way."

"We can solve this, Ang," Sullivan intervened firmly, before Shannon could answer her husband. "You said it's only off at that one corner by six inches. We can take down the framing for that corner and move it inward . . . round off the corner, or install triangular glass bricks so the dragon vein will pass right through them."

Ang smiled. "I was just about to suggest that. And I can show you how to direct the energy, once it's inside the house, to maximize its power for the occupants."

Michael grimaced. "Triangular glass bricks? How much is *that* going to set us back?"

"Oh, honey, but just think about how great that's going to be! We'll have a *major* dragon vein, running right through our house!"

"Your profit will increase tenfold from such a wonderful thing," Ang exclaimed.

"Really? Oh, Ang! Thank you so much!" Shannon rushed over to him to give him a hug. "You're such a godsend!" She dashed back up to her husband and gave his arm a squeeze. "We don't have to redo the addition. Isn't that great?"

"Triangular glass bricks?" he said again, his eyes desperate as he looked at Sullivan and me.

Doing some quick geometry, I said, "As long as they're at least nine inches long and wide, we should be able to use regular glass blocks. They'll be clear, so their corners won't affect the energy lines. We'll just incorporate that contemporary style into our design."

"And everybody is happy," Ang concluded, flashing a smile at Shannon and Michael. "This is what happens when you listen to your Mother Earth."

"Provided we *also* listen to our budget," Michael countered evenly.

"We'll get to work on the alterations," Sullivan said, "incorporating a glass column at the corner. And maybe we can turn your front room into both a gallery and a living space."

"Wonderful," Shannon said. But her attention was once again focused on the roofline across the street. "And let's hope that David can get the reflective window glass installed for us."

Ang said good-bye to the Youngs and left. Shannon and Michael went back inside with nary a word to Sullivan and me. As they shut the door, I told him, "Kudos for your remarkable restraint at resisting any *Crouching Tiger, Hidden Dragon* jokes."

He grinned. "That was only because I can never remember which creature's doing what."

"Way to pull us out of the fire with the glass bricks idea. Too bad Shannon gave all the credit to Ang."

"Yeah. Maybe I should start wearing silk pajamas all the time to get her attention." He frowned. "You ready to go?"

"In a minute. I need to say good-bye to Taylor."

He pulled out his cell phone. "Take your time. I'm going to tell David about the glass bricks so he can order them and figure out how to frame around them. We need to make sure Ang can't claim the foundation has to be made of glass, too. Bet the jerk's charging by the hour... supposedly supervising every minute of the construction. That way he profits every time he throws a monkey wrench into our plans."

Sullivan was probably right, I thought as I rounded the house once more. Ang was probably bleeding Michael and Shannon dry by creating all this confusion. Taylor was hard at work but stopped and listened as I explained about the column of glass bricks. "From now on," I told him, "get everything in writing from David and Ang. Have them make a note on the blueprint, and then get each of them to initial any changes."

"Yeah, right. I got so much power, *I* can tell *them* to write stuff down."

"*I'll* tell them that I'm insisting on that procedure from now on."

"I don't need my sister to bail me out."

"Jeez, Taylor! You complain that you don't have the authority to fix your problems, yet you don't want me to use *mine*!"

He grinned at me. "I'm getting your goat already, aren't I? See? This is why siblings can't work together."

I had to laugh, and he did, too.

"Hey, Erin?"

Our eyes met, and a rare flicker of emotion registered on his features before his tough-guy mask slipped back in place. I could swear the emotion I glimpsed looked a lot like fear. My heartbeat quickened.

"Earlier?" Taylor said. "What I said about our needing to stick together? I'm... getting set up."

"Go on."

"Last week, I walk into Dave Lewis's office and tell him all about my past, right? How I'm just out of prison and everything... and I'm willing to start at the bottom. And he says, 'I need a new foreman.' Puts me in charge of four carpenters. What does that tell you?"

"That David saw something in you. And he wanted to give you a break."

He chuckled and shook his head. "Come off it, sis. What planet are *you* living on?"

I didn't answer. In truth, he had an excellent point. Maybe Shannon was right. Maybe David *was* trying to sabotage this job. But why?

"If something feels suspicious to you, for heaven's sake, Taylor, just *quit*. You've been in too much trouble already. If your instincts are telling you you're getting into more now, why risk it?"

"You figure it's easy to find work in a town like Crestview with a criminal record?"

"No, but you could—"

"Forget I said anything," he snarled. "Just do your thing, and I'll do mine, and everything will be cool."

There seemed little point in arguing with him about this right now. We had a dragon's vein to unsever. "Okay, Taylor. Good seeing you again."

"Yeah. Say hi to Mom when you see her."

"You're probably going to see her before I will."

He shook his head. "I want to wait till I've got some money together. It'd be nice to take my mom out to a fancy restaurant... treat her right for once, you know?"

I was touched and meant to tell him so, but he turned on the noisy table saw before I could reply.

The next morning was a Saturday, but Sullivan and I were working a half day. While Sullivan was driving us to a prospective client's house, Taylor called me on my cell phone. "Erin. I managed to get some proof. You know, of what's really going on." He sounded tense and almost breathless.

"At Shannon and Michael's house, you mean?"

"Yeah."

"What is it?"

"I took some pictures. And some other stuff."

"No, I mean, what's really going on there?"

There was a thud like a door slam in the background, and Taylor said stiffly, "Yeah, of course I've got lunchtime off. I gotta eat, don't I? Can you be at your office at noon?"

"Uh, sure. I take it someone's eavesdropping. We've moved into Sullivan's office, you know. I'm still on Opal, but a block farther east."

"No problem. I'll see you then." The line went dead.

Sullivan glanced over at me. "What was that all about?"

"A weird call from Taylor. He says he has proof about some trouble at the Youngs' house. He wants to meet me at noon."

"We were supposed to measure that kitchen in Longmont." I said nothing, and he sighed. "However. Have tape, will measure. I'll take care of it."

"Thanks."

He sighed again. "Sure wish Duncan wasn't our foreman. Especially not *there.* Shannon's not the most easygoing of people."

"No kidding. But I've got to say, he seems to really have matured."

"Prison probably ages a person pretty quick."

"I think he really is trying to get his act together now."

"Good. But don't go getting all sisterly on me and insist that we use him on a regular basis. There are too many good carpenters out there who *don't* mouth off to clients."

"Such as *my* regular contractor's crew. Which is who we should have hired at Shannon's. I'd already won the coin flip. Remember?"

He raked his hand through his hair. "If it makes you feel any better, *I* wish we'd hired your regular crew for Shannon's job, too. Lately, David seems to be burned out. I'm thinking this should be his last gig with us, for a while at least. But he'd lobbied hard for this job, so what could I do?"

"You could have assured him that we'd catch him the next time around . . . but that we needed someone else on this one."

Sullivan made no reply.

When Taylor still hadn't shown up at my office by twelve-twenty, I scanned my list of "incoming calls," found Taylor's, and called that number. It was his cell phone. It quickly switched to his message box, which meant his phone was turned off. I left a message that I was waiting for him as we'd agreed.

By twelve forty-five, however, I was growing concerned. I debated calling Emily to ask if she had a second number for Taylor, but my being worried was enough; I didn't want to worry her as well. He'd mentioned that he had "lunchtime off," as if he was at work. But it was Saturday. He must be moonlighting someplace. On the chance he was at Shannon's house, I called her number. I hung up when the recorder answered.

Not knowing what else to do and increasingly uneasy about Taylor, I drove out to her house. Taylor's beat-up pickup truck was parked at the curb.

I rang the doorbell. No answer. Every instinct was screaming at me that something was dreadfully wrong. Unfortunately, all too often of late, even my most irrational fears proved to be justified. I rang the doorbell a second time then pounded on the door for extra measure. It swung open under my fist.

I stepped inside, calling "Shannon?" as I did so.

On the floor near the front door, Taylor's body was sprawled. His head lay in a pool of blood. A nail gun lay beside him. What seemed to be the head of a nail was lodged in my brother's temple.

I staggered backward onto the porch. Everything went black.

chapter 3

S*omebody was shaking me and calling my name. I* opened my eyes and slowly realized that Rebecca Berringer—Audrey's and my rival—was bending over me. It was freezing. My head hurt, and I was lying on a really hard surface. Was this a bad dream? Where was I?

"Yes, she seems to be okay," Rebecca said into her cell phone. She looked pale and anxious. Keeping her blue eyes riveted to mine, she listened, then said firmly, "No, I *won't* stay on the line." She dropped her phone back into a compartment in her purse. "That was nine-one-one. My God, Erin! It's like a scene from a horror movie in there. How did that poor guy manage to do that to himself?"

"Taylor. Oh, my God." The hideous memory hit me as

I struggled to sit upright. I had stumbled out Shannon's door. After seeing him. And the blood. My poor brother! Poor Emily! This was going to break her heart!

"I just happened to be leaving Pate's house when I saw you collapse," Rebecca told me. "I ran over here, and I . . . saw him lying there, through the doorway." She shuddered. "I pulled the door closed."

"The police . . ."

"I just told you. I called nine-one-one. They're on the way. You sure you're okay? It looked like you had a pretty hard landing. You must have fainted."

I heard the crunch of gravel beneath tire wheels. I tried to stand up, but thought better of it when my vision swam.

"Oh, here he is," Rebecca said. "That gorgeous partner of yours has arrived." She clicked her tongue and muttered, "You are *so* lucky, Erin."

This is one of my luckiest hours, all right. I blinked back tears.

She raced down the steps toward him. "Oh, wait right there, Steve. Please. You don't want to see inside. It's all just too horrible to believe." She hid her face against his chest.

Rebecca really *was* the world's biggest flirt. Just on the other side of the door, Taylor lay dead on the floor. He'd told me yesterday that she'd been flirting with him. If she'd had anything to do with his death, I'd kill her! I glared at the back of her blond head.

"Erin? Are you all right?" Sullivan, despite the fact that Rebecca was pressed against him, was peering at me.

I finally managed to get to my feet. "How did you hear?"

"Hear *what*? You weren't at our office when I got back, and I figured this is where you'd be. What's going on?"

Rebecca stepped back, proving herself astonishingly

capable of standing upright without Sullivan's support. "That big galoot you've got working over here had a fatal accident with a nail gun. Erin found him and the poor thing fainted dead away. I called the police." She paused, and the first sounds of sirens in the distance could be heard. "Here they come now."

"Taylor Duncan is my brother." *And no way was his death an accident!*

She spun around and gaped at me. "You're kidding me!"

"Does it look like I'm kidding?"

"Oh, Erin. Good Lord! He was your brother? I am so, so sorry. No wonder you passed out."

She gasped and turned to Sullivan. "Oh, dear God. I just thought of something!" She clenched his arm. "The feng shui! The forces are really powerful. It's not *my* fault, is it? You don't think I'm responsible for this, do you? I couldn't have known . . . I was just following my client's instructions!"

"You're worried that your client's feng shui arrows did this?" Sullivan looked bewildered. "Nobody's going to die from having a roofline pointed his direction. I mean, come on, Rebecca."

"No, you're right. Of course you're right."

Two Crestview police cars pulled into the driveway. I was shivering uncontrollably. I leaned against the house to steady myself. The first officer who started toward us did a double take at her. Was it because he'd noticed how pretty she was? Or because he recognized her from her TV show? "Are you Rebecca Berringer?" His awed tone indicated the answer to my questions: both.

"Yes, I am." She sniffled. "I'm sorry. I'm a little . . . shaken up. This has been such a shock."

The officer continued to stare, starstruck, or at least thoroughly dazzled, by her. "Understandable, miss. If you can just come with me, we can sit down together in the squad car, and I'll get your statement. But you take as long as you need. Don't try to push yourself too hard, Miss Berringer."

Never had the police treated me as gently as this officer was treating her. With my luck, it would be Detective O'Reilly who'd appear next and insist upon being the one to grill me. O'Reilly was the single most unpleasant policeman I'd met in Crestview. The second officer called to me, "You okay, ma'am?"

Ma'am?! "Yeah, thanks. I'm—"

"She fainted," Rebecca interjected. "You need to take care of her. I'm fine. The man who was killed . . . it's her brother."

"What's happening?" a male voice called. Pate Hamlin was striding across the street toward us. "Rebecca? You okay?"

"I'm fine, Pate. There's been a terrible accident. Involving a carpenter."

"Go back in your house, sir," the officer said. "We'll be—"

Pate ignored him. "He gonna be all right?" he asked Rebecca.

"No, he's dead. I think his name was Duncan."

"*Taylor* Duncan?"

"Please, sir! We need to clear the scene so we can do our jobs."

"He's Erin Gilbert's brother," Rebecca told Pate. "And Erin works with Shannon's designer, Steve Sullivan."

Another officer sauntered toward us. With a bearing that signaled he was top dog, he barked, "You people need to move away from the house and stand by the patrol cars. Sir," he thundered at Pate, "go back into your house."

"Actually, I've got to head into town." Pate pulled a

business card out of his pocket. "If you have any questions, you can reach me at this number. But I won't be much help. I didn't know anything was wrong till I saw the police cars. Didn't hear anything, didn't see anything."

He trotted away. Ten minutes later, as Sullivan, Rebecca, and I were being ushered away from the door, Pate drove off in a red sports car—a Corvette, I was guessing. A pair of officers entered Shannon's house.

While I was answering some questions for the officer who'd called me "ma'am," a tan sedan drove up and parked in the road. I groaned. Detective O'Reilly's vision locked on mine. His jaw muscles were working. He was no doubt envisioning himself chewing my head off in an icy cold interrogation room. A uniformed policeman emerged from Shannon's house and spoke quietly with the detective, probably filling him in on the grotesque scene inside. After their conversation, O'Reilly sauntered toward me. "Miss Gilbert. Again. I might have known."

"Detective O'Reilly." *Again! I* did *know!*

He shook his head. "Unbelievable."

"Just what I was thinking."

"You found the body? *Again?*"

"Yes. It was Taylor Duncan. My half brother."

"Huh. Figures. We've had more than our fair share of run-ins with Mr. Duncan."

"He'd been trying to clean up his act, Detective," I growled.

"Uh-huh."

Shannon's silver Lexus neared the driveway; Michael's black BMW followed. At the sight of all the emergency vehicles, they both barely pulled over before deserting their cars in the road. "Oh, my God! Erin? What's going on?" Shannon called.

"Why are the police here? What's wrong?" Michael

rushed up beside his wife and put an arm around her protectively.

"Do you live here, ma'am?" O'Reilly asked.

"Yes. I'm Shannon Dupree Young. And this is my husband, Michael Young. Why are you here? What's happened?"

"Apparently one of the men working on your, uh, project had an accident. Do you know why there was only one carpenter here?"

"*None* of them were supposed to be here today," Michael answered. "It's Saturday. The crew don't work on weekends."

"Oh, honey," Shannon said. "Didn't I tell you? The foreman asked me yesterday if he could put in some overtime this morning. He wanted to get us back on schedule. I told him yes, because we wouldn't be here anyway."

Michael took in this information without comment, then returned his attention back to O'Reilly. "My wife was the keynote speaker at a luncheon at the Royala. It just ended. Shannon, are you saying you just *gave* this man our key?"

"No," she said petulantly. "I told him the combination to the garage-door opener. Like I did for Gilbert and Sullivan. And David Lewis. Are you sure it was a *carpenter*, Detective? Not a burglar, or something?"

"It was Taylor Duncan. The foreman," I said. "He was murdered."

"Oh, dear Lord!" Shannon cried.

"That real big guy, you mean?" Michael asked.

"I need to get your statement, Miss Gilbert." O'Reilly grabbed my elbow. "Excuse us, Mr. and Mrs. Young."

"What... do we do now?" Michael asked in bewilderment. "Can we get into our house?"

"No. Talk to one of the officers. They can give you a

number for Crestview Victims' Advocates. They can help get you set up in a hotel for the night."

Shannon sent a string of protests trailing the detective, but O'Reilly led me away as though he hadn't heard her. He asked me quietly, "So, let's hear it: Why were *you* here on a Saturday?"

"Designers work on weekends when that's what our clients need us to do."

He cocked an eyebrow as he led me to his sedan. "Okay, but in this case, your clients weren't even home. Did you come with your brother?"

"No. I was looking for my brother and hoped he might be here." The police must have pried Sullivan free of Rebecca's grasp. She was talking to one of the officers in his squad car, while Sullivan and a second policeman stood at the foot of the drive. Sullivan gave me a reassuring smile, but I couldn't return it.

After what could only be considered a ridiculously lengthy interrogation, O'Reilly let me go. By then, Steve and Rebecca were sitting next to each other in the back of the van, their legs dangling from the side doorway facing the house. The sight of their too-cozy seating arrangement instantly irked me. Granted, for the sake of our fledgling business, Sullivan and I had vowed to keep our relationship strictly professional. And the man was something of a natural flirt; he was *very* charming, which often worked wonders in winning over new clients. But in *this* case, he was literally flirting with the enemy, and I despised him for it.

They both hopped to their feet as I approached. "Hi, Erin," Rebecca murmured in a sicky-sweet-I'm-oh-so-concerned voice. "I didn't want to take off before I knew that you were all right."

"I'm fine."

"I just...feel so terrible that I called your half brother a 'big galoot.' I never would have been so heartless if I'd had any idea—"

"That's okay," I interrupted, though I'd noticed two things. One, that she now knew Taylor was my *half* brother. Two, that she was watching Sullivan out of the corner of her eye.

"As I've been saying to Steve"—she glanced over at him with lust-filled eyes—"I hate it that circumstances beyond any of our control have forced us into such adversarial roles. Let's hope that this tragedy will bring an end to the hostilities between our clients."

"That'd be great. Will Taylor's death make Pate Hamlin decide not to buy the Youngs' house out from under them, do you suppose? Or maybe Pate will stop trying to make Shannon's life so miserable that he simply drives her from the neighborhood."

The sharpness of my tone wasn't lost on Rebecca. She averted her eyes and said gently, "Pate's not a bad man, Erin."

"Merely ruthless."

She gave me a wry smile, squeezed my arm, and announced—I was certain—for the benefit of Steve's ears more so than mine, "I'm terribly sorry for your loss." She added solemnly, "Call me if you'd like some company, Steve."

I glared at her as she strolled down the driveway. Quietly, Sullivan said to me, "Want to go someplace and talk? I'll buy you lunch."

I shook my head, unable to meet his gaze. I was dangerously close to tears. "I think I need to take off."

"Of course. You going home?"

Again, I shook my head. "I'm going to tell our mother about Taylor."

"Do you want me to come with you?"

"No. But thanks for offering."

"No problem," he said sadly. "I just wish..." He didn't finish the sentence.

I struggled to get my thoughts together as I drove out to my mother's house, which was in a neighboring town, twenty minutes from Crestview. I didn't know what to say to her, but I did know that I had to do this in person.

Emily Blaire was a truly nice woman, if at times a tad self-absorbed. She ran a fitness studio in town, and I tried to get together with her at least once a month. It had been a strange shock last year to meet my birth mother out of the blue for essentially the first time. These days I was working hard at getting Sullivan's and my new business venture going; Emily was now dating a man who she thought was "the real thing." Both of our lives were hectic. Taylor, with his drug-abuse problems and constant brushes with the law, had been a source of contention in our relationship. There was no telling whether his death would push us further apart or bring us closer together.

The drive went much too quickly, and I soon found myself walking up to her small but cozy ranch-style brick house. My heart was pounding. I began to panic and now prayed that she wouldn't answer the doorbell. No such luck. I heard her melodious, "Just a moment," and she swept the door open moments later. "Erin!" she exclaimed. Then her smile faded. "What's wrong?"

My eyes were tearing up. "Can I come in, Emily?"

"Oh, my God. It's Taylor, isn't it." It wasn't a question.

Emily cried. She dropped one damp white tissue after another, until they surrounded her like the petals from a dying flower. I sat beside her on the sofa. Gently, I explained how and why I'd found him, and that I knew very little else. I also told her about my friend in the police department—Officer Linda Delgardio—and that I hoped Linda would keep me up to speed with the investigation. My heart ached, and I found myself half regretting that Detective O'Reilly had allowed me to be the one to give Emily the horrible news; he'd agreed to wait an hour or two before he or anyone else from the department spoke to her.

Finally, she'd collected herself enough to speak. "This was the one thing I prayed would never happen.... I never wanted to outlive my child. It was bad enough that I never had the chance to watch you grow up, Erin. Now I've lost my only son."

"I'm so sorry—"

"I wish I'd been a better parent to him. I never knew what to do when he started hanging out with the wrong crowd. I made him change schools. He found an even worse crowd. We moved. Same results. I pleaded. I nagged. I wept. I ignored. I fawned. Nothing worked! I finally went with tough love. I banished him from the house. Six months ago, I turned him into the authorities when I found out he was using again."

"I know, Mom."

She met my eyes, startled. That I'd inadvertently called her "Mom" was equally startling to me; it seemed disloyal to my adoptive mom's memory; she'd died after a lingering illness three years ago. I continued, "You did everything you could do. You couldn't live his life for him. Taylor seemed a lot more together when I spoke with him yesterday than he's ever been."

"Somebody did this to him! He's been using power tools and nail guns since he was ten years old. He's never hurt himself. Not once. He was murdered, Erin. You've been through this before. You found your father's killer."

"The police did," I reminded her.

"And they wouldn't have if it weren't for you. The police are never going to put full effort into finding Taylor's killer. They'll just assume it was drug-related. If they run into any dead ends, they'll just quit."

"No, they won't. They'll treat Taylor like they would anyone else, and they'll solve it." I realized at once that I'd spoken with a confidence I didn't feel.

Emily picked up on my hesitancy. "Erin. Please. You know as well as I do what will happen. They'll look at this and say, 'Here's a dead twenty-year-old handyman with a drug record who tripped over his own nail gun. Tragic accident.' And that'll be the end of it."

A pang of guilt melded with my sorrow. I'd missed Taylor's twentieth birthday. Now he was dead. There was no way to make up for that now.

An idea struck me. "Remember how Taylor had that hiding place in your old house, between the studs?"

"Sure. He was always one for building hiding places. Especially when he was using drugs."

"Did he have a hiding place in this house?"

"Yes, unfortunately."

"Has he hidden anything there since he got out of prison?"

"No. It was emptied out when he went to jail, and he hasn't been living here since he got out. He rented a room east of downtown Crestview. We agreed that'd be best... if he was living on his own. But he had an old paint can in the garage where he hid things before he..."

went away. And he did visit me once. Earlier this week... Monday or Tuesday. I can't remember right now."

"You should tell the police about his hiding place when they get here."

"Which I'm sure will be soon...and that they'll accuse him of dealing drugs again, or something." She rose. "Let's go look now and make sure his hiding spot is still empty."

She led me to her garage. She looked, frankly, like walking death, and I asked if she wanted to be doing this now. She nodded grimly. "To the police, he was just a punk with a record, Erin, but he was my baby. You need to make sure the police get to the bottom of this. Promise me, Erin."

"I will. I'll do my best."

"Thank you," she said in a broken whisper. An array of cans lined the shelves along the back wall. She reached for a paint can.

"Wait! Fingerprints could be significant."

"Mine and his will already be on it." Despite her words, she used a plastic trash bag as a mitt to handle the paint can. She pried off the lid with a screwdriver. "He keeps some sand in the bottom of the can so it doesn't feel empty." A look of enormous pain passed across her features; she must have suffered from the realization that she should have used the past tense just now. She muffled a sob.

She stared in surprise. "My God. It's not empty."

"You never let on to him that you'd found his hiding place?" I asked.

She shook her head. "It was the best way I could keep tabs on him."

Using the bag to avoid ruining the evidence, she removed an envelope. It had been curled to fit inside the can. Her hands were trembling. She shook the contents of the envelope onto the concrete garage floor.

Four photographs landed faceup. Each showed a couple in the throes of passion in a silver sedan. I recognized the car immediately. A moment later, I realized that I recognized the couple, as well.

"What had he gotten himself into?" Emily murmured. "Pornography?"

"More likely he was collecting evidence."

"Evidence? For blackmail?"

I hesitated, not wanting to answer, for there was no other easy explanation. "Maybe."

"Do you recognize these people? It's got to be related to Taylor's murder, don't you think? That he was maybe keeping these pictures hidden to protect him from somebody?"

"Let's not jump to conclusions. I'll take this to the police. We'll let them handle this."

"Wait, Erin! I've seen that blonde before! She's got that television show in the mornings. That she copycatted from Audrey's *Domestic Bliss* show. Isn't that her?"

"Rebecca Berringer, yes. And that's Chef Michael from Audrey's show." My client.

chapter 4

Our homes are what restore us, reveal our inner selves, and celebrate not only who we are, but who we hope to become.

—*Audrey Munroe*

Although I had every intention of taking the photographs directly to the Crestview Police Department, I didn't. I simply couldn't face the prospect of going from the heartbroken grief of my biological mother's house straight to the sterile coldness of the police station in general, and of Detective O'Reilly in particular. I first needed to go home and shore up my flagging spirits.

My whole body was trembling as I parked near the slate walkway. Just the sight of the regal stone exterior of the mansion that I was lucky to call my home gave me some solace. As I opened the carved oak door, I desperately hoped Audrey would be here.

I immediately noticed a new bouquet of

pristine white calla lilies in the Waterford vase. The vase sparkled with captured yellow light from the chandelier. Seeing such a pretty sight at such a bleak time made my eyes mist again. I took a moment to drink in the atmosphere. I loved every square inch of this entranceway, from the high-coved ceiling to the travertine tile floor—the succulent smoky green wall paint, the roomy coat closet with its paneled doors, the quiet elegance of the precise trim.

Now, however, what I loved most of all was my view through the French doors into the messy parlor. Audrey sat on the Oriental rug, ensconced in some art project for her show. My black cat, Hildi, sat beside her, scrutinizing her every move.

I shed my coat and stepped forward. Audrey's smile faded as she studied my features. "Erin?"

"The worst thing has happened. Taylor Duncan was killed." Feeling as though I was in some kind of a stupor, I watched as Hildi leapt onto a cushion of the sofa, apparently wanting to race me to my favorite seat.

"Oh, my God." Audrey sprang to her feet, showing the grace that had been her hallmark as a former ballerina decades ago. "Sit down."

I obeyed. She wrapped a feather-soft chenille comforter around my shoulders, swept up my startled kitty from her perch on the cushion, plopped her down in my lap, then took a seat beside me on the sage-colored sofa. "Tell me everything," my landlady said.

When I glanced at my watch, I was surprised to see that an hour had passed since I'd begun pouring my heart out to Audrey. Hildi, who only ever stayed where she'd gone of her own volition, had long since left my lap. Having finally talked myself out, I slid the throw from my shoulders and started to rise. "Thanks for listening."

"Where are you going?"

"The police station. To give them those photos."

"That can wait. You look like you've been hit by a train. You shouldn't be driving."

"I'll be fine."

"Maybe so, but I need to understand. This feng shui practice . . . isn't it supposed to be used for self-defense, like karate? And for the betterment of the soul and body? It sounds to me like Rebecca Berringer is using it for evil."

"That's a bit of an overstatement. But I agree with the gist."

"Rumor is she was bragging on her TV show about the whole nasty feng shui battle with the neighbor."

"Oh, really?" I feigned ignorance; I knew Audrey secretly recorded Rebecca's shows, but I wasn't about to force her to acknowledge that fact—and what it revealed about her deep insecurity regarding their rivalry.

"Somebody should de-feng that woman." A frown marred her patrician features. "Rebecca's making a mockery of the philosophies. Although I have to admit, her brash statements on her show have piqued even *my* interest." She hesitated. "According to *my friend's* stories about the show, that is."

I thought about how Ang Chung was obviously conning Shannon. "Did you know that some practitioners say that they can predict natural disasters for buildings that have bad feng shui?"

Audrey replied, "I've heard that, yes, but I'm more than a little skeptical."

"Me, too. There's also a Westernized, modern approach to feng shui that I personally can really appreciate. One that takes a common-sense approach to the whole thing."

"Is that what you practice in your designs?"

Audrey, I realized, was trying to keep me talking in order to get my mind off my half brother's murder, and I loved her for doing so. "Yes. I tend to use intuitive feng shui—to look at what works for my clients."

"For example?" she prompted.

"In traditional feng shui, only square-shaped houses are considered lucky. Nowadays, we have attached garages, mud rooms, home offices, and so forth, so designing strictly square homes is rather difficult. Shannon has this lovely work area in a separate wing of the house, which is perfect for her lifestyle, but now she thinks that's bad feng shui. So Sullivan and I have designed the front deck and a courtyard—including a gazebo—to give the house a square footprint. Without having to actually square off all the external walls."

"Doesn't it irk you that you have to jump through hoops for her?" Audrey asked, frowning.

"Not at all. If she hadn't gotten so concerned about bad energy, she might never have considered remodeling, and then I wouldn't have been hired. And you'd be surprised how well our design ideas mesh with feng shui. It is wonderfully instructive when it comes to furniture placement, and for reminding you to balance and harmonize rooms with a wide range of textures and materials. Also to bring the outdoors into your rooms. Everyone knows to use greens and blues to cool rooms and reds and yellows to warm them. A feng shui consultant would suggest the very same thing with colors for the exact same reason, but he'd call them yin and yang."

"Which reminds me," Audrey said, racing over to snatch up her Tiffany notebook and pen from the side table. "You once gave me that quick rundown on dos and don'ts of color. I was going to talk about color on my show next week."

"You're reaching deep for diversions now, Audrey." I gave her a sad smile.

"But I really want to hear your answer, Erin."

"Use reds in dining rooms and kitchens, because it flatters both foods and people's complexions. Blue isn't good for dining rooms. It's a yin—cooling—color that's great for bedrooms and to calm the spirit. Greens are also cool and soothing and yet rejuvenating, because they're natural, outdoorsy hues. Yellows aren't good for complexions. So you want to avoid using them in super-small bathrooms, but otherwise they warm and cheer rooms. Purple's good for meditation, spirituality, deep thinking. Pink is the most sedative of all colors. Which is why it's also great for bedrooms. Orange is good for gathering places because it stimulates and sustains conversation." I sighed. "I think that's the rainbow in a nutshell."

She studied me anxiously. "Did you want me to go with you to the police? Give you a little support?"

"No, thanks, Audrey. I'm fine. Really." But my thoughts flashed to the sight of poor Taylor on the Youngs' foyer floor, and tears burned my eyes. "I just... He was so young. He didn't deserve this."

"As we both know, my dear, life isn't fair. All we can do is treat others with loving care, and try to make ourselves as receptive to loving care as we can."

"Nobody treated Taylor with loving care. That's why he's dead. And if *loving care* toward him was the measure I should have used, I failed him miserably."

"So you're discounting how hard you and Emily worked together to try to keep him out of jail and off drugs last year? You know, Erin, in any given day, we can always focus on our failures and on the countless things we wished we'd done... what we *would* have done if only we'd been clairvoyant. The fact of the matter is, sometimes even our best still isn't good enough. Often, the hardest person to treat with loving care is yourself."

I thanked her for her advice. Frankly, though, I doubted it was even possible to treat myself with "loving care" under these circumstances. It felt as though I had a cavernous hole in my heart. The only way I could imagine myself ever closing that wound was to see Taylor's killer behind bars.

chapter 5

The *Crestview police station was an austere, white* stucco building a couple of miles east of downtown. Before getting out of my van, I donned leather gloves to avoid getting fingerprints on what I hoped would be crucial evidence. An officer showed me to Detective O'Reilly's desk. O'Reilly, in turn, ignored me and completed his phone conversation, although his scowl deepened at my presence. While he spoke his noncommittal *I sees* and *Sures* into the handset, I set the paint can on his desk and lined up the four photographs to face him.

His work space was every bit as drab and colorless as he was. His institutional, fake-wood Formica desktop was bare except for two pens, his computer screen and keyboard, a few papers and notepads, and one of those hand-sized squeeze balls for relieving stress. There were no photographs of family members or pets, no cartoons tacked to the blue-gray carrel wall behind him. Even his coffee mug was plain white. I studied the not unattractive streaks of clotting cream within the inch or so of coffee at the bottom of his cup. Those mocha hues would look quite fetching on the walls in Shannon's family room.

He finally hung up and gestured for me to take a seat. "What's this?" he asked, his voice flat. He eyed the photographs without reaction.

"Emily Blaire, Taylor's mother, gave them to me to give to you. Taylor hid them in her garage. I've made sure I didn't get my fingerprints on them. And I brought the hiding place with me as well."

"The paint can?"

I resisted the temptation to reply that, no, I'd brought him a can of magenta paint so that he could spruce up the police station. "Yes. It was on the shelf among the actual partially full ones."

"Good hiding place. How'd it get discovered?"

"Emily had been trying to keep tabs on him, and she found it."

I expected him to give me a hard time about my not having left this "hiding place" for the police to discover for themselves, but he said nothing, merely examined the photographs with new interest.

He arched an eyebrow. "This is that Berringer woman, who's got some dopey housewives' show on local TV, right?"

"Her show is about interior design and lifestyle tips."

"Yeah. And this is the guy I talked to today. The owner of the house you're working on." He smirked. "Wonder if the wife knows."

"My guess is that she doesn't."

He stared into my eyes and said nastily, "And let's try 'n' keep it that way, okay, Miss Gilbert?"

"I told Emily not to tell anyone about the photographs, and I'll do the same."

Well, not counting Audrey. And Steve Sullivan. He and I were partners. Keeping him up to speed was the least I should do. Not to mention that watching Rebecca flirt with him had galled me, so how bad could my showing him her true colors be?

"Thanks for bringing this in." O'Reilly grabbed the top sheet of paper from his kneehole drawer and focused his attention on that. I'd been dismissed.

"You're being almost nice to me, Detective. What's up?"

He looked up and held my gaze for an uncomfortably long time. Finally, he sighed. "Erin, you do realize this is almost certainly an accident?"

He had suddenly put me on a first-name basis, which made his statement all the more grating. "No, Detective O'Reilly. I *don't* realize any such thing!"

"Hey, I'm not saying we won't investigate thoroughly, I'm—"

"Good. Because Taylor was murdered. He called me with *evidence*. He said he'd *figured out* what was going on. I told you that when I gave you my statement. Don't you think it was terribly convenient that, right after he'd arranged to give me this evidence, he had a fatal *accident*? While he was supposedly at work? On a Saturday—his day off?"

O'Reilly leaned back in his chair and laced his fingers behind his head, scowling at me. "You *also* told me he was short on money and was on the outs with his boss. Which could explain why he was putting in some overtime. And my hunch is his tox screens will come back positive. That'll prove he was stoned out of his gourd. While using dangerous tools."

I shook my head stubbornly. "He'd sounded lucid when he called me just a couple of hours before it happened."

Again, O'Reilly released a weary sigh, then snatched his notepad from the pocket of his brown suit jacket. He scanned his notes. "You didn't describe him as 'lucid,' Miss Gilbert. You said he sounded 'out of breath' and 'anxious.' "

"So? I'm telling you now that he *also* sounded lucid. And his being a little anxious is a far cry from sounding 'stoned out of his gourd'!"

"We'll investigate his death, Miss Gilbert." His tone was patronizing. And infuriating. "I'm just trying to let you know how I'm reading things at this particular juncture."

"Good thing you're keeping such an open mind, Detective." I left without awaiting his reply.

The next morning, my heart wasn't up for one of my favorite activities—perusing the furniture and home improvement fliers in the Sunday paper. I ate breakfast with Audrey, but then went back to bed while she went to church. The phone rang, jarring me awake. I grabbed for the handset, feeling groggy and disoriented. It was Sullivan, who promptly asked how I was. "Fine," I mumbled.

"Somebody once told me what 'fine' really means: Feelings Internal, Not Expressed."

I had no response to that remark.

When the silence grew heavy, he asked, "How'd things go at your . . . at Emily's house?"

"It was difficult."

"She going to be all right?"

"I hope so. She's fairly strong. She's endured more than her fair share of tough times already."

"You're thinking this was murder, I take it."

"Of *course* I am! Taylor was shot with a nail in the side of his head! Did you think he put it there himself?"

"It's possible. It could have been an accident." His gentle tone of voice was maddening. I wanted to fight. I wanted somebody to be as angry with me as *I* was with me for . . . not being clairvoyant.

"That's stupid! Have you been talking to the police? Is that what you told them yesterday?"

"No, Erin. I'm just saying . . . things like that have happened before. A nail gun was fired through a hollow wall a few years ago and killed a young carpenter at a distance of twenty-plus feet. I read about it on the Internet last night. I couldn't sleep, so I did some research. There've been a handful of accidental deaths from nail guns."

"Well, please spare me any more of your research. This is my *brother* we're talking about, Sullivan. Granted, we weren't close. We barely knew each other, in fact. But I don't want to talk about his death as if it's some 'Story of the Weird.'" (That was a column that the *Crestview Sentinel* ran every Sunday.)

"Sorry."

I sighed. Snarking at Sullivan wasn't helping me feel any better.

Come to think of it, Audrey had ferreted away the front section of the newspaper before I could read it. Probably trying to spare me the headlines about Taylor's death.

"Erin? You still there?"

"Yes. I'm going to solve this murder without the police if I have to. I promised Emily. And I promised myself."

"I'll do everything I can to help you," Sullivan said, without hesitation.

I spent much of Monday afternoon with Emily, helping her with funeral arrangements.

Sullivan was already hard at work, revising Shannon's presentation boards, when I arrived at our office early Tuesday morning. I wheeled my red leather desk chair beside his, and we brainstormed. We both had a tendency to overstate our objections to each other's ideas and take polar positions, but would then find compromises that captured the best in both of our tastes.

The design of our office was the perfect example. His decorating style was purely masculine—sleek, simple lines, heavy on the mahogany hues and burnished steel. You half expected him to offer you bourbon and a cigar when you sat down in front of his exquisite knotty-alder desk. My style was more feminine—I loved vertical lines, asymmetrical balance, soft luxurious fabrics, a wide-ranging palette of colors and textures—yum!

Even so, we'd succeeded in blending our tastes beautifully. Upholstered in a delicate print, my slipper chairs were invitingly placed in front of his tiger maple coffee table. My vases and glass accent pieces warmed and added sparkle to the room. When spouses whined that their styles were in such opposition that the situation was hopeless, we merely had to show them this space. We'd tell them honestly about how we'd been in despair at first. (Although the truth was, *I'd* been in despair. Whereas Sullivan had been in an angry funk.) When we'd finished cramming my stuff in, he had stormed out the door, announcing we were going to have to lease a bigger office. I'd worked feverishly, and when he returned an hour later, he scanned the space in obvious surprise and said, "Huh. I didn't realize you were *this* good." Considering the source, that was the highest compliment I'd ever received.

The phone rang. It was Shannon, saying she needed to schedule "an emergency meeting as soon as possible."

My thoughts immediately went to the photographs of her husband and Rebecca. Had Detective O'Reilly already spilled the beans? "Is everything all right?"

"Of course not," Shannon shrilled at me. "What part of 'emergency meeting' did you fail to understand?"

I took a quick calming breath. "I meant that I hope you and Michael aren't sick or injured, or something." Sullivan looked up from his drawing and watched me in curiosity.

"We're fine. How soon can you get here?"

I relayed that question to Sullivan, and we agreed on noon. Shannon was irritated that we couldn't come any sooner. She gave me a curt "Thanks" and hung up.

"Any idea what the emergency's about?" Sullivan asked.

"Not really. She said 'we,' so I doubt it's a marital crisis."

"Why would you immediately suspect *that*?"

"I meant to tell you yesterday... Taylor had apparently snapped some very suggestive Polaroids of Michael and Rebecca Berringer. Emily and I found them tucked away in Taylor's hiding spot."

"You're sure that it was Rebecca and Michael?"

"I'm one hundred percent sure. I gave the photographs to Detective O'Reilly. He said to keep the story quiet, so whatever you do, don't tell Rebecca, please... or anyone else, about them."

"Goes without saying," he grumbled.

His mood had darkened considerably. I couldn't help but wonder if that was because he was disappointed that Rebecca's flirtations hadn't been reserved for him alone.

Michael greeted us when we arrived. The look on his face—and the cloud of Shannon's cigarette smoke—told us all we needed to know: Shannon had gotten herself worked into a major stew.

My eyes, however, immediately drifted to the spot where I'd last seen my brother's body. There was a stain—a shadow of darker color on the once-white portion of the checkerboard floor pattern. Michael read my mind and murmured, "We're having the carpenters pull up all the linoleum today. We were going to do that soon enough anyway."

He put his hands on my shoulders. Disgusted by his infidelity, it was all I could do not to shudder and pull away. He didn't seem to notice. "I'm so sorry for your loss, Erin. I had no idea Taylor was your brother. I tried to tell Shannon it was cruel to expect you to come here today, but she—"

"Thanks, Michael, but I'm fine. Really." The last thing I wanted now was to alienate Shannon or Michael and get fired from this job; I'd be hindered when poking around into the circumstances of Taylor's murder. "I barely knew him, to be honest with you. I was adopted. We were raised by different parents, halfway across the country from each other."

"Oh. Still. I'm sure—"

"Erin. Steve." Shannon whisked into the room as though fueled by her jet trail of cigarette smoke. The thought of what her husband was doing behind her back gnawed at me. I felt a pang of empathy for Shannon. "Thank God you're finally here! Have you read the papers this morning?"

"No, I—"

"Have you heard about Pate Hamlin?"

"About Pate?" *My God. Had he been killed too?*

"There's a big story on him this morning. As it turns out, Pate is one of the *owners* of BaseMart."

"The discount-store chain?" Sullivan asked.

"Right. The very one that Erin's landlady, Audrey, and I have been working our asses off to keep *out* of Crestview."

"Oh, that's right. You and she are on that 'No Big Boxes' committee together," I recalled.

"They're co-chairs," Michael interjected. "And speaking of chairs, Shannon, how about allowing our guests to sit down?"

She sighed and whirled on a heel. "Let's go into the living room. Now that all the hammering and sawing's stopped. Lunch break. They can never follow any kind of a schedule, except when it comes to stopping work. Noon to one every day, it's quiet as a church around here. And by four P.M. on the dot, they pack up and race out."

"Can I get you anything to drink?" Michael asked us. "Water? Coffee? Jim Beam?"

"No, thanks," we answered in unison.

To Shannon I said, "Audrey had mentioned last week that you'd managed to block BaseMart from moving into city limits."

"Right. But, of course, the city council has no control over Crestview County, which is precisely where that chunk of property's located. Not to mention my *home*!"

"I'm confused," I admitted. "I didn't see the newspaper article. What chunk of property?"

"Pate wants to put his store in that big open field behind his house," Michael explained.

"I remember that they were trying to get the rights to build that area into a store, but—"

"He wants to put a store *in his own backyard?*" Sullivan interrupted, incredulous.

"It was front-page news. I'll show you." Michael began to rummage through the red woven basket that was beside his wife's feet.

I massaged my forehead. It was a struggle to care about this, when we were sitting just a room away from the very place where I'd found poor Taylor's body.

"Erin, are you all right?" Shannon asked.

"I'm fine. I'm just trying to think, that's all."

"You've dragged her out here three days after discovering her brother *died* in our house," Michael told her as he handed a newspaper to Steve. "Remember?"

"I'm sorry, Erin," she managed. "I truly am. And I really wish this could wait, but once Pate breaks ground for BaseMart, the energy lines will be so vile, this house will be cursed *forever.*"

There was a noise in the attic over my head. It sounded like a squirrel or something, scampering across the floor. "As I said earlier, I didn't know Taylor at all, really, but he's still my brother. It's been extremely upsetting."

"Oh, I know," Shannon replied. "Imagine how it's been for us. It happened in our home, after all." She peered at my face as though it was smudged. "I should call Ang Chung to come speak with you. He does these Taoist mediation sessions, too, that are nice and relaxing."

"That's okay. But, getting back to your problem, frankly, if Pate builds a megastore across the street, there isn't much Steve and I can do to help you."

"Short of physically moving your house," Sullivan muttered under his breath.

Shannon hopped to her feet. "That's it! We'll move our whole house! That's our only hope!"

"Shannon!" Michael scolded. He fired a quick, penetrating glare in Sullivan's direction. "We can't afford that!"

As though she hadn't heard, Shannon paced excitedly around her chocolate leather coffee table and prattled on. "It's the *perfect* solution. We've got lots of acreage to work with. Oh, I wish Ang were here! He'd be able to tell us precisely where we should relocate."

"But... what happened to stopping Pate's store from expanding into the Crestview area?" Michael asked his wife. "You've been worrying about how the store's going to suck away all the money from downtown Crestview. That all the shops and galleries will go out of business."

Sullivan was scanning the newspaper article. "According to this quote, Pate insists that's a 'small price to pay' in exchange for bringing cruddy goods to the town at cheap prices. Claims it's going to be fabulous for our local economy."

"It sure won't be great for our *personal* economy," Michael said, "no matter whether we move this house or not. Hon, even if we put it on the back corner of our property line, we're going to have a huge, ugly store, right across the street from us!"

"We can plant a big copse of trees in the front and install a long, meandering driveway through them," Shannon said promptly. But she plopped down on the sofa with an air of defeat.

"Pate might be bluffing," Sullivan suggested. "He'll lose hundreds of thousands of dollars in property value himself. The store would be even closer to his house than to yours, so—"

"Oh, they'll be bulldozing his house down as well, but he doesn't care about any of that. He just wants to force me to sell to him. That's why he's putting in that hideous porch roof and all sorts of god-awful things. Next he'll be moving in a trailer. You watch. What does he care? He's a millionaire many times over. He intends to hang out here in Crestview, till he drains this town dry of every drop of cultural interest and integrity and character. He's plotting to put a BaseMart auto-repair shop right where we're *sitting*!" she wailed.

The rustling above our heads was growing more and more distracting. "What's that noise?" I asked, looking at the ceiling.

"It's nothing," Shannon replied. "Those darned raccoons must be back."

"Raccoons?"

"We've had a problem with them off and on for years," Michael told us. "But *she* doesn't want me to call the exterminator." He waggled his thumb at his wife.

"We hardly ever go up there. And it's not like they bother us. Other than making the occasional scurrying sounds."

The noise was growing louder. "It sounds as if the whole extended raccoon family must have moved up there," I pointed out.

"But getting back to my problem, Erin, there has to be *something* we can do . . . other than moving the house itself. Even Ang says he's stumped."

"Shannon, a big store locating across the street is a bit beyond the limitations of what interior design can do for you," I replied bluntly.

"I know." She sighed. "It's going to be a total disaster. Regardless of whether we move the house to the far corner of our property or not, we'll still be stuck with the entrance road to BaseMart as a dead end, directly in front of our property. You might as well put a cemetery there, for all the bad energy bombarding us."

"Honey?" Michael said. "Much as I hate to say it, maybe it's time we consider taking Pate up on his offer."

"Sell him our home? Over my dead body! How can you even suggest such a thing?"

"If we sell now, our property value will still be high. If we wait and Pate gets the okay from the county to build—"

"No! If that happens, we'll get a new foundation built where Ang tells us to relocate. They moved that lighthouse in North Carolina's Outer Banks that was too near the ocean. Compared to that, moving our house will be a *snap*."

"But that's going to cost us more than this house is worth, Shannon! That's crazy!" Michael protested.

The racket above our heads was still increasing. Sullivan said, "Sounds like your raccoons are break-dancing up there."

"They do seem to be a little more rambunctious than normal," Shannon replied.

To me, it sounded like the raccoons were about to crash through the ceiling. Enough was enough. "I'm going to go take a look." I left the room and headed for the attic door, which had been built into the tongue-and-groove wood ceiling in their family room.

I glared at the badly designed two-foot-by-three-foot door in the ceiling. The wood door had been hinged incorrectly—so that it had to be pushed open into the attic instead of simply pulled down. The flap was easy enough to open when climbing up; not so easy to close when coming back down. Well, if I had to be the one to confront a dozen break-dancing raccoons, two-timing *Michael* could handle the challenge afterward of shoving the pull-down ladder back into place, all the while keeping the door flap only partially closed.

I centered a wood splat-back chair underneath the opening, climbed onto the chair, and threw the door wide open with so much force that it bounced a little on its rubber bumpers. I reached up and grabbed the ladder and tugged it into place. The wood rung felt strangely hot. There was a strange flickering light above me. Now that the door was open, I smelled something that made my heart race. "My God," I cried. "I think your attic is on fire!"

"That's insane," Shannon retorted.

"Insane or not..." I took a couple of steps up the ladder. I ducked as a small section of a joist on the roof cracked off, shooting down a cascade of hot embers. The noise had been crackling wood. Thick smoke stung my eyes. "Oh, God! The whole attic's in flames!"

I had to get the door shut or the fire would spread

downstairs along the ceiling! The far edge of the door was dangerously close to the fire—too close for me to climb up there and swing it toward the opening. I tried to grip the edges on either side of the hinge and shut it, but it was much too heavy to lift. I had to climb farther up the ladder.

Standing as high on the ladder as I dared, I yanked on the door. It wouldn't budge.

"Erin!" a voice cried. Probably Sullivan, but I was too frantic to care. "Get down from there!"

I wasted precious oxygen to shout: "Just a second!" I had to find a way to shut this damned door! The added oxygen flow would only help fuel the flames.

Roiling mountains of thick black smoke clogged my vision and my throat.

"I'm calling nine-one-one!" someone cried—Michael, I realized.

I ducked, took a deep gulp of air, and tried once more to pry the door flap back toward the stairs. Again, it wouldn't budge.

Without warning, something grabbed me by the waist. I was lifted and pulled off the stairs. I yelled, "Let go of me!" In one swift clean-and-jerk motion, Sullivan lifted me off the stairs and deposited me on the floor. Then he raced up the ladder, pulled the trap door partially shut, lowered himself onto the chair, then heaved the ladder back up as the door dropped into place.

"Let's get out of here! Now!" he shouted.

"Somebody already alerted the police," Michael announced. "Fire trucks are on the way." He glanced anxiously at the ceiling.

"My artwork! I can't leave it! Mike," Shannon cried to her husband, "carry these pieces out. I'll get the ones on the far wall—"

"No! Shannon, get a grip!" he snapped. "You can redo

the paintings, if you have to. We're all leaving this house *now*!"

"Fine! Fine!" she shrieked. But she didn't move an inch closer to the door. "So we'll all just grab a *pair* of paintings and go. Come on, people!" she cried over her shoulder as she dashed into her studio. "Let's move! Each of you grab one of these paintings against the wall. Now! Hurry!"

The three of us exchanged shocked looks, but then raced after her. Michael reached for an oil painting near the door. Shannon cried, "No, not those! They're not my best work! I said the ones against the wall."

Figuring it would take longer to chastise her than to grab a painting or two, I complied, as did her husband and a glowering Sullivan. Dragging as many of the awkward wood-frame-backed canvases as we could, the four of us finally made it out of the house. Shannon set her two paintings down on the front lawn. "Put them here, everyone. We'll stack them up. They should be safe this far away from the house."

But Sullivan didn't move to obey. Instead he was eyeing Pate, who was standing on his porch, speaking on his cell phone as he watched the Youngs' roof. I turned to look. Six-foot-high flames were shooting out into the deep blue sky.

Shannon tore across the street toward him.

"I called nine-one-one." He pocketed his cell phone. "They were already on the way."

"You bastard!" Shannon screamed at him.

Pate took a step back. "What!?"

"You did this!" Shannon shrieked. She started to pummel his chest with her fists. "You set fire to my house! You're trying to *kill* me!"

chapter 6

Michael dragged Shannon away from Pate and tried in vain to get her to calm down. Within minutes, sirens were once again wailing. Two chartreuse fire trucks arrived, along with a smaller emergency vehicle. A team of firefighters hooked up a hose to a hydrant. Soon a steady blast of water slashed across the flames. Shannon was in tears, all the while harping at the firefighters: "Save the *north* side of the house first! That's where I do my painting!"

Though my client's wishes were paramount, *my* heart was invested in the new construction on the southwest side. David's team had started in on the "deconstruction" (as I liked to call it), which would allow us to install the column of glass bricks. Sullivan and I had redesigned the room as a combination art showroom/living room, and it was going to look amazing.

Provided it wasn't burned to the ground.

In any case, that skuzzy Ang Chung was going to be doing his happy dance at how badly this fire would delay the remodel. I couldn't help but wonder if he'd sunk so low as to torch it himself. That was a preposterous notion, though. How could he have gotten away with climbing into the attic this morning, unnoticed?

The temperature had dropped rapidly. Sullivan and I huddled together for warmth as we stood watching on the front lawn—a not entirely unpleasant sensation. Michael, the two-timing hypocrite, kept trying to coax his wife into his arms. She wasn't even wearing a coat. Maybe her adrenaline was keeping her sufficiently warm.

Minutes later, the leaping flames had been extinguished, and the firemen were entering the house. The charred, gaping holes were sorry evidence that the roof had sustained considerable damage. Thankfully, judging from what I could glimpse through the open front door, the blaze hadn't spread into the Youngs' living quarters.

A police car parked in front of the house. Shannon dashed over to the first officer as he emerged. Pointing at Pate, still standing on his porch, she shouted, "*That's* the man who set my house on fire! Arrest him!"

"Hey! Whoa!" Pate said, holding up his palms as he walked toward us. "I had nothing to do with this fire, Officer."

"He's been sneaking around in my home! He got to be buddies with one of my construction workers—and *that* guy wound up dead in my foyer! Just three days ago!"

Michael had been talking with a firefighter, but now he trotted toward his wife. "Shannon! Get ahold of yourself! Sorry, Officer. My wife is a passionate person.

Sometimes she lets her emotions get the best of her and doesn't think things through."

"Michael!"

"She doesn't mean to be *officially* accusing our neighbor, Mr. Hamlin, of committing a *crime*," he persisted. "She's merely speculating."

Shannon glared at him. "Way to play Benedict Arnold! What's the matter? Are you afraid Pate's going to sue us? He doesn't scare *me*!"

To his credit, Pate didn't say a word.

"Did you see this man setting fire to your house, ma'am?" the first officer asked calmly, indicating Pate.

"Well... no. But I'm also not 'merely speculating.' I have plenty of good reasons to suspect him."

"None of which amount to anything, I assure you, Officers, because I'm innocent." Pate's deep voice was calm, in striking contrast to Shannon's. "I did *not* set your house on fire, Miss Dupree."

"It's Mrs. Young to you! I only use my maiden name professionally!"

"The very last thing I would do at this particular time would be to commit arson," Pate assured the officer. He then focused his gaze on Shannon. "Think about it. The *Sentinel* already spread the word that I'm trying to build on a tract of land behind my house. Do you really think I'd be stupid enough to set fire to your home *now?* While my financial future is in the hands of local government officials?"

"I wouldn't put it past you. Just look at that jutting roof, Officers! He *aimed* it right at my house! If that's not proof that the man is trying to destroy my house, I don't know what is!"

The two officers looked where Shannon was pointing, clearly baffled by her accusation.

"Bad feng shui," Pate explained, incorrectly pronouncing "*feng*." "You know... the Chinese art?"

"*Feng* shui literally translates to wind and water," I interjected. "It got that name because, with China's geography, building a structure on high ground meant battling strong winds. Lowlands meant flooding."

"Oh, right," the one officer said, grinning. "Ya know, my wife got into that for a while. She even bought this ugly ceramic turtle and stuck it near our door. Said it'd protect the house." He chuckled. "Here she *lives* with a cop, but she figures she needs a turtle statue to..." He let his voice fade as he watched a firefighter run past us, apparently only then remembering the situation's gravity.

"So that porch roof across the street is bad for you?" a second officer asked Shannon.

"Of course it is! It's shaped like a dagger! And it's pointing at the window of my art studio!"

Pate grinned. "Personally, I happen to like the way it makes my porch look. Kind of dramatic and different. Don't you think?" He glanced at Sullivan and me for confirmation. Under Shannon's watchful eye, I didn't dare blink. Truth be told, from purely an aesthetical standpoint, Pate's roof had a certain appeal. He strode toward Steve, his hand extended. "I owe you an apology, Mr. Sullivan. I should have heard you out when you wanted to discuss my porch roof. I'm not real patient these days. I'm in the middle of a nasty divorce. Whole thing's running me ragged."

"No problem."

As the men shook hands, Shannon grunted in disgust. "You sure were right about Pate being the megamacho type, Erin."

Pate overheard and gave us a wry smile. He stepped toward me, and our gazes met. I was startled. The man had Paul Newman–like blue eyes. He clasped my hand in his. "Miss Gilbert, I just wanted to tell you how very sorry I am about your brother." He gave my hand a gentle squeeze, then released it. "Taylor had a terrific sense of humor and a refreshing openness. His death at such a young age is tragic."

"Thank you." As I studied his handsome features, I realized that the white hair had fooled me. Pate was probably only in his early forties. Maybe even his late thirties.

"Taylor spoke highly of you," Pate continued. "He told me how much he was looking forward to getting to know you better. I'm sorry the Fates robbed you both of that opportunity."

Now I had to avert my gaze from his or risk tearing up. I didn't dare look at Shannon; my brief, civil exchange with Pate Hamlin had no doubt already painted me with the same "traitor" brush she'd applied to her husband. (Although she was correct where *he* was concerned.) I turned toward Sullivan instead, only to discover that *he* was glaring at me. I glared back, willing him to telepathically hear me retort: *What!?* You *can cozy up to the designer who's sleeping with our client's husband, but* I *can't accept the condolences of the homeowner the slut works for?* And then I noticed Pate Hamlin was staring at me intently, looking sincerely concerned. Impulsively, I found myself giving him an appreciative smile.

The firefighters emerged from the house. "Everything's under control. The fire's out."

Michael sighed with relief. "Thank God for that much."

"How bad's the damage from smoke and water?" Shannon asked.

"Hard to say. Your insurance agent can probably judge that better'n I could."

"I should head home," Pate said abruptly. "Good to see you again, Mr. Sullivan." He nodded at me. "And to meet you, Miss Gilbert. Though I'm sorry about the circumstances. If your family needs any help with funeral arrangements, I'm friends with the best mortician in Crestview. I'd be happy to pull some strings for you."

"Um, thanks, but... that's not necessary."

He searched my eyes, nodded, then turned and walked to his house with a confident stride.

"So we can go back inside now, right?" Michael was asking the fireman who appeared to be in charge.

He rubbed his craggy chin, then frowned. "You can go in and pack up some things, sure. But it's probably going to be a long time till you can live there again."

"What!?" Shannon shrieked.

"You need a new roof. 'Fraid you'll have to move into a hotel. Your homeowner's insurance should cover it. There's a place this side of town that has full kitchens and two-bedroom suites. Won't be home sweet home, but it'll be better than nothing. And it's only a matter of time till your place is good as new."

"But I have to be allowed to work in my studio during the day! Ask my designers. Erin? Steve? Tell them how I *have* to be here in my workspace! Everyone who's ever met me knows that much about me!"

"You've already got a contractor and his team working here," Sullivan reassured her. "That's the one good thing. It'll cut your repair time in half. At least."

"It doesn't look like there's any damage to the roof over her studio," I said to the fireman. "So surely she can continue to occupy that space during the day, right?"

"Absolutely." He turned to face Shannon. "In fact, after the fire marshal's checked things out, you can have free rein of the place. So long as it passes the safety inspection. And provided you can make do without heat or electricity."

"Fine," Shannon sniffed. "I can work in the cold

during the day." She was so flustered she kept dragging her fingers through her windblown hair and getting them stuck in the process. "And . . . and we'll just . . . survive this somehow. What choice do we have?"

Michael shrugged. "It could be worse."

"Don't say that, Michael! Whenever anyone puts those kinds of vibrations out into the universe . . . well, it's like you're issuing a *challenge*. Next thing you know, things *do* get worse."

"I just mean that our living quarters didn't catch fire. Your paintings are fine. Nobody got injured."

"True." She clicked her tongue. "At least *this* time, there are no dead carpenters by the front door, thank God."

"This is the same house where that guy managed to kill himself with a nail gun?" a fireman quietly asked the police officer next to me.

I balled my fists but kept silent. Overhearing the question seemed to agitate Shannon once more. She stomped her foot. "Officers, you need to find the person who's trying to destroy me! Don't go giving us any stories about that Duncan man's death being an accident, and the house *accidentally* catching on fire three days later. Somebody's hell-bent on destroying me. If it's not Pate Hamlin, it's got to be some crazed maniac who's jealous of my artistic successes. My choice of careers tends to appeal to the nutcases in this world."

There was an awkward pause. "Was anyone smoking in the attic at any point today?" a firefighter asked.

"No! I never even go up there! This is *exactly* what I *just* told you not to do!" She was literally hopping mad. "I did *not* accidentally drop a lit cigarette and burn my house down!"

"Ma'am," the firefighter said gently, "you'd really be

helping us out here if you all could vacate the premises for the time being."

"You and your people are going to be tromping through my home once we're gone?"

"The fire marshal needs to determine the cause of the blaze."

Shannon started to cry. After just a few seconds she sniffled and asked, "Can't that wait till tomorrow? Please? I need to recuperate in private."

He sighed. "Al? Charlie?" he called over his shoulder to a pair of firemen standing near the small rescue trucks. "How 'bout lending the homeowners a hand? They've gotta grab some personal items." He returned his attention to Shannon. "We have to make sure nobody's going up in the attic till the investigator can check it out. But you can lock up now, and meet him back here around eight or nine tomorrow morning. Okay?"

"Fine, fine," she said through clenched teeth. She dried her eyes. All but two firemen returned to their truck and drove away. Shannon gestured at the heavens and let her hands flop to her sides. "Michael? We need to pack up my plates."

"You're bringing our dishes to the hotel with us?" he asked in dismay.

"No! Not our *dishes*! The heirloom plates in the family room!" She looked back at Sullivan and me and explained unnecessarily, "My ancestors brought those over from Europe in the early 1800s. They came clear across the country on wagon trains. I'm not going to risk having some fireman knock them off the mantelpiece."

"I'll go get them right away," Michael said. He bustled inside.

Steve and I lingered for a moment; we needed to discuss a course of action in private. Shannon hefted up a painting from the lawn and demanded, "Erin? Steve?

And, uh, you two firemen? Help me move my paintings back where we got them."

The five of us collected her art pieces and quickly fell into a step-march, with Shannon leading the way through the front door. She crossed the foyer toward the studio. "I'm going to deadbolt the door to my studio, as well as to the front door. That way I'll know that—"

A crash emanated from the family room. It sounded eerily like a plate shattering. Shannon froze, then leaned face-first against the wall, moaning, "Oh, God. Too much. I can't handle this." She stayed there, her forehead pressed against the brilliant tomato-red surface. Wordlessly, we all set to work putting Shannon's paintings against the wall beside her.

After what felt like a full minute or two, Michael finally emerged from the family room. He was hanging his head. His ears were crimson. In his hands were plate shards. I caught a glimpse of yellow-ochre glaze. Shannon had had three plates that showed oak leaves painted on a solid background. The one he'd broken was the most striking of the three. "Er, Shannon?" Michael said sheepishly. "I'm really, really sorry. It slipped right out of my hand."

She straightened her shoulders, but kept her eyes squeezed tight. "Which plate was it? The lavender, the melon, or the ochre?"

"Well... they all had leaves on them, but this one's yellow."

"My favorite!" she groaned. "Perfect. Emblematic for what's happening to my life."

"I'm sorry, hon."

Sullivan caught my eye. He tapped his watch. I winced; we were late for an appointment to discuss a kitchen remodel with a prospective customer. "Unfortunately, we've got no choice but to get going," he said to the Youngs. "We'll keep in touch on your cell phone. And we'll come out here tomorrow to discuss the roof construction with David."

Shannon gave us a vacant stare. "Fine," she said flatly. "We'll see you tomorrow then. Meanwhile, we can hope that the earth doesn't crack open and fill our home with poisonous snakes."

Audrey phoned as we drove to our appointment to ask what time I'd be home. When I told her five, she said, "Excellent. I'll see you promptly at five."

Her "promptly" seemed odd, but I chose not to explain that "five" had been a rough estimate.

To my enormous surprise, when I walked into my house a few minutes after five, there sat Shannon Young, chatting in the parlor with Audrey Munroe. "Hi, Erin," Audrey said. "We're holding our meeting of the No Big Boxes cochairs here tonight."

"My hosting it suddenly didn't seem appropriate." Shannon mustered a smile.

Hildi meowed at me as she trotted into the room.

"Are you settled in at the hotel, Shannon?" I asked.

"Yes. Me, my husband, and my two remaining heirlooms." She drained the contents of her wineglass and commented to Audrey, "My husband found an appalling time to suddenly become clumsy with plates."

Audrey clucked sympathetically. "On top of getting burned out of your house and home. You really should have allowed Tracy and me to handle this thing ourselves."

Who's Tracy? Handle what *thing, exactly?*

"This is hardly an act of martyrdom," Shannon replied, sounding exactly like a martyr as she refilled her glass from a half-empty bottle of Chianti on the coffee table. "I have more at stake than anyone on the planet... as it turns out." She grimaced. "Apparently, Pate figured if he couldn't buy me out, he'd burn me down."

"A new meaning for the term 'Fire Sale,'" Audrey cracked. Being sympathetic for any length of time has never been one of my landlady's strong points.

"Just you two are meeting tonight?" I asked.

They exchanged glances. "Actually, it's not really a meeting," Audrey replied.

Uh-oh. Audrey was up to something. Whenever she acted mysterious like this, she was usually gearing up to ask a favor that would put me on the spot.

"And there are three of us," she continued. Another woman entered the room, from the direction of the nearest bathroom. "Here she is now. Erin, I'd like you to meet Tracy Osgood. Tracy, this is Erin Gilbert."

The thirtyish woman was pretty, although she was wearing a lot of makeup and too much gardenia-scented perfume. Her smile, however, was warming. "Hi, Erin. We were just talking about you." She spoke with a Texas twang.

"Oh?"

"Did y'all ask her yet?" Tracy perched on the far end of the sofa.

"I was just about to," Audrey replied.

"I have a feeling I should sit down before I hear this," I muttered, as I slipped onto the Queen Anne settee beside me.

"Shannon and I have hatched a plan that involves you, Erin," Audrey began.

"Do tell."

"We'd like you to speak at the Crestview City Council meeting tonight. It starts in two hours. And I've already got dinner for the four of us in the oven."

Shannon said, "Yes, Erin. It would help us all out if

you'd plead our case to the board. After all, if BaseMart really does put a megastore in the field behind my neighborhood, it's going to be terrible for Crestview. And you already know what a disaster it is for me personally. At the hotel after you left, Michael was urging me to sell so he could get a new restaurant going."

"He *was?*"

Audrey sighed. "He misses having his own restaurant. He's told me that before . . . how much he dreams of seeing 'Michael Young's' on the marquee once more."

"I have dreams, too, you know," Shannon snapped. "And none of them involve keeping my husband's business afloat by selling my home and moving into a trailer park. We have a wonderful life that we built for ourselves. I want to be able to enjoy the rewards."

The image of Rebecca in Michael's arms appeared front and center in my mind's eye. Shannon's husband was seemingly far less invested in their "wonderful life" together than she was.

"So are you willing to help us out, Erin?" Shannon wanted to know.

I grimaced at the thought of public speaking. Tracy was nervously fidgeting with her nails. When our eyes met, she gave me a smile. "The rest of us have already spoken out against BaseMart," she told me. "And you're in a profession where you travel to people's homes, all throughout Crestview. The town board will really respect the opinion of someone with your unique perspective."

I sighed. "I'll give it my best shot. I'd feel terrible if I sat back and did nothing. And I do side strongly with you all on this issue."

"Thank you, Erin." Audrey was beaming at me. "I *knew* you wouldn't let us down."

Which brought to mind the possibility that I could

very well make a blathering idiot of myself and "let down" the entire town of Crestview.

Two hours later, my stomach was doing flip-flops. There were at least a hundred people in the small auditorium at the city building. Worse yet, I would be forced to use a microphone. My every little quaver was going to be amplified. I was going to sound like a sick warbler!

The nine council members were seated in front, facing the rows and rows of arena-style seats. The microphone stand was at the front of the center aisle, just five or six feet away from the council president. The good thing about the seating arrangement was that the members of the audience, including Audrey, Shannon, and Michael, would be behind my back. To keep my nerves at bay, I decided to engage myself in some heavy-duty denial. I would pretend that there was no audience, and that I was merely making an appeal for a design job to a family of nine. All of whom happened to be middle-aged and seated in a straight row like judges. And that a couple of them had short-term memory loss, so they were simply *recording* my voice, and hence the need for a microphone. And this family had such a short attention span that my presentation had to take sixty seconds or less.... Yep. Just one big, bizarre, dysfunctional family.

When Audrey rose and announced that I, as a "highly regarded interior designer," would be speaking on behalf of the group, I took a couple of gulps of water and made my way to the microphone. I wished I'd forgone the water; I felt the sudden need to run to the bathroom. A quick confidence-and-optimism mantra did the trick. Introducing myself, I said, "It's easy enough to discover what's happened in the towns that BaseMart has moved into in the last ten years since the chain's inception. A few minutes of research on the Internet will paint a dismal story for you." I was speaking too rapidly, I realized, and scolded myself to slow down. My knees were trembling so badly that I was afraid I'd set my whole body in motion—clatter my way right out the door like a windup toy. "When BaseMart moves into a town, all of the mom-and-pop stores are driven out. BaseMart employees are paid minimum wage, and often as part-timers, so the corporation doesn't have to pay their fair share of benefits.

"What happened to every single one of those towns will happen to our beloved Crestview. In exchange for our thirty pieces of silver—or rather, for our tax-base incentives—Crestview's identity will be destroyed, including the quaint charm that's made it a tourist spot. When we say 'No Big Boxes,' the ultimate 'big box' is the coffin that Crestview will be building for itself."

I took what felt like my first breath of air since I'd started talking, and returned to my seat, between Audrey and Michael Young. Audrey whispered, "That was very good, Erin. Well done."

"Thanks."

Michael whispered into my ear, "I think you convinced the majority of holdouts on the board." He patted my hand, which made me cringe.

"Oh, come now," Pate cried, rising. He didn't go to the microphone and was clearly speaking out of turn. "If BaseMart was such a terrible thing for Colorado, why would I be putting the store in *my own backyard*? I know better than anyone else the congestion and decrease in property value that the store will cause. That's why I've offered to buy out my neighbor's property."

He'd fallen for my trap! I sprang to my feet. "Is that so, Mr. Hamlin? Maybe, then, you can explain why it is that this is the *fifth* house that you've owned, which borders on the property line of the *fifth* upcoming store. In each case, you bought the house a year or two before the proposed store site was announced. Then, three of those four previous times, you *bulldozed* your own house!"

Pate's jaw dropped. He stammered, "I don't intend to do that this time. Those places were different. Crestview is my *home*."

The audience mumbled and stirred in their seats as if with collective skepticism.

The president pounded his gavel and told us to take our seats. I felt too giddy to listen as a dozen other citizens rose to speak against BaseMart; nobody spoke in its favor. After several minutes of deliberation, the council voted to give the county officials "our strongest recommendation" that BaseMart not be allowed to erect a store in Crestview. Tracy Osgood shrieked with joy, hugged each of us, then all but skipped ahead of us and out the double doors. Pate, all the while, sat glowering at her. I avoided his gaze and tried to leave quietly while the board meeting continued to other matters.

I sensed a man's forceful strides catching up to me as I crossed the lobby. Before I could reach the door, a deep voice said, "Congratulations, Erin." I stopped and turned. Pate's handsome features were stony. "Quite the effective speech you gave just now. How did you get your information?"

I squared my shoulders. "Power of the Internet. I looked up the street addresses of the neighborhoods where you've built your stores and compared them to phone directories. Then I placed a couple of phone calls. Local residents were all too happy to tell me precisely what went on in their neighborhoods."

"You're a regular Sherlock Holmes, Miss Gilbert."

"I doubt Holmes would have cared much for Internet research. Too easy." Our gazes locked. It was unfortunate that he was such a dynamic, attractive man. It made the struggle of being on opposite sides that much harder. "In any case, I was simply reporting the truth."

"The 'truth' can look very different according to the beholder, Miss Gilbert. You've won the first round tonight, but I was expecting that to happen. I haven't even brought in my corporate-lawyer big guns."

"When all else fails, throw legalese at 'em."

He sighed. "There's always somebody like you, in every town. Somebody who thinks they can play the little Dutch boy and plug the hole in the dike. But you can't stop us, and you shouldn't try. BaseMart *isn't* a flood, Erin. Nor a hurricane. There's no feng shui involved. There's only the march of progress, and the future of American commerce."

"I can't tell you how strongly I hope you're wrong about this country's future. But good for you to finally have learned how to pronounce feng shui." *If none of its lessons.*

With startling intensity, he held my gaze and said calmly, "Like it or not, Miss Gilbert, I always win in the end."

It isn't healthy to take one's diet so seriously as to be made miserable. Chocolate comes from beans, which are vegetables, and wine comes from grapes. That's two servings of vegetables and fruit right there!

—Audrey Munroe

Though I felt physically exhausted, I lay awake for well over an hour after we'd returned home from the city council meeting. Below me I could hear Audrey rattling around. It sounded as though she might be moving some furniture. Hildi, who was curled on the pillow beside me, looked at me as I propped myself up on my elbows. We shared a common thought. "Time for some warm milk, isn't it, sweetie?"

She purred her agreement. I rose and donned my dusty-rose robe and tan slippers. She raced me down the stairs.

Audrey was indeed moving furniture—putting a blockade of the kitchen stools in front of the refrigerator. "Oh, I'm sorry, Erin. Did I wake you?" she asked when she spotted me in the doorway.

"No, my brain seems to be wide awake when the rest of me is exhausted. Which makes you kind of wonder where one's common sense is supposed to reside."

She angled a fourth barstool on its side atop the other three stools as I spoke. Audrey was perfectly proportioned, but must have gained a couple of pounds lately. Once or twice a year, Chef Michael made one too many rich entrees on her show, "Domestic Bliss with Audrey Munroe," and she insisted she either had to lose weight or risk being replaced by someone thinner. "Going on a diet?"

"Yes. And I read in one of your feng shui books that putting furniture in your path to the refrigerator gives your will power a chance to kick into gear."

"That's true, but your choice of furniture and placement needs adjusting. Now we have no place to sit at the island, plus Hildi and I need access to the milk." My kitty, to her credit, had curled up on the moon-and-star patterned rug by the back door and was licking her paws patiently. We'd recently installed a small cat door there, which Hildi had taken to sitting next to, at least, although she almost never actually used the thing.

Audrey examined her arrangement of stools and sighed. "Too extreme?"

"By a factor of four." I walked to the far side of the kitchen table. "All we need to do is move the table over by two feet and swing it around by a quarter turn. Then we'll have to round the table every time we want to reach the refrigerator."

She frowned. "When we're coming from the main

entrance, that's true. But not when I'm coming home and entering through the back door."

"We're moving the captain's chair to handle that, as well. Grab the other side of the table."

She hesitated and her frown grew deeper. "But it'll take no time at all to walk around the table."

"Moving a piece of furniture into your path isn't intended to form an obstacle course, Audrey. It's simply a psychological trick—a mental memory jog. This way, you walk into the kitchen, and you see the table. That gives your will power an extra second to kick in, which is all you need to do the trick, if you really want it to. Better yet, you'll see the nice, inviting table, and you'll pull out a chair, sit down, and read the newspaper."

"I prefer to sit at the kitchen island when I read the paper."

I gestured at the barstools. "Your seats are currently forming a blockade."

She sighed, unconvinced.

"Audrey, the point is that we all tend to be drawn to the first thing that we see when we walk into a room. That's why, when you walk into your office, for example, you want your desk to be the first thing you see, so that you go right over to it and get straight to work."

I lifted my end of the table. Audrey was still not budging. Hildi released a plaintive meow. I winked at her to silently signal that it wouldn't be much longer.

"If we move the table, the pendant light will be off-kilter," she whined.

"We can attach a ceiling hook temporarily and

lengthen the chain. And it beats stacking the barstools. Seriously, Audrey. If this were a segment on your show, would *that* be the solution you'd recommend?"

"No," she said forlornly. "But I like the table where it is. And having the captain's chair in the corner, as well."

"Audrey. You're creating more fictitious obstacles than four barstools and all the furniture in this room combined. Plus, I already promised Hildi some milk."

She put her hands on her hips. "Well, *I* can't remove the stools, or I'll be standing at the refrigerator, with full access!"

I took a moment to stay calm, then returned the four barstools to their logical places.

As I moved the last stool, Audrey clicked her tongue. "Honestly, Erin. You're a wizard when it comes to dreaming up creative solutions for your difficult clients. You're not giving up on me this easily, are you? What about a big potted plant in front of the fridge?"

"There was an article in last month's 'Arts and Living' section of the *Sentinel* that said red wine was being tested for its powers for negating calories. Remember?"

"Oh, that's right! I *do* remember that article. See? *Now* you're talking." She gleefully crossed the room and flicked on the light to head downstairs to her wonderful wine cellar. As she descended the stairs, she called after her, "Oh, Erin? Since you're getting the milk out anyway, would you please get me the brie? And a box of crackers?"

chapter 8

Sullivan and I joined the Youngs at their house the following morning—to be supportive if nothing else—while the fire investigator went to work. Every creaking floorboard above our heads made me flinch, half expecting him to come crashing down. My eyes stung from the lingering odors of yesterday's fire and Shannon's cigarette smoke. There was considerable water damage to the drywall in the hallway and the den, but that could easily be replaced. Otherwise, except for the odor, the main level was in remarkably good shape.

We sat in the kitchen and silently nursed cups of takeout coffee, which Sullivan and I had supplied. This was currently my second-favorite room in the house (after the art studio). The stainless-steel appliances and elegant appointments throughout were top of the line. Walnut cabinetry warmed the black granite countertops and backsplashes. The walls were a lovely sage, and the cream-colored ceramic tiles lent this space a timeless, classic character. The built-in kitchen table was hand-planed to look antique, with surprisingly comfortable solid pine benches; the kitchen was relatively small, and by eliminating seatbacks, the owners garnered precious inches from the pathway into the formal dining room.

Yesterday, Sullivan and I had completed the reworked design for Shannon and Michael's remodel, which was going to bring the entire house up to the graceful beauty of the kitchen and studio. But the Youngs were too tense and distracted with the fire investigator in the house for any kind of meaningful design discussion right now.

At length, the investigator—a heavyset man with a slight limp and beady eyes—came into the kitchen. Michael rose and offered him a cup of coffee, which he declined. "I determined the cause of the blaze," he announced. "Faulty wiring."

"But what *caused* the faulty wiring?" Michael asked, still standing, his hands jammed into the back pockets of his black chinos. "Was it one of our workmen?"

The investigator peered at him. "Why? Did you have an electrician out here recently?"

"No. But how else could our wiring just suddenly go bad?"

"You've obviously had some trouble with critters up there. One of 'em could have gnawed through the shielding on your wires, causing a short."

"*Or* it could have been someone deliberately tampering with our wires," Shannon interjected.

The inspector frowned at her. "No accelerant was

used, ma'am. It's many times more likely that this was an accident."

Which meant he wasn't ruling out arson completely.

"That's a relief," Michael said.

"We'll need to get a time estimate on the repairs," I said, glancing at Sullivan. *Plus I need to look for clues about who might have been up there recently.* "Is it safe to go into the attic? As long as we only step on the joists?"

"S'pose so. You won't want to trust the pull-down ladder. Otherwise, the floor is structurally sound. Most of the damage was along the east wall where the blaze started. And the roof itself."

"Getting back to my point about the wires," Shannon persisted, "wouldn't tampering with them *without* a telltale accelerant be the smart way to start a fire and not get caught?"

"You'd have to have a solid base of knowledge about electricity and electrical fires. Ma'am, I can tell for a fact there was a short between a hot wire and a ground wire, which can only happen when the shielding between 'em is missing. That eventually created a hot spot and a fire."

"So that's the end of that," Michael stated, casting a stern glance in his wife's direction. Shannon curled her lip and grumbled unintelligibly into her coffee cup. After thanking him again, Michael ushered the investigator to the door.

In a low voice, Shannon informed me, "The police made the same noises about your brother's death . . . that it was most likely an accident. But the shielding could have been deliberately stripped off. I can't buy that we coincidentally had two freak accidents within three days of each other. Obviously, someone out there will stop at nothing to drive me out of my home. And I just know it's that damned Pate Hamlin!"

I said gently, "Maybe so, but I've got to say that Pate

made a good point when he told the police about his having too much to lose."

"Erin!" She banged her fist on the table. "Pate's a ruthless son of a bitch who doesn't care about anybody but himself! As far as he's concerned, we either get out of his way or he'll run right over us!"

I held my tongue and felt the heat of both her and Sullivan's glares. I couldn't argue with her statement—especially not after experiencing Pate's veiled threats at the council meeting last night—but I was certain that the man wasn't just a heartless, egocentric jerk. And yet, among my mental list of people with the opportunity to have taken my brother's life, Pate Hamlin was the wealthiest and had the most public exposure. That surely meant he would fall the hardest if Taylor had somehow collected evidence that could ruin him.

No sooner had Michael reclaimed his seat than someone knocked on the door. He promptly went to answer and, a moment later, brought David Lewis into the kitchen. Michael was saying to him, "The arson investigator was just here. The fire was an accident. Bad wiring."

"Thank God. So there's no chance one of my men loused up the wiring and started the fire?"

"The investigator seemed to think it was an animal gnawing on the wires."

"Good."

"Why were you worried it was one of your men?" Shannon wanted to know.

David looked at her, then cast a guilty glance in my direction. "Well, um, Taylor went up there a couple days back. Must've been Friday morning. Said a fuse had blown, and he wanted to double-check everything."

"This is the first time you've mentioned that." Michael's tone was skeptical.

"Yeah, I know. But... if the expert thinks it was accidental, it must be. I don't see how fiddling with wires on a Friday could've started a fire on Tuesday."

Nor would my poor, hapless brother have had the slightest motive to start one.

Sullivan said, "We brought the updated plans for the remodel, David. After we develop an action plan for repairing the roof and the attic, let's go over them."

"Sure thing."

Sullivan left to fetch the designs. I rose and threw out my styrofoam cup. "I need to take a look at your attic. To see how much work needs to be done. Can I borrow a ladder?"

Shannon got to her feet. "There's one in the garage. Michael can get it for you." Michael had only just now reclaimed his seat and took a slurp of coffee. Shannon clicked her tongue, then said, "Hon? Did you hear me?"

"Oh, right. I'll go get the ladder." He started to rise.

"Nah. Stay put, Michael," David said, heading for the door. "I'll just get mine off my truck. That'll be faster."

"Thanks, but let me come give you a hand."

Shannon winced as the door banged shut behind the men.

A split second later, Michael called, "Sorry, sweetie." My hunch was that his door slams were a pet peeve of hers.

"I'm sure our Christmas decorations and old clothes upstairs are history," Shannon told me glumly.

"Probably so," I muttered, distracted. With David and Michael fetching a ladder, they'd be intent upon climbing into the attic immediately. That would prevent me from searching up there first.

All three men returned and quickly set up the ladder.

"I'm the lightest and should inspect the area first," I interposed hastily.

David dismissed my suggestion with the groaner "Age before beauty," and climbed the rungs.

"Go ahead," Sullivan said to me with a mischievous wink.

Luckily, I'd anticipated having to climb a ladder today and was wearing slacks. Even so, I said, "No, you go first. We might as well stick with our macho-before-magnificent battle plan."

Michael chuckled. Sullivan merely smirked. I gave him a quick signal with my eyes and hoped he understood that he should hurry up there and keep an eye on David while I made a search. Sullivan climbed the ladder. I went up last. As I gingerly stepped off the ladder, I spotted something nestled among the ashes and soot: a black, silk-covered button.

Ang Chung was apparently missing a button from his favorite robe.

We already knew that two rooms' worth of Sheetrock needed to be replaced. The attic would need to be gutted and rebuilt. The roof would also need to be razed and rebuilt. The triangular roof supports had to be replaced, which would be the most time-consuming part of the process. Several boxes along the opposite wall had survived the blaze, though Shannon and Michael were going to have to inspect their contents to see if they'd been irreparably damaged even so.

Both David and Steve got busy on the phones trying to tap into their substantial connections in the construction world to find a means to get Shannon's roof repaired as quickly as possible. They soon hit pay dirt: A local roofing subcontractor that David frequently used had been stiffed on a multiple-house job. As a result, he already had the major support structures in stock that Shannon's house needed. Despite his previous record of foot-dragging, David was now apparently going to more than make amends. He estimated that he could install a whole new roof in less than two weeks. A time frame like that was utterly unheard of for such a big job, especially when insurance companies were involved.

As we left the Youngs' house and got into the van, Sullivan grinned at me. "We finally caught a break on Shannon's house. It's amazing that David's going to be able to fix the place that quick."

"Yes, it is. Although I'm less convinced than ever before that the fire was a mere accident. Take a look at this." I pulled the button from my pocket. "I found that in the attic, right next to the ladder."

"Gotta be Ang's."

"Right. And why would a feng shui consultant be climbing around in a storage attic?"

"Other than to set fire to the house, you mean?" He handed me back the button and started the engine. "Thing is, that'd be real incriminating, if we were talking about a reputable consultant. But this is Ang Chung. He'll say anything to explain this away. The guy churns out more pure fiction than Stephen King." He backed out of the driveway and onto the road.

I sighed. "True. All the button really proves is that Ang was recently in that attic. And he'll claim he went up there to get a reading on the *ba-guas* or something." (*Ba-guas* are the octagonal shapes that determine the optimal locations for various types of activities in a building.)

"Even so, you should give it to the police."

"Oh, jeez! I'm such an idiot! Chain of evidence! I removed the evidence from the scene of the crime! Now it really *is* worthless!"

"Ouch," Sullivan muttered quietly. He patted my

thigh—to be reassuring, I'm sure, though I was a little startled by the gesture.

Discouraged, I vowed to give Linda Delgardio the silk-covered button as soon as I could.

Sullivan and I went our separate ways during lunch. I grabbed a salad and joined a couple of girlfriends at the gym for a yoga class. Far from being able to relax, my brain was filled with images of Ang creeping around in Shannon's attic and messing with the wiring. Reportedly, the *ba-gua* could be used to predict the future of a home and its occupants. If only we'd been working with an authentic master instead of with Ang Chung, perhaps that ancient art could somehow reveal the home's secrets. Such as who had murdered my brother within its walls and had set fire to its roof.

chapter 9

R*emembering Taylor's funeral was in a mere two* hours, my mood was decidedly low when I returned to the office. Sullivan was there, hard at work at his desk. Unexpectedly, I suddenly found myself wishing he and I were better friends. In the past three years, my adoptive mother had died, my biological father had died, and now so had my half brother. I was starting to feel like the last remaining duck at a shooting gallery. I would have loved to find reassurance and comfort in Sullivan's arms, I thought as I hung up my coat.

"How come you didn't tell me about your speech at the city council meeting last night?" Sullivan snarled at me in lieu of a greeting. He didn't even look up.

That statement was about as far from what I needed to hear from him at that moment as imaginable. Then again, "Drop dead" would have been worse—a realization that cheered me somewhat.

I'd been in no hurry to bring up the subject of the council board meeting. Pate was the second man I'd considered an archrival, yet found myself strongly attracted to nevertheless. Sullivan had been the first. No doubt a good psychotherapist would have a field day with that. It probably had something to do with my father deserting my mother—my adoptive mother, that is—and me. But if so, I detested discovering that my behavior was predictable.

"Erin?" His hazel eyes challenged mine.

"I should have mentioned it. Sorry. Though it wasn't exactly a speech. Just thirty seconds of my opinions."

Sullivan scowled at me.

"Did they cover the council meeting in today's paper?" I asked.

"I don't know. I dropped my subscription and haven't read it. Got my info over the phone in this case. Pate's on the warpath."

"Uh-oh." I sat down. We'd arranged our desks in an L-shape with our backs to adjacent walls. Pate was likely going to *figuratively* put our backs to the wall, now that I'd publicly blasted his BaseMart empire. "He kind of warned me last night that he wasn't thrilled. Did he call during lunch, wanting to curse me out, or something?"

He nodded. "About twenty minutes ago. Though he wasn't cursing. Just said that you wasted your breath last night."

"He's probably right. All that happened is the city council voted to recommend to the county officials that they deny BaseMart's building permits. That's really the extent of the city's power over the county."

"Well, Pate claims he's got enough influence with government officials to get the go-ahead to build."

"Let's hope he's bluffing."

"No kidding." Sullivan's eyes flashed with anger. "Pate claims that the most the *city* officials can do to him is force him to put the entrance to BaseMart on the opposite side of that huge land parcel he owns behind his house. Which will tick off the homeowners in both Creekside Estates and Wellshire Manors. *And* he says that the word's already out among those homeowners that it was partly *your* fault that he had to redesign the access to his store."

My heart sank. Sullivan had just named two of the ritziest neighborhoods in all of Crestview County, which also meant they were two of the most lucrative locales for interior design jobs. He continued, "He's threatening to begin a door-to-door campaign, letting everyone in Wellshire and Creekside know that he'll surround BaseMart with tree-filled parks to hide their view of the store. But only—"

I groaned and held up a hand. "Don't tell me. But only if he can put the main entrance—and the BaseMart Auto Repair Shop—on *Shannon's* property."

"Correct. Give that little lady a cigar."

I sighed. "We can always spin it that I was merely being loyal to my client's needs by speaking up to prevent her home from getting flattened. Surely the homeowners in Wellshire and Creekside will appreciate my dedication to our clients?"

"On an intellectual level, sure. But when they're dealing with traffic noise and lowered property values, they—"

Rebecca Berringer barged through the door. She smiled sweetly at Sullivan. "Good afternoon, Steve. I'm afraid I have something *personal* to discuss with your business partner." She indicated me with a flick of her wrist, but her blue eyes remained fixed on him.

"No problem," he replied graciously. "I was just about to head out for a latte, anyway. Can I get you ladies anything?"

"No, thanks," we replied simultaneously. "But you don't have to be the one to leave, Steve," I said, rising. "I'll just step outside with Rebecca for a minute."

"That's okay. I'll be right back. Call my cell if you change your mind about wanting something."

"Thanks so much," Rebecca cooed to him, stroking his arm as he walked past her. *Gag me! Rebecca was beautiful, and she knew it. She was making my client's life miserable, my beloved landlady miserable, and I didn't want her within fifty yards of my business partner!*

She watched him leave, then leveled a glare at me the instant the door shut behind him. "I just had an upsetting conversation with two police officers, thanks to you."

Uh-oh. The photographs. "What about?"

"They told me that 'an anonymous source' gave them some suggestive pictures that they're certain were taken by Taylor Duncan."

"I don't follow."

She rolled her eyes. "Don't play games with me, Erin. You know full well what I'm talking about. Yes, I was having an affair with Michael Young, but I ended it *weeks* ago. It was a dead-end relationship. Michael will never leave Shannon. Besides which, I told him the truth... that I've fallen for somebody else."

"That really isn't any of my business." *Although she was lying. "Weeks" ago, Taylor had still been in jail, unable to photograph their tryst with his Polaroid.*

"No, it *isn't* your business," she said sharply. "Which is exactly my point. It wasn't hard to figure out who the 'anonymous source' was who gave pictures to the police that Taylor shot of me and Michael. Considering Taylor was *your* brother."

"We all have a civic duty to give any possible evidence from a crime to the police—"

"Oh, please, Erin," she cut in. "Civic duty was hardly your motive."

"Of course it was! I want the police to arrest whoever killed my brother!"

"My *private affair*, which, again, had already *ended*, has *nothing* to do with your stupid brother accidentally or intentionally shooting a nail into his skull."

"Taylor did no such thing. But he *might* have tried to blackmail you or Michael with those pictures. And *that* could have been a motive for killing him."

"Give me a break! In this day and age? Blackmailing a two-bit chef for having an affair with a *single* woman? No way! But you go right ahead, Erin. Tell yourself you were just being a good citizen. *I*, for one, am very aware how badly you want to get me out of the picture."

"What are you talking about?"

She gave a haughty toss of her head. "I'm your biggest rival for Steve Sullivan's heart. You want him all for yourself."

I felt a pang that I hoped wasn't a stab of recognition at being so bluntly confronted with what I feared was the truth. "Sullivan can make his own decisions about his personal life," I fired back. "But I'm not about to sit back and watch you fawn all over him, while you're fooling around with my client's husband. Sullivan's a friend. He deserves better than you."

She looked angry enough to hit me. I half wanted her to, so I could hit her back. "Erin, I'd focus first on my own behavior, if I were you."

"*I* haven't done anything to be ashamed of."

"Oh, no? A police officer told me he saw you blatantly

flirting with *my* client after the fire yesterday! Pate's a married man, too, you know. He and his wife have separated, but they're not divorced."

"That police officer was spouting nonsense... probably to get *you* rattled enough to say something incriminating! I *haven't* been flirting with Pate. And *we* certainly haven't been having an affair. We've barely exchanged two sentences. And those weren't even friendly, let alone flirtatious."

"Bull!" she snorted. "Get with the program, Erin! Just who do you think you're dealing with here? You can't treat me like this, you know!" She wagged a finger in my face. "I wield a lot more power than *you* do in this town. Guess who is now in charge of Crestview's branch of the I.D.A.?"

I.D.A. stood for Interior Designers Association. "Oooo," I said in mock fright. "Heaven save me from Crestview's designers. They're almost as powerful as the N.R.A."

"When things get ugly, Erin, just remember: You started this. You turned those embarrassing photos into the police. If you'd had any decency, you'd have given them to me."

"The photos were *evidence*! In a *murder!*"

"The only thing those pictures revealed was that your brother was a peeping Tom. Before I'm through with you you're going to find yourself struggling to get jobs designing *outhouses*!" She whirled and headed for the door, but then stopped. Slowly, she turned and grinned at me while reaching into her coat pocket. She snatched up her cell phone and dialed. With infuriating casualness, she leaned back against the wall.

After a moment, she straightened and cooed into her phone, "Hi, Steve? It's Rebecca. I've changed my mind about having you get me a latte. In fact, I have something important to talk to you about. I'll be right there." She cast a triumphant smile over her shoulder at me as she trotted out the door.

The phone rang an instant later, and I was so distracted I growled "Gilbert and Sullivan" by mistake.

"Erin? It's Shannon," our client sobbed. "I've got to talk to you. Now!"

"What's wrong?"

"It's Pate. He's running a smear campaign against us! He's talking to all my neighbors! And all this pounding on my roof is killing me! It sounds like they're dropping pianos up there, every few seconds!"

He was already *lobbying his neighbors against us?!* "Why don't you go back to your hotel and try to—"

"I *can't!* Somebody has to keep an eye on my artwork! And it sure as hell isn't going to be Michael!"

"Fine. I'll . . . be right there."

I weighed calling Sullivan, but figured he had his hands full with Rebecca Berringer at the moment. (I could only hope not literally.) So I tore out of the office, leaving it unlocked, and raced to Shannon's house.

The gist of Shannon's lamentations was exactly as Sullivan had forewarned. Pate was taking his case to the homeowners on the opposite side of the enormous land parcel he'd purchased for BaseMart. Those neighborhoods would be adversely affected by BaseMart if Shannon's property remained unscathed. Yet, there also was some conflicting information floating around. As best we could gather, Pate was now pitching an either-or ultimatum: He was threatening to develop *either* a BaseMart—which he'd surround with mature landscaping—*or* high-density housing, meaning condos or apartment complexes, with no parklike buffer zones.

Shannon was in a frenzy, saying we should "just give up and burn my house to the ground! Let the bad guy win!"

Nothing I did or said could calm her. Finally I vowed to discuss the matter with Pate and headed alone across the street. As I made the short journey, I bypassed my usual confidence-and-optimism mantra and repeated to myself: *He's not all* that *handsome. . . .*

By the time I rang his doorbell, I'd convinced myself that he was a conniving, heartless, money-grubbing S.O.B. The door opened. My jaw dropped. It wasn't Pate. It was Tracy Osgood—the woman Audrey and Shannon had trusted to manage the finances for the No Big Boxes campaign.

"Tracy?" I said, stunned.

"Hi, Erin." She came outside and shut the door behind her. She was wearing a snug-fitting angora sweater and black slacks tucked into her knee-high black cowboy boots embossed with silver lassoes. "This is really unfortunate timing. I'm hardly ever here. This is only the third or fourth time I've been inside this house in my entire life."

"And yet you're here now, because . . . ? Oh, my God. Are *you* Pate's wife?"

Even beneath all that makeup, her cheeks grew rosier. "We're legally separated . . . and our divorce will be finalized very soon."

"Is he here now?"

"Pate's on the phone?" She seemed to be flustered; her Texas accent was ratcheted up a notch, and she'd turned her statement into a question. She glanced over her shoulder at the closed door. "He'll probably come out any second to check up on me."

"Why are you working for No Big Boxes? To get back at your estranged husband?"

She shook her head. "I wanted to stop Pate from destroying the neighborhood. I'm fixin' to take ownership of this house, so as I can live in Crestview permanently. I like it much better than my current home in Denver. The bastard built a BaseMart right behind it. *After* he'd moved out himself. When I found out he was fixin' to do the same thing here, I was fit to be tied. Figured I'd best pitch in at No Big Boxes to—"

She broke off and whirled around as the door opened. Ignoring her, Pate said, "Hello, Erin. Are you here to see my ex-wife?" He was dressed casually—leather sandals, gray slacks, and a bright sea-foam–colored long-sleeve shirt. I'd obviously caught him at a bad time; his face was flushed, and his tone chill. "I saw you two conferring at the meeting last night." He seemed to have deliberately angled himself so that he wouldn't have to face Tracy.

"No. I didn't even know that she... was here." My cheeks were blazing. I hoped he didn't realize how shocked I was at Tracy's decision not to tell me or, apparently, her fellow members of No Big Boxes that she just happened to be married to their archnemesis.

"I see. In that case, you must have come over because Shannon told you my latest plans. I'm giving our neighbors the choice between BaseMart and a huge condo development."

"You're thinking of putting in a bunch of *condos* now?" Tracy cried. "So *I* lose out either way? How dare you!"

"Give me a break!" Pate glowered at her. "Our agreement states clearly that I can develop the land behind this property. You can stay put in the house in Denver if you don't approve of my plans for *my* land."

"I like this house better. Especially now that you built a BaseMart in the backyard of *my* home! I should've known you'd go right ahead and destroy this home too! I should have demanded a cash buyout!"

Someone gasped behind me. Shannon was standing in the middle of the street, staring up at us. "Tracy! What are you doing here?"

"My ex-wife is trying to stake a claim on her territory," Pate declared with a laser-hot glare to Tracy, "which includes half the house, but *not* the land parcel behind it."

Before Shannon could reply, he added, "I was just discussing my new idea about the condos with Erin, Shannon. I'm afraid your property value has just plummetted. It's probably worth only about half what it was last week, before my development proposal to the county became fodder for the general public. But I'd be willing to split the difference if you'd like to sell. Shall we say... seventy-five percent of my original offer?"

"I'm going to *kill* you for this!" she shrilled.

I grabbed her arm. "Come on, Shannon. Let's go back over to your home and discuss strategies."

Red-faced and cursing, she let me lead her back home. As I ushered her through the door, she wailed, "*Now* do you see what a horrid, hateful man he is?"

"Yes, but there *were* extenuating circumstances. Apparently I interrupted him in the middle of an argument with his estranged wife. So we can't really expect him to be—"

"Well? *Do* something, Erin! Get me out of this mess! Otherwise, I'm going to have no choice but to cave in and sell my house *and* my soul to that devil of a man!"

"We're not out of options, Shannon. I'm going to tell Audrey about Pate's latest plot. She has a lot of influential friends around town. She might be able to get someone with power to pull some strings and rezone that property. Maybe we can declare it as a wetland, or something, and get it protected."

"Oh, sure." She rolled her eyes. "A wetland. Which is bone dry. In the meantime, I'll start packing."

Her cell phone chirped. "About time!" she said to me as she glanced down at her phone. "It's Michael calling me back on his cell." She pressed a button with her thumb. "Hi. What took you so long?" She listened, then told me, "He's on his way home now." To Michael, she said, "I was getting some good work done, till Jerk-face Hamlin showed up at the door. If he can't construct a BaseMart, he's threatening to build hundreds of condos on his property. Apparently the main entrance would be where his house sits now." Pause. "*I'll* say it is! We'll be facing a heavily traveled T in the road, Michael! That's hideous feng shui. And he dropped his offer to buy our place to seventy-five percent of his original offer." She drew a halting breath. "He still wants to put a car repair garage on my property. A *garage*, Michael! Right where I've created my artwork throughout my entire life!" She was in tears. To her husband's reply, she cried, "You should have listened to me! I've told you all along he wasn't a *nice guy*. Ang Chung warned me about Pate's terrible tao vibrations."

Tears streaming, she listened, and her wet eyes widened. "You mean, you're willing to stand up to him, after all? Really?" She gave me a tentative smile. "Okay, then. I will. . . . I love you, too." She hung up and gave me her first real smile in days. "Erin, go talk to Audrey like you said. No need for me to start packing. I'm going to build myself a slingshot, instead. We'll be David, and we'll take on Goliath."

"That's great news. Audrey and I will help in any way we can." I glanced at the thick plastic sheeting that separated the addition from the rest of the house. "How's the construction for the new room coming along?"

She grinned. "Oh, Erin. It's just fabulous! Ang's idea for the glass column just *utterly* makes the room!"

I pushed the plastic aside and entered the room to see for myself, saying, "It's great that the column is working so well, Shannon, but I have to say that Ang didn't..." I let my voice fade, distracted. Indeed, the glass column looked spectacular. It glowed with a nearly ethereal light. However, a rumbling engine outside was only growing louder by the second. And the plywood floor was shaking.

It sounded as if some heavy machinery was headed straight at me. I bolted out of the room, pushing Shannon back through the plastic in the entranceway with me.

A horrific crash resounded behind us. I whirled around. Shannon let out a piercing scream. The wood supporting the plastic sheeting snapped, and the plastic fell away, giving us a clear view of the devastation.

As if the sturdy new walls were merely balsa wood, the room crumpled. An enormous bulldozer burst through the wall. The seat of the huge yellow machine was empty. And it was heading our way.

chapter 10

h*uddled together, Shannon and I watched* helplessly as the north and west walls and the ceiling of the new room collapsed. The glorious column of glass bricks shattered. The plywood subflooring buckled.

I had to find a way to get to the controls! Just then a man bolted inside through the gaping hole where the glass-brick corner once stood. Cursing profusely, he scrambled up into the seat and fumbled with the controls. The growling machine fell silent.

We stood there in shock as the dust settled. It looked as though we stood inside a gingerbread house and some giant ogre had taken a big bite from one corner.

"Is everybody all right?" the bulldozer operator asked. If I remembered correctly from the six weeks ago that we'd been introduced, his name was Hal. Or maybe Hank.

"I think so," I answered. *Except that all of our hard work is now in ruins.*

"Thank God for that much," he muttered as he jumped down from the machine. The color had drained from his face. His belt was unfastened. He'd apparently been indisposed when someone had started up the heavy vehicle's engine.

A pair of workmen trotted partway toward us and silently surveyed the damage from the front yard, perhaps afraid to come closer. Hal or Hank turned and yelled at them. "Who the hell turned on my dozer and set the throttle lock?"

Both men pleaded innocent. Michael suddenly charged inside through the garage door. "My God! I heard the crash from the garage. I thought a bomb had dropped! Is everybody all right? Shannon?"

"We're fine," I answered. His wife was still clinging to me, trembling. She made no move to go to him.

"Who's responsible for this?" he demanded of the workmen.

Hal or Hank said, "It's my dozer. But it was turned off."

David Lewis arrived on the scene. Panting, he shoved his men aside and stepped into the wake of the bulldozer's damage. "Jeez! What the—"

"Where've you been?" Michael snapped at him.

"I was outside on a ladder, inspecting the work on the roof. What the hell happened here? Hank! How could you plow into the house like this?"

"I *didn't*! Somebody started it up and engaged the throttle lock."

"And where were *you?*" David shouted. "Why'd you leave the key in the ignition?"

Hank's beet-red cheeks colored another ten percent. "Er, I... was in the can."

"So nobody saw anything? Somebody just hopped into the dozer and started it up?"

The men all muttered excuses to their boss, shuffling uneasily under his furious glare. In the meantime, the trauma finally sank in for Shannon. "Oh, Michael," she whimpered. "First our roof. Now this! Look at our house!"

He put an arm around her shoulder protectively. "It's okay. It doesn't matter. It was just the new construction. We're not even staying here at night. The team will rebuild. That's all there is to it."

"Erin and I were in that room *seconds* before it happened. A bulldozer nearly mowed us both down, Michael! This is outrageous!"

"You're right, Shannon," David interjected. "It is." He glared at Hank and stabbed a finger at the yellow bulldozer. "Get that thing out of here. *Now!* We're all working overtime and getting this mess cleaned up and rebuilt pronto. So you'd all better call your families and tell 'em you'll be late for dinner. And maybe for breakfast tomorrow morning."

The men exchanged anxious gazes. "But... we were shutting things down an hour early today," Hank protested. "The funeral. Remember?"

Oh, jeez! Taylor's service! I'd lost track of the time! I'd promised Emily I'd pick her up!

David winced, then nodded. "Right. Of course."

"You can't all leave me with this mess!" Shannon protested. Just then, both Rebecca Berringer and Pate Hamlin approached, stopping at a respectful distance at the edge of the lawn. "What do *you* think you're looking at!" Shannon shrilled at them.

"We just wanted to make sure everyone's all right," Rebecca called back.

"Yes, we're fine. You missed me again, Pate," Shannon sniped.

Rebecca snorted and turned away. But Pate stayed his ground for a moment, gazing at me. He looked sad.

"Shannon, Michael," I said gently, "I'm so sorry, but I have to go pick up my mother for Taylor's service. I hate to leave you now, but—"

"We're fine. Just go. We were planning on going, too, but now..." Michael stared at the gaping hole in the wall. "Looks like we'll be filling out insurance forms all afternoon instead."

"And talking to the police," I agreed. "This had to have been deliberate."

The Gilbert and Sullivan tune "Little Buttercup" had begun to play. I realized with a start that the song had to be coming from *my* cell phone; Sullivan must have sneaked my phone out of my purse yesterday and downloaded the song. I'd mentioned to him a few weeks ago that I'd been searching for that particular ring tone, because the tune "never failed to make me smile." I'd spoken too soon; that was before Taylor had been murdered. Now I dashed to my purse and swept up the phone. Sullivan's name was displayed as the caller, and my "Hello" was crankier than I'd intended.

"Hey, Gilbert. Your mom... I mean *Emily* called the office just now, looking for you. I told her you were on your way to get her."

"I'm just about to get into the car now. I ran into a delay. A bulldozer, actually."

"Pardon?"

"Shannon's house got hit with a renegade bulldozer... right while we were standing in the room."

"Jeez! Are you all right?"

"Yeah."

He sighed. "A runaway bulldozer. Just another day in the life of Sullivan and Gilbert, Incorporated. Did you want me to go pick Emily up for you?"

I thanked him but declined his offer and disconnected. Next, I reiterated my sincere apologies and regrets to my dazed clients for having to desert them. Then I dashed into my van.

As I drove to my mother's house, I tried to calm my shattered nerves by mentally replaying my recent phone call with Sullivan. That had been so thoughtful of him to load the "Buttercup" tune without even mentioning that he'd done it. Rebecca had been right about one thing: Steve really was an amazingly good business partner. Make that *two* things she'd gotten right. I also truly *did* want to keep her "out of the picture." Far, far away from the picture *gallery*, even.

Taylor's funeral proceeded without incident. I'd met only about a dozen of the attendees beforehand, a list which included David Lewis and his employees. In the receiving line, David praised Taylor at length to Emily, which she tearfully appreciated.

She and I had decided to forgo the usual sad gathering afterward. After thanking the thirty or so attendees, she and I went on a long walk together instead. We'd chosen one of Crestview's lesser-known trails, one that looped around a rather uninteresting hill east of town, not all that far from Shannon's house.

Drying her eyes, Emily told me softly, "I can't help but wonder if Taylor would have been better off if I'd put him up for adoption, too. You turned out so well, and he just... could never make the right decisions... could never stay out of trouble."

"Emily, please don't be so hard on yourself."

"I tried my best with Taylor." She sighed. "I guess I just wasn't up to the task."

"You could have been an absolutely perfect mother to him, and he *still* might have fallen in with a bad crowd and gotten into drugs. There's no direct connection between being a perfect parent and raising a perfect child."

"Oh, I realize that. Believe me, Erin. I've been around long enough to see plenty of good kids from semi-negligent parents, and vice versa. But I knew all along that I had to be an extra-good parent to compensate for his father. He was not the best of people, let's say."

I'd never met the man, but she'd told me yesterday that she'd finally managed to locate him to tell him about his son's funeral. He was living in Anchorage. He'd told her he was "sorry to hear that," but there was no way he could afford to come all that way just for the service. He offered to pay for half of the tombstone, which she told me was "generous, by his standards."

"I just wasn't up to the task," she repeated. "Taylor was my responsibility. I couldn't protect him the way a parent needs to."

I had no way of measuring how accurate her harsh self-appraisal was. I felt chilled, nevertheless. How different might my life have been if Emily had retained custody of me? Although my adoptive father had pretty much removed himself from my life when I was twelve, my adoptive mother had been a gentle, loving soul. Not a single day went by when I didn't miss her. "It all seems so random... a person's lot in life," I told Emily. "Some people never seem to have a fair shot."

She nodded, reaching for her handkerchief again.

"That's why I couldn't stand to have a gathering afterward. I don't care for many of Taylor's friends. The majority of them are in worse shape than *he* was before he got sent to jail."

I had no response.

After a weighty pause, Emily cleared her throat. "Erin, maybe you can do something for Taylor now, for his memory."

"You want me to set up some sort of memorial in his name, you mean?"

She shook her head. "Did he ever mention the big project he'd been working on for the past year or so?"

"No. Tell me about it."

"I'll show you when we get back."

She'd raised my curiosity. When we returned to her house, she led me down to her unfinished basement. There, she unfurled a rolled-up blueprint. "This is some sort of a computer desk?" I asked as I bent over the drawings.

"It's a full-function computer workstation," Emily explained. "It's especially good for people with back problems. Taylor put quite a bit of money... which was mine, actually... into getting the design checked by an orthopedic doctor."

These blueprints were much more precise and professional than anything I would have expected from Taylor's hand. Having worked with him a year ago, Sullivan and I had concluded that my half brother was some sort of carpentry idiot savant; he ignored instructions and measurements, but he eventually managed to build what you wanted.

Emily seemed to be almost holding her breath as she waited for my reaction.

"I have to tell you honestly, Emily. There are a zillion

different designs for workstations already out on the marketplace. . . .”

“I know that. And so did Taylor. But what makes his unique is that the desk and the seat and footrest are all easily adjustable so you can customize it for your exact body dimensions. He was envisioning an advanced model having memory capability so that it would switch between the settings for two users with the push of a button.”

“The price points would have been a big problem for him. It's bulky and awkward, and the manufacturing would be complex. So the challenge would be finding an investor willing to assume the considerable up-front costs. And then hiring someone who could market it to the stores.”

She searched my features, and I knew her well enough to cringe a little; she was about to ask me for a big favor. “That's where I'm hoping you can come in, Erin . . . convincing furniture-store owners to stock Taylor's invention. I urged him to go to you for advice before, but he was too shy.”

I doubted that it was shyness as much as pride and obstinacy that had prevented him, but that was no longer the point. “This is way out of my area of expertise, Emily. I wouldn't have the first idea how to go about finding an investor and a manufacturer, or even how to develop a prototype.”

“Oh, the prototype is already done,” she assured me, brightening.

Inwardly I kicked myself. Of *course* building the prototype would be the phase that Taylor would complete on his own. “That's great, but frankly, this isn't nearly as big a hurdle as everything else is. With this type of product . . . with any product, really, the key is mass production . . . developing something that can be built on an assembly line at a low per-item cost.”

Ignoring me, Emily said, "It's right here, in the corner of the basement." She pointed. "Underneath the tarp. Taylor hadn't wanted to keep it out in the open. He used to like to tell his friends about it, then bring them down here and whisk the tarp off, saying 'Tah-dah' like a magician. He was so proud of it."

She was starting to cry again. She crossed the relatively tidy concrete floor toward her son's prototype. Although I was beginning to feel like a total heel, I desperately didn't want to get involved with this. Any start-up venture is risky by its very nature. A terrific design wasn't enough these days; the concept of an adjustable workstation just wasn't sexy enough to sell big.

I had a horrible vision of Emily losing all of her personal savings in an attempt to redeem Taylor posthumously. It would kill me to be the one who couldn't pull off this venture for her. "I'm really not the right person for—"

"Please, Erin. Just think about it. If you really can't help me, all I'll really need from you is a name or two of someone who can. After all, you work with furniture manufacturers and distributors all the time. Surely you can come up with someone I could talk to who can take this to the next level." She jerked the army-khaki green tarp away and chucked it to one side.

At first glance, Taylor's creation was high on mechanical adjustments and low on aesthetics. But beneath the rawness was a surprisingly brilliant design. Emily showed me how both its desktop and the keyboard stand could be quickly and independently adjusted for height. As she'd claimed, the range of heights was astonishing. It would work for a six-foot man to set this up at his standing height—with no chair whatsoever—or equally well as a miniature computer desk where a ten-year-old child could be seated with his elbows and knees at the ideal angles. A third flat surface could also be independently set to serve as a shelf for a printer or a writing surface. Emily explained that the bookcase that was currently atop this surface was removable and could be placed on the floor as a small freestanding shelf unit. Taylor had ingeniously managed all of this versatility with a combination of levers and metal rails that looked like big Erector set pieces but were more likely salvaged from adjustable exercise equipment.

Emily was wringing her hands and watching me expectantly as I finally turned away from the computer station. "I'm sure I can manage at least to come up with some names of marketers and furniture manufacturers," I told her, feeling a pang of guilt. Taylor had clearly worked very hard on this, and Emily needed my help. "And I'll try my best to figure out how I can make a bigger contribution."

"Thank you." She gave me a radiant smile, then retrieved the tarp. I grabbed the opposite end of the plastic-coated fabric and helped put it back in place. "Taylor would have liked to know you thought it was a worthy product, Erin. He told me he was really making progress and couldn't wait to show you what he'd done."

"He did a remarkable job."

"Well. This was his baby. Just a year ago, he was so into building it that I let myself hope that he'd gotten over the hump... that his energy was so focused on it that he'd finally found what he needed. That he wouldn't feel the need to get back into drugs."

"Did something specific happen? Which made him slip into his old bad habits?"

She sighed and nodded as she ushered me back upstairs. "He'd gotten discouraged. I think he'd run into somebody who crushed his hopes... and his spirit. All I know is, a month or two before I found out he was using and dealing drugs again, he'd had a couple of meetings with someone he'd been sure was going to make him an offer of a partnership. Then I came home one night and he was drunk. He kept saying his workstation was crap, and he should never have bothered." A tear slipped down her cheek. "That was the beginning of the end for him. Till he got the job working with you."

The second pang of guilt was so fierce that my eyes filled with tears.

chapter 11

t*he next morning, Sullivan and I went back to the* Youngs' house. We were hoping against logic and past experience that David had succeeded in lighting a fire under his crew—so to speak—and that the damage done by the runaway bulldozer had been repaired overnight. No such luck.

"Damn it," Sullivan cursed from the passenger seat as I turned off the engine of my van. "All they did was nail plywood over the hole!"

"Yeah. But David and his crew were all at Taylor's funeral yesterday. They were really kind to my mother. I know she appreciated it."

"Guess it's too much to expect them to go back to work afterward," he grumbled.

We knocked on the door. Michael greeted us, explaining that Shannon was lying down. "Whoever started up that bulldozer really seems to have taken the fight out of her," he remarked sadly.

Although I'd already given Sullivan my version of the incident, he asked Michael, "You just happened to arrive right as the dozer was heading toward the house? And you didn't see anybody near it?"

"Correct on both counts. And that sounds kind of suspicious, I know. The police questioned me on that very point." He turned to me. "After you left, Erin, we decided you were right about calling the police. I was afraid for a minute there that they were going to arrest me right on the spot. Except that'd mean I was damaging my own property. And obviously I have no reason to do such a thing."

Unless his motive had been to kill me or, more likely, Shannon. He'd recently been cheating on his wife. And yet for all I knew they had an open marriage and Shannon knew all about his infidelity. In any case, Audrey was friends with the man, so I hated to think that he was cooking up not only dishes on her show, but murder attempts, too.

"So you didn't see anybody at all in the immediate area at the time?" Sullivan asked him again.

"There were plenty of folks who could have started up the bulldozer—one of the workmen, David, Pate . . ."

"Or Rebecca Berringer," I interjected impulsively, testing Michael's reaction.

"Rebecca?" Michael echoed as though I must be daft. "Would *you* know how to set a bulldozer into cruise control, Erin?"

"No, but I doubt that's innate knowledge that comes only with the Y chromosome."

Michael rocked on his heels, but made no comment. "By the way, Ang Chung showed up just after you left for the funeral. He seemed to think that we should scrap the idea of the glass bricks, now that the front wall had been all but flattened anyway."

"He wants to shorten the room again?" I asked through gritted teeth. "And Shannon agrees?"

He shook his head. "She really liked the glass bricks, and so did I. She merely agreed to postpone our decision till this afternoon. Ang can take more readings, which he said he could only do at high noon, or some such hooey. Maybe that geo . . . something-or-other compass he uses is solar-powered."

Shannon shuffled toward us, wearing jeans and a CU sweatshirt. She was also wearing a pair of purple-tinted, octagonal, wire-rimmed glasses that looked like a throwback from the sixties. I'd never seen her wear glasses before. As Michael had forewarned, I'd also never seen her look this listless. "Ang's still not here?" she asked with a sigh. "I hope he hurries. I'm half ready to chuck this whole remodel."

"We can do that, you know, honey," Michael replied.

"Oh, sure," she snapped. "We'll just leave a smooshed shell of a room out front, maybe hang a garland or two on the Porta Potti, and then we'll be all set for a big bash to celebrate our wonderful remodel!"

Shannon may have *looked* listless, but she was as sharp-tongued as ever, I silently noted.

Michael didn't seem to mind, however. He replied gently, "We can figure out the best way to put the house back together again . . . maybe just scale back on the size of the addition. I'm sure Gilbert and Sullivan can help us."

Sullivan frowned at my name having come ahead of his. I grinned and winked at him.

"Whatever we do," Shannon responded wearily, "we can't afford to keep paying David and crew to sit around, twiddling their thumbs."

"There's no excuse for that," I interjected. "There's scads of work yet to be done. Even if everything else is done, they could be working on the back of the house." Shannon's devotion to feng shui had inspired her to commission a partially covered courtyard that would effectively square off the ell wing of the studio, making the house more rectangular and more in line with feng shui principles. "I'll go speak to David."

I headed out the door. Ang's Toyota was now parked alongside my van. He was nowhere in sight. Must have been wandering around someplace with his compass, looking for more dragon tails.

I decided to cross the street to take a good look at the front of the house. I could see right away that it might indeed be possible to "scale back" on the size of the addition as Michael had wanted. We could fill in and hide the excessive foundation beneath the wraparound deck.

Either way, I'd grown enamored with the idea of glass bricks in the southwest corner of the room. Sullivan and I had truly turned lemons into delicious lemonade with our plans. The room was going to be spectacular. It would irk me to no end if this bulldozer "accident" forced Shannon to settle for a smaller, ordinary room with no glass column.

A cynical thought gripped me: Could Michael have been desperate enough to save money—and get a payoff from his insurance—to have aimed the bulldozer at his own house? Surely not. That would be pointless. Michael wanted his home to be worth as much money as possible.

I rounded the house in search of David Lewis. I hesitated when I heard a male voice speaking in hushed, secretive tones. I peeked around the corner. David, his back to me, was using his cell phone. I ducked out of sight.

"Yeah. I got it all handled," he was saying. "So you owe me every penny you promised."

My stomach clenched. His words could be innocent. But they could also mean that he'd been promised money for sabotaging this job. Such as by plowing an unmanned bulldozer into the house.

"Look, my friend. Somebody already wound up dead. That was *not* what I signed up for." He paused. "I'm not saying you *did*. But you need to understand. If I pull one more stunt, my ass is going to be in a sling. I'm not letting our little agreement wind up putting me in jail."

David was all but confessing to a crime!

"And what about the bulldozer? . . . No, I didn't have anything to do with that! I figured *you* did! . . . In *that* case, I'm doubling my fee! . . . Why? Because someone *else* is messing with this job! It's out of control! No way am I taking the fall. Look, I gotta go. We'll talk again later."

Furious at the implications of what I'd just overheard, I tore around the corner and shouted, "Wait, David! Who were you talking to just now?"

"I was talking to another home owner, a guy who's trying to stiff me. Why?"

"You're lying! You were talking to someone who hired you to wreck this house!"

"No way! Check my phone log if you don't believe me!" He thrust the phone at me.

"No, let me see the one you're trying to hide in your hand."

He froze. For a second I had a vision of him striking me and fleeing.

Ang Chung strode across the Youngs' backyard toward us. "Pardon me," Ang said with a deferential bow, apparently reverting to his pseudo-Asian roots. "Can I have my phone back?"

"It's not what you think, Erin," David said. "I was pretending to be Ang Chung just now. That's why I borrowed *his* cell phone to call Rebecca Berringer. I wanted to see if she would admit to knowing anything about his ruining my work."

"Your voices are hardly similar," I said.

"But there's lousy reception here," he countered with a shrug.

Ang's jaw had dropped. "You asked to borrow my phone so that you could *impersonate* me? I'll have your head on a platter for this!"

David said to him, "Hey, buddy. Don't go making threats to me! I just found out that *you're* getting paid off by Rebecca."

"That's a lie!" Ang turned to me. "He was using my phone, yes. But he was speaking for *himself*. Not for me."

"Let's get Rebecca over here to answer for herself," I said, "shall we?"

"She'll lie," David exclaimed. "She's the one paying off Ang, so that she can mess with Shannon's mind."

"You miserable, lying piece of crap!" Ang growled.

"You're calling me names," David said with a sneer. "Not very enlightened-Asian of you."

"You're right. And neither is this!" To my complete surprise, Ang braced himself and punched David's stomach. With a groan, David doubled over. Ang grinned triumphantly. Seconds later, however, David dived at Ang's knees. Ang went flying to the ground. Each man flailed at the other, struggling to land solid blows.

Three of David's crew members appeared, but none of them wanted to break up the fight and instead proceeded to cheer their boss on. "Steve! Help!" I yelled.

The back door flew open. "Break it up, guys!" Steve grabbed the closest man, which happened to be Ang, and tried to pry him off of David. Michael had followed Steve outside and helped break up the altercation by grabbing David around the waist. Soon the two men were crimson-faced and gasping for air, but were no longer fighting.

Shannon rushed outside. "What on earth is going on here?"

"Get back to work! Now!" David snarled at his employees, ignoring her. The crew slowly shuffled off.

I explained to Shannon, "David borrowed Ang's cell phone and claims to have called Rebecca Berringer. Supposedly this was in order to impersonate Ang and find out if he was accepting bribes from her. If David's lying, he has been sabotaging the work here himself. Sullivan and I will probably have to fire him right now, and—"

"What? You can't do that!" David objected furiously. "I haven't 'sabotaged' a thing!"

"But Rebecca *did* know she was talking to you," I said. "Otherwise you'd have kept your answers really short. That way she wouldn't be able to detect the difference between your voice and his."

He scowled and brushed off his dusty blue jeans. "The truth is, all I'm doing is telling her what's going on here. With the feng shui. She promised to do the same for me at Pate's house. In exchange. That's all. Once Taylor had the accident, I wanted to call a stop to it. And that's when I found out that Ang is being paid to slow us down."

"Lies!" Ang hollered. "All lies!"

"This is ridiculous," Michael intervened. "Shannon,

this is our home. We need to fire both of them...Ang and David."

She shook her head adamantly. "I'm not going to do that. Ang predicted all of this would happen. That the people working on this house would fight amongst themselves. So nobody is to blame. It's the malevolent energy lines. Our house is in a terrible cycle right now. We're all falling victim to those dangerous forces. It's just lucky that you and I aren't living here right now. We're less under the pull of the bad energy." She crossed her arms and said to Ang, "This is the last straw. We need to hire you to do an exorcism."

"A what!?" Michael bellowed. "Now you think our house is *haunted*?"

"No, no. Not by ghosts, but by the bad natural forces at play."

"It's not natural forces! Both of these creeps are taking us for fools!" Michael gestured at Ang and David, "One of them probably put a nail in the foreman's head!"

"I did no such thing!" David protested just as Ang chimed in: "That's untrue!"

Michael tried to shout over their voices. "And plowed a bulldozer into our house! And set fire to our attic!"

"What we need to do is to regroup," Shannon continued, suddenly sounding calm and collected, now that her husband was the one in hysterics. "That's what I've had to do many times as an artist. Some piece I've devoted months or even years to just isn't coming together. So I meditate, and I'm patient. I listen to what the world is trying to tell me. Then, and only then, do I take action."

The word "patient" wouldn't leap to my mind when describing Shannon. She must hold her saintly attributes in reserve for her artwork.

"You really want to just let this go?" Steve asked her.

"You're letting both of these jerks get away with cheating us?" Michael asked more pointedly.

"We don't know that either one is cheating us," she retorted. "In any case, Ang and David are grown men, not little boys who need to be reassigned to new classrooms."

"The least we should do is contact Rebecca and ask her who she was talking to just now," I suggested.

"Yes. Let's," David piped in.

"Fine by me," Ang said. Then he furrowed his brow. "On the other hand, we both *have* been exposing ourselves to terrible I Ching here. That would cause anyone's tempers to erupt." He held out his hand to David and gave a slight bow. "Mr. Lewis, I understand your desire to find peace with a warring force. I blame the impact of those malevolent forces for making you unjustly accuse me of wrongdoings."

David groaned.

"Shake hands, gentlemen," Shannon instructed, "or I'll have to let both of you go."

Reluctantly, David shook Ang's hand.

"All right, then," Michael said, but his voice was simmering with frustration. "We'll try and carry on."

Sullivan glanced at me, probably expecting me to speak up, but I'd decided to stay silent this time and for once let this play out however our clients wished. "Shannon," he said, "this is a mistake."

"No, it is not, Mr. Sullivan," Ang said sharply. "Or are you saying you can't remain on this job?"

"Sullivan and Gilbert are the only ones who deserve to stay on, if you ask me," Michael said. "Unfortunately," he added, glaring at his wife, "*nobody* did."

After a few minutes of grudging silence, the men seemed to accept Shannon's questionable decision. We all sat down at Michael and Shannon's large, country-style dining table to discuss rebuilding the front room.

We quickly reached a consensus. We would stick with our original plans, including the glass column in the corner. David got his crew back to work, and Sullivan and I drove off.

The moment we were safely away from the house, I said, "Things are way too strained between David and us. I can't imagine how we can keep working with him."

"Yeah. Plus I'm thinking Ang Chung is crossing our names off his Christmas card list, right about now."

I tried to brake for the yellow light, but nothing happened. I gasped and veered around the car ahead of me to make a hair-raising right turn. I pumped the brakes wildly. Nothing!

"Jeez, Gilbert! Slow down!"

"I'm *trying* to!" I pulled on the emergency brake. Still nothing! There was no pressure there whatsoever! It felt like I'd just adjusted the windshield visor, for all the effect that it had on our speed.

"Oh, God! Steve! The brakes are out!"

chapter 12

S*omehow I had to get away from traffic. The wheels* squealed as I made a right turn. "We've got to find a ditch!"

"Shift into low gear!" Sullivan demanded. He grabbed the steering wheel.

"Let go! I can steer! I just can't *stop!*"

We were speeding toward a clot of cars. We both started cursing.

"Turn! Field!" He pointed across the oncoming lane of traffic. A car was heading toward us. I didn't have time to wait for it to pass. I jerked the wheel. That car's brakes screamed, and the driver leaned on the horn. We barely missed colliding. An instant later we all but flew over a ditch and crashed through a barbed-wire fence. I flattened a flimsy metal post in the process.

We bounced across the bumps and ruts in the old corn field at a teeth-breaking pace. A copse of Russian olive trees was up ahead, then a farmhouse.

"Get down!" Sullivan shouted. I ignored him. He again grabbed the wheel and cranked it toward him. We made a sharp turn in the soggy field. He was sending us back toward the intersection!

"What the—"

"I'm trying to stop us on the bank of the damn ditch!"

I screamed as the van started to tip. Steve cursed repeatedly. The van righted itself. We crashed through the barbed-wire fence a second time. All that separated us from traffic was a line of saplings alongside an irrigation ditch.

"The bank's not steep enough! Keep us off the road!" I cried.

He aimed us directly at the trees. Sullivan pulled me toward him to shield me. A moment later the windshield shattered. The airbags inflated. One hit my forehead with the force of a solid right cross.

Seconds later, the airbags sank away. Mercifully, we'd come to a complete stop.

"Erin. Are you all right?" Sullivan asked.

"I think so. You?"

"Fine."

I had a vision of the car catching fire, which always seemed to happen in Hollywood movies. I tried to get out. "My door's stuck."

Steve climbed out and dashed to my side of the van. He easily opened my door and took my hand to help me down. Our eyes met as I stepped onto the ground in front of him. He pulled me into a hug. I buried my face against his chest. I could hear and feel his heart pounding.

"Is everybody okay?" a man was calling from the road.

Sullivan abruptly ended our embrace and stepped back, as if embarrassed and anxious to get away from me. Affronted, I turned toward the voice. A celery-green SUV had pulled over. "We're fine," Sullivan said. "Our brakes failed."

"I've got nine-one-one on the line," the woman beside the driver said, waving her cell phone.

I glanced at my van. The windshield was cracked, and the bumper was bound to be badly damaged; I couldn't see it from this angle.

"You sure you're okay?" Sullivan asked me again.

"I'm doing a lot better than my van is." At my mention of the van, I remembered something: When we'd left the Youngs' house, I'd stepped over a puddle, which appeared to have spread from underneath my vehicle. Now that I thought back, I hadn't needed to avoid any puddles while getting *out* of my van.

"This was no accident, Steve. Somebody drained my brake fluid."

A pair of traffic patrol officers arrived and took notes as we recounted the incident to them. They helped us to contact an auto body shop, which sent a tow truck. The patrol officers waited with us as the paunchy, grizzled truck operator hooked my vehicle onto his. He was staring underneath the chassis of my van, and he called the officers over to see for themselves. The moment the officers had slipped into their car, I said to the tow-truck driver, "The brake line was cut, wasn't it?"

"Yep. Cut through, clean as a whistle."

"I told you so!" I promptly told Sullivan. "Somebody tried to kill us!"

"Might not have been after *both* of us," he intoned. "Since it's your van, *you* were the likely target."

"Maybe so, but the passenger side isn't known as the death seat for nothing."

"Which I came uncomfortably close to discovering," he muttered, staring past my shoulder at the road. Linda and her partner were walking toward us. They must have intercepted a call from the patrolmen.

After a few minutes of deliberation, Sullivan and I found ourselves in the back seat of Linda's patrol car as we followed the tow truck. Linda listened to me while her partner "Manny"—Officer Mansfield—drove. I repeated what the tow-truck driver had said about my brake line having been cut. She asked, "How long would you say that the Youngs were out of sight, from the time you arrived to when you left?"

Sullivan and I exchanged glances. "Half an hour, maybe?" he guessed with a shrug.

"At least twenty minutes, for sure."

"And were they gone separately, or together?"

"Separately," I answered. "It was like they were on a tag team for a while. One would leave the room when the other arrived."

Sullivan added, "But neither of them was there when we were in back, talking to David Lewis."

"The contractor," Linda muttered as she jotted something down. "So could *he* have slipped away long enough to tamper with your brakes?"

"Easily," I answered with a nod. "All the carpenters are mostly working in back of the house today. And Ang Chung arrived at some point."

"Plus Pate Hamlin seems to be home more often than not," Sullivan said. "And he's right across the street."

"He works out of his home office, so of course he's there." I felt a little annoyed at how eagerly Sullivan seemed to throw Pate's name into the circle of suspects.

"For all we know, Rebecca Berringer could have spotted my van, done the deed, then left."

"So could Pate's ex-wife."

I frowned. "That's a stretch. Yesterday was the only time I've seen Tracy at the house."

"But it's still possible," Sullivan countered.

Linda was flipping back through her notes, no doubt to reference Tracy Osgood. It felt as though Sullivan had offered her up to the investigators to protect Rebecca. "Sure. And it's *also* possible that a perfect stranger could have slashed my brake line. But there's a certain *lack of motive* where either Tracy Osgood or a stranger is concerned."

"Anyone else you can think of?" Linda intervened, before we could start squabbling. "We'll talk to all the workmen, too, of course. Have you had any unpleasant encounters with one of them?"

"No," we said in unison.

"Did Taylor Duncan have troubles with anyone on the crew?"

"Not that I know of," I replied. "Not counting his prickly relationship with his boss, David Lewis. They were all at his funeral yesterday, though, and spoke highly of Taylor afterward."

She nodded and said nothing.

"By the way. Detective O'Reilly hasn't said a word to me lately, though I told him I wanted to know the results of Taylor's autopsy."

Linda kept her face impassive, but I thought I saw a flicker of annoyance in her eyes. "He must have forgotten to call you. The tox screens were all negative. No drugs or alcohol whatsoever were in his system."

I settled on a white Saturn sedan as my temporary replacement for the van. Sullivan joked that my first order of business should be getting an enormous magnet to stick on the car door that read *Sullivan & Gilbert Designs*. He volunteered to handle the remainder of our appointments for the evening, which I gladly accepted, then headed home.

Some aches and pains in numerous parts of my body were starting to make themselves known as I made my way up the slate walkway. Despite my world weariness—or perhaps because of it—the approach to the house looked extra lovely and welcoming, like a Hallmark housewarming card. The darkening sky formed a striking indigo background for Audrey's regal stone house. I marveled at how the yellow glow through the transom and sidelights from the crystal chandelier beckoned. The crisp, pine-scented air mingled gently with warm lavender and eucalyptus scent as I stepped over the threshold into the picture-perfect foyer.

Through the French doors, I could see Audrey pacing in the parlor. That was not a good sign. She'd quite possibly reached the limit of her nurturing skills over my loss, and this evening was going to be All About Audrey. It would be wise for me to wait my turn to tell her about my car accident.

She faced me the moment I opened the door. "Erin, I'm in real trouble here. I need your help."

"Why? What's wrong?" Hildi, meanwhile, meowed a greeting from her perch on the sofa.

"It's that dreadful Rebecca Berringer's fault. Or at least her hyperactive publicist's."

I clucked in an advanced show of sympathy and settled into the comfy Ultrasuede cushion beside Hildi. I stroked her soft, black fur. She rumbled with a contented purr.

"They've been advertising Rebecca's show everywhere," Audrey continued. "The *Sentinel*, the *Post*, the

News, the sides of buses, magazines, store windows... you name a large, vertical surface in this town, and Rebecca's face is on it. My numbers are dropping. The station says that's because her show is hipper and fresher than mine. Which, by the way, is their way of tactfully pointing out that she's forty years younger than I am."

"But you're the one she's copying. You're the Domestic Bliss Goddess herself. There's no way she can overtake your loyal audience and your credibility."

"True, but let's recap, shall we? Forty years younger than me. A *television* show. She's got the higher percentage of eighteen-to-twenty-eight-year-olds. That's the market everyone wants. It has the most clout because of its high percentage of disposable income. The advertisers consider it their bread and butter."

"But for a show about interior design, airing at nine in the morning, your and Rebecca's audience is basically the same as Martha Stewart's. And she's *your* age." More or less. Lately Audrey had vowed to assign herself negative numbers for her birthdays, so she was supposedly getting younger with each passing year.

Audrey put her hands on her hips and lifted her chin. "Be that as it may, my numbers are dropping, Erin, and either I get them up or the station drops *me*."

"Uh-oh," I muttered, now certain that I knew where this conversation was heading.

"I have to bring in younger, fresher guests. I need you to get over your silly TV phobia, Erin, and do a segment on the show. Immediately."

I had fought off this request mightily ever since we'd first met. One glance at her face told me that this was her Waterloo. (Or was that her Alamo? I meant whichever battle was shorthand for *I won't take no for an answer*. Sadly, my knowledge of history began and ended with architecture and furniture periods.)

"Okay, Audrey. If it's that important to you, I'll do my best," I promised. "But let's please start me out with as short a segment as possible. That way, if my stage fright forces me into a state of shock, your viewers will only have to stare at your catatonic guest for a couple of minutes. You can wheel me out of there afterward during a commercial break."

"Fine. I'll put you on with Chef Michael, who's always popular. He agreed to bring along a feng shui expert that Shannon knows. I'm sure he'll be a big hit as well."

I grimaced. "Ang Chung?"

"Yes. Why the face? Doesn't the man speak English, or something?"

"Perfectly. He's an American. He doesn't seem to have any Asian whatsoever in him. I think he changed his name when he started practicing feng shui because it was good for business."

"You don't sound fond of him."

"I'm not. I think he might have killed Taylor."

"That's a problem. Well. Murderer or no, it's too late to change my guests around for tomorrow's taping. I've got everything confirmed already with the producers."

"*Tomorrow!?*" I shot to my feet, Hildi emitting a *rr-r-r* of protest. "You scheduled me for *tomorrow*? Before you even *talked* to me about it?"

"I knew I'd be able to count on you when the chips were down. Which they are now."

"I just hope I don't lay an egg. Heaven knows Rebecca Berringer is far from one of my favorite people. I'd love to see your show outshine hers and drive her back into the B-leagues, where she belongs."

Audrey grinned at me. "There's the spirit! So let's sit down and discuss what your topic will be for tomorrow."

Sullivan okayed my forcing him to cover for me yet again. That was my last hope for bailing out on Audrey. The next morning I rode down to the TV studio with her. Ang was in the greenroom when I arrived. He was wearing all black silk, but his Nehru jacket was an upgrade from the usual one. Audrey's greenroom was literally that; she'd requested that the walls here be painted a lovely mint green. Ang did a double take as I entered. He studied my features as I took a seat in the exquisite overstuffed beige jacquard chair across from him.

"Erin? Are you all right?"

I tried to force a smile, but felt too nauseated to be successful. "I guess they call it the greenroom because the future TV people can get so nervous that they turn green."

Ang arched an eyebrow. "You're nervous? You should put yourself in the southwest corner and breathe in the winds of change."

I oriented myself mentally and realized I was sitting near the north wall. "I don't feel like moving at the moment."

"That's a mistake. Feng shui should never be dismissed out of hand."

"I use intuitive feng shui myself in my designs, Ang. But I don't want to be breathing in any winds just now. I'm already feeling blown away by my stage fright."

He chuckled. "You poor thing. Wish I could help. I'd suggest that you allow me to guide you in some meditations, but I'm next on camera."

Just then, Audrey's assistant came in—a rail-thin young thing who seemed overcaffeinated—and informed Ang that they were "ready for him." The wording gave me an image of an execution chamber being prepared for us, and I nearly fainted.

On his way to the door, Ang patted me on top of my

head as though I were a cocker spaniel. "As they say in show biz, break a leg. And reconsider your cavalier attitude about feng shui. You're up right after me, and you're running out of time to pull yourself together."

His smug attitude was intolerable. I snarled at him, "I like your new jacket. You lost a button from your other one, didn't you?"

"No. Why?"

"I found one that looked like it came from your black robe. In the Youngs' attic. Right after the fire. I gave it to the police."

The assistant was now jiggling anxiously. She urged him on with a tight smile. Ang's dark eyes flashed in anger, but he clenched his jaw and left with her.

Okay, that was mean of me to bring up the button just then. It was also unwise, in general, to prod a potential killer. Figuring it couldn't hurt, I moved to the southwest corner and breathed deeply. Where Ang Chung was concerned, there was no telling if "winds of change" were truly what I was inhaling, but I could sure smell the cheese danish from the snack tray, and that wasn't helping my nausea.

I watched on the monitor while Ang lectured the audience in that infuriating calm demeanor of his, demonstrating the nine "rooms" of the "house" in feng shui, and explaining how each can have an effect on a person's life.

"For example, your next guest is shaking in her boots, she's so frightened to be out here on stage."

"Oh, thanks for bringing that up in front of the audience!" I grumbled to myself. Payback for mentioning giving the button to the police, I supposed.

I turned off the TV and sat there, staring straight ahead. After a minute or two, Michael Young arrived.

"Erin! My God. You look like you've been running a marathon. What happened? Food poisoning?"

"No. Stage fright."

"Really? Can't relate, to tell you the truth. I just pretend Audrey's the only one there, and there's nothing to get nervous about around Audrey."

"But she's *not* alone," I reminded him sourly. "There's an audience. And a camera."

Miss Pencil stepped across the threshold. "Are you ready to go, Ms. Gilbert?"

I think my heart stopped. "I . . . no, I'm not."

She looked confused. "But . . . that was just a rhetorical question. You *have* to be ready. Nobody ever says no."

"They *would* if you asked them the right question," I babbled, stalling for all I was worth. 'Do you want to fall flat on your face on stage?' for example. If you asked *that*, the guests would say no."

She blinked at me. "You *have* to come with me," she insisted. "Right now."

Michael rose. "Erin needs a couple more minutes to compose herself. I'll go first."

"But Ms. Munroe just announced that it was going to be the interior designer up next," she whined.

"The show's taped anyway, so they can just edit the guest appearances in whatever order they want afterward."

"Okay, I guess, but . . ."

I got to my feet. "Thanks anyway, Michael. I'd better get this over with now before I talk myself into going AWOL, which Audrey would never forgive."

"Tell you what, Erin." Michael took my elbow. "They film your segment in the quote-unquote living room, and they film mine in the kitchen. We'll both go onstage at once. If you get nervous, just look at me, and I'll give you the thumbs-up and beam at you for all I'm worth."

The assistant was peering at my face and, when we

stepped into the hallway, she suggested, "How about a quick visit with the makeup artist?"

I agreed, and the "artist," who doubled as a camerawoman, dabbed artificial tawny colors onto my face.

By the time I sat down in Audrey's pseudo living room, I was going through hot flashes and cold chills and could only think that if this had been the Middle Ages, someone would have decided I had the plague and I'd have been dragged off and put out of my misery. Audrey did everything she possibly could to calm me down, and when the assistant asked if there was anything she could get me, I said, "Beta blockers? Valium?"

"Sorry. I can't give you my prescription meds. It's illegal. How about some *water*?"

"Could you spike it?"

She raised her eyebrow. "Of course. By 'water,' I meant 'vodka.' Or would you prefer gin?"

"Never mind. I'll take the actual water. *Tap* water."

She trotted away, and I started to worry if "tap water" was a code name for some sort of illegal substance. I never should have joked about pills.

A moment later, the crew turned up the stage lights. I felt like an ant beneath the burning hot ray of a prism. The assistant gave me a dainty cup and saucer for my water. When I tried to take a sip, my hands shook so badly that I sloshed water over the rim. My cup chattering against its saucer sounded as loud as a typewriter.

I dimly realized that Audrey was staring at me as though she'd asked me a question. After a horrifying pause, I mumbled, "Yes, indeed," figuring I had a fifty-fifty shot at that being a reasonable answer. The flicker of concern across her features and the guffaw backstage from Ang Chung let me know that I'd missed the mark.

"Erin decorated this studio," Audrey said in an aside to her audience. "Didn't she do a *fabulous* job?"

There was a nice applause, driven, no doubt by the "applause" light that was flashing. I muttered, "Thank you."

"Getting back to my question, what are the most common mistakes that homeowners make when they're decorating their new homes?"

Blank. My God! My mind was a total blank! I was turning into a tawny-painted zombie!

"Other than not hiring you, I mean," Audrey said, with a wink to the camera.

Still nothing.

"Is it color clashing? Lack of focus? Too much trendiness? Too little attention to detail?"

"Scale can be a big challenge with a new home. The sofa that looked huge in the old apartment can be dwarfed in the new living room, or the table that looks perfect in the showroom can barely fit in your actual dining room."

"So you recommend that home owners measure everything very carefully?"

"That's always important, yes. But also, colors can go a long way to fixing the problems in scale and in harmonizing the visuals of the room." I was sounding as stuffy as a closed casket.

"What do you mean by that? Give us an example."

With the aplomb of an elephant on roller skates, I trudged on with my answers to her questions. An eternity later, Audrey was thanking me, and I was finally able to leave the stage. There was a commercial break afterward, and Michael promptly gushed, "You did great, Erin."

"That's nice of you to say."

"I'm sure he meant it," Audrey said, coming backstage to check on me, probably to make sure that I wasn't trying to hang myself in her greenroom. "You did a fine job."

"I was shaking like a leaf the whole time!"

"The TV audience won't notice. They'll think it was the camera that was shaking."

"Oh, sure," I moaned.

Audrey said, "You got off to a rough start, but your information was excellent, and you were charming. The only problem was you shook too much. You'll do better next time."

"This was a one-shot, Audrey. There isn't going to be a next time."

She gave me a quick squeeze. "Wait for me, dear. We'll celebrate your appearance on the show with a nice lunch when we get back to Crestview."

"*Celebrate?!*" I squawked.

"You can also look at this as a recovery meal, if you prefer. In any case, it's a business expense, so you'd be foolish not to take me up on the offer."

"I'd really rather—"

"Hold that thought. Watch Michael and me do our thing. I'll be right back."

Now that I was off camera, the next fifteen minutes of listening to Michael and Audrey's easy banter was actually great fun. Chef Michael was demonstrating how to make a pasta salad, and they were both so warm and witty that I'd soon forgotten my troubles. Michael said, "I want to take this opportunity to reveal a new invention for the kitchen."

"I can't wait!" Audrey cried. Michael gave a grin to the camera as though he expected to cut to a commercial, but Audrey said, "No, I mean that literally. Go ahead and show us right now, Michael."

He chuckled and drew something out of a canvas shopping bag that he'd carried onstage. "When you're tired of looking around for a pepper mill for your salad, here's the perfect solution. It's a combination salad tongs *and* pepper mill."

"You're serious?" Audrey exclaimed.

"Dead serious," Michael replied, losing his smile. "Let me demonstrate." With a flourish, he unsnapped the plastic tongs at their pivot point, and then unsnapped the handles from both sides of the tongs. "These simply snap together. You unsnap the spoon side from its handle, and it becomes a shaker for some zesty accoutrement, such as Parmesan cheese or salad spices. You unsnap the handle of the fork and, voilà, you've got a pepper mill." He shook the Parmesan cheese out, he twisted the pepper mill portion, and beamed proudly at Audrey.

She laughed. "That's wonderful, Michael." She flashed him her television smile, then glanced at her producer. Sotto voce, she told Michael, "But you've got four pieces of plastic that might be coated in salad dressing. You're going to get that salad dressing all over your fingers as you snap them apart and put them back together, when what you really want to be doing is eating your delicious salad. . . ."

Michael's face was growing an ominously dark shade of magenta. "But it's all so handy. You've got everything you need to serve your salad in one small utensil."

"Well, that's nice, Michael. Except, what if you've made a big salad so that everyone can serve themselves? Suppose one guest doesn't want pepper, and the next guest does? Is each guest going to take apart and then reassemble the salad tongs?"

"It won't take any more time than passing the salt and pepper does."

"Which will already be on the table, because you're *not* going to have a salad tong sitting there throughout the meal." She laughed again. "Let's all give a hand to our wonderful Chef Michael-turned-inventor, shall we?"

The audience applauded on cue, and she turned back smoothly to the camera. "We'll be right back after the next commercial."

"Not *all* of us will be," Michael growled the instant the red light went out on the camera. He yanked off his apron and threw it down on the counter.

"Oh, dear," Audrey said, grabbing his arm just as he tried to brush past me. "I didn't mean to upset you. It's just that . . . your invention is stupid. But we all have bad ideas from time to time. Just ask Erin."

"Pardon?" I said, bewildered.

"Tell him about how I turned the one bathtub in the house into a terrarium."

Michael put his hands on his hips and glared down at her. "And did a *host* make fun of *you* on TV afterward?"

"Absolutely. Of course, *I* was the host, so I was the butt of my own joke. Which, granted, isn't the same thing. Again, I apologize, Michael. You should have told me you were going to be promoting an invention of yours on the show. I would have voiced my concerns *then.* But don't worry . . . I'll ask my producer to edit my reaction out of the broadcast. Honestly, Michael. Do you truly think the world needs a combination salad tong/pepper mill?"

Michael stormed off the set.

Audrey was unusually quiet during our lunch at the restaurant of her choice, which, as it turned out, was the nicest one in Crestview. I finally asked what was wrong. She said, "I think Chef Michael set me up. I can't believe that he honestly believed in his ridiculous invention. I'll bet you anything that, after all his years on the show, Chef Michael is going to dump me in favor of Rebecca."

"You're probably right."

"Thanks for the vote of confidence," she said glumly.

"Well, Rebecca is willing to go the extra mile, after all. She slept with him."

Audrey shrugged. "He's attractive. Who's to say *I* wouldn't be willing to go that same extra mile?"

"He's a married man."

"Oh, that's right! What was I thinking? Shannon's his wife. No, I'd never go so far as to be with a married man just to keep him on my show. Regardless of the extra viewers his segments bring me. I don't believe it! That slime bucket," she muttered, staring over my shoulder.

"No kidding. Here he is, having an affair, right as he and Shannon are undergoing a big remodel."

"Not Michael. Your partner. Steve Sullivan. *He's* cheating on you. *And* on me!"

I turned around and followed her steely glare. Steve Sullivan and Rebecca Berringer had entered the restaurant. She was holding his arm and smiling as he whispered into her ear. They looked like longtime lovers.

chapter 13

Sullivan's face fell when he spotted us. With the maitre d' leading them right past our table, however, he had no choice but to acknowledge us. He gave us a feeble: "Hey, Gilbert. Hello, Audrey."

"Well, hello, Mr. Sullivan," Audrey called with her fakest of smiles. "And Rebecca."

"Fancy running into you two here," Rebecca chirped. "Erin, I heard that you're appearing on Audrey's show. I'll be looking forward to watching your performance when it airs."

"Thanks," I mumbled, wishing I didn't have a full afternoon of work ahead of me so that I could order something stronger than iced tea.

She clutched Sullivan's arm and gazed lovingly up at him. "Our table's ready."

As they took their seats a few tables away from ours, the waitress arrived with our entrees. I blurted out, "I'd like a glass of Chablis, please."

"Make that two," Audrey told her.

I had a blessedly uneventful weekend. I vowed, no mat-ter what, to steer clear of anything police investigation- or work-related, and, most importantly, not to waste another precious second of my life thinking about Steve Sullivan. Saturday, Audrey and I spent a glorious afternoon perusing the exquisite showrooms at the Denver Design Center, and we went to an estate sale on Sunday. (Granted, those were still design-related activities, but even on camping trips I spend a portion of my time creating an aesthetically pleasing interior to my tent.)

Monday morning, Sullivan and I pulled into our parking spaces at the same time. We exchanged cool "heys" as we emerged from our respective vehicles. I asked how his weekend was while we walked toward our office building. He replied, "I had a good, laid-back weekend. You?"

What I *heard*, alas, was: "I got laid by Rebecca. You?"

So I ignored the question and asked, "And how was your lunch at the Chez Friday?"

"Good. Yours?"

"Good."

"Rebecca and I are *not* dating, you know."

"Right. You're just sitting at the same table in a restaurant and eating at the same time. And walking arm in arm as you crossed the floor."

"I guess she *was* being a bit flirtatious. But that's the way she is. It was just a business lunch."

"And what kind of business were you partaking in, pray tell?"

"Rebecca wants to convince me to join her on her show."

I stopped walking abruptly. "You do realize how badly you'd be giving Audrey the shaft if you were to agree to that, don't you?"

"Sure, but I'm playing along till Taylor's murder is solved. Rebecca's the best resource we've got if we want to keep track of the prime suspect."

"And by prime suspect, do you mean her or Pate?" I asked as I brushed past him.

"*Pate*. You suspect *Rebecca?*"

"I think that woman's capable of doing almost anything to get what she wants. And, by the way, what she wants at the moment is *you.*"

"No way."

"She told me so herself!"

"If that's true, I'll just have to try and resist her considerable charms. While I cleverly ply her for information."

"You'd better," I snapped. "Because she could very well have killed my—" I froze and stared at our front entrance, not believing my eyes. The lock was in pieces. The door had been jimmied. "Oh, my God! Somebody's broken in!"

Sullivan flung open the door and uttered a couple of quite vivid profanities. "Somebody trashed our office!"

I stepped beside him and surveyed the destruction. The desk and file cabinet drawers had been dumped out. All of our personal belongs—our coffee mugs, photos, and bric-a-brac—were now on the floor. Curiously, at first glance at least, nothing had been broken. The sofa cushions had been pulled off and tossed into one corner and the coffee table upended. Our computers had been left running, as if to announce that they'd been searched.

"Jeez," I muttered. "I hope she didn't figure out our passwords."

Sullivan's brow furrowed. "*She?*"

"I... guess that just popped out because we'd been talking about Rebecca. But, yes, that's who I suspect."

"Come on! Rebecca's got too much at stake to do something dumb like this. If she were to get caught, she'd be history. Her TV contract would get canceled, and she'd lose her clients, as well."

"Maybe she felt she had too much on the line *not* to do it. She figures she has to find whatever evidence I have in my computer."

"*What* evidence?" he demanded.

"Maybe Taylor had more photographs hidden in a different spot. Ones that were more incriminating. In any case, this has something to do with my brother's murder. I'm sure of that much."

Sullivan called the police. When he hung up, he warned me that Detective O'Reilly had said that he'd be the one to come out and investigate.

By the time O'Reilly arrived, a half an hour later, we were anxious to restore a little order to our office. Fortunately, no clients had dropped by in the meantime; we'd had visions of having to say: No, really, this is from a burglary. Our workspace is usually much cleaner than this. O'Reilly, however, promptly tried to convince us that we had to leave it in this state until the crime scene investigators could arrive at some indefinite time, "but before the end of the day, for sure." We insisted that we couldn't wait and also needed to take inventory of everything, so he grudgingly allowed us to don gloves and then refile all our papers in the cabinets and desk drawers.

Sullivan and O'Reilly quickly fell into a friendly patter as we worked, but it felt like macho posturing to me. When they finally allowed me to speak, I told the detective that it seemed odd to me that there was so little damage and no "significant" theft. He cut me off mid-sentence and asked me, "Did you have an insignificant theft?"

"Yes. I'm missing one of my billing files. As bills come in, I stick them in one file, and then as I pay them, I stick the receipts in a temporary 'paid' file."

"A temporary file?" Sullivan asked.

"Yeah. Which I use for a couple of months. Till I get the chance to file them."

"That sounds like a wasted step," O'Reilly said to him.

"My point exactly," he replied.

"Be that as it may," I said sharply, "the file is missing."

"What would anybody want with your receipts?" O'Reilly asked.

"They didn't take the receipts. I found *those* on the floor."

"They just took the *empty* folder?" O'Reilly asked.

"Yes. It's this drab olive color, like the others. See?" I opened a drawer and lifted one of the files to show him.

O'Reilly gave me an exaggerated solemn nod and made a notation in his pad. "I'll put out an APB and alert the media."

Sullivan, the jackass, chuckled. I growled, "Detective O'Reilly, you need to know what was taken, and *that's* what's missing!"

"Nothing else? No pens, pencils, paper clips?"

"Not as far as I can tell, no," I replied through clenched teeth.

He grinned at Sullivan. "Are *you* missing anything? Significant or otherwise?"

"Nope. Not a thing."

Through a tight jaw, I asked, "Any theories about why someone would break into our office just to steal an empty folder?"

Detective O'Reilly shrugged. "My hunch is it was some teens blowing off steam. Maybe they were clowning around with the folder. Or it was a frat party, having a treasure hunt, and they had to collect a folder marked 'paid.'"

"A scavenger hunt, you mean? Were there any other break-ins last night?"

"No. Guess it's more likely that someone cut himself and got blood on your folder... figured we'd run a DNA test and track him down."

"Oh. So, for that theory to be valid, you're assuming the culprit is someone who *isn't* familiar with the Crestview police. Who might mistakenly think that you'd treat this break-in seriously."

He glared at me with laserlike eyes. With a chill, I realized I'd gone too far. "I assure you, Miss Gilbert, we *are* taking this matter very seriously. And if *you* had wanted us to handle everything by the book, you should have left everything exactly as it was till CSI could arrive."

Sullivan explained, "We get walk-in customers sometimes. And that would have been lousy for business. Nobody hires interior designers who can't keep their own office tidy."

"We'd have put up yellow plastic crime-scene tape," O'Reilly countered with a shrug.

"That's not exactly a big draw for potential customers, either," I muttered.

He scowled at me, then grumbled in Sullivan's direction, "My fault. I should have insisted. Miss Gilbert here has so many dealings with the police, I tend to cut her slack. Kind of like a repeat-customer's discount."

I gritted my teeth to keep my mouth from getting me into deeper trouble.

O'Reilly scanned the room. "You have a cleaning crew come into your office?"

"Every two weeks," I replied. "They're scheduled to come in again tonight."

"Damn. We could get someplace if they'd come Sunday, instead. Got a rough estimate of how many people would have been in the room in the past two weeks?"

Sullivan and I exchanged glances. "Twelve, maybe? We had those reps here last week."

O'Reilly's scowl deepened. "The door and most of the furniture's going to be useless, in that case. We can test for fingerprints on your files, though. Maybe something will show up there. Got to warn you. Procedure's messy. And we'll need to boot you out for a couple of hours. I know that won't sit well with all your . . . walk-in customers."

"You should go ahead, just in case," I said. "As long as you've already taken the suspects' prints."

"*Suspects*?" he barked at me. "You mean for your brother's apparent accidental death?"

"My brother was murdered, Detective," I said firmly.

"Actually, we *do* have some fingerprint evidence. So we're going to want to pull the prints here, just in case."

My thoughts raced. There was only one location at my brother's murder scene in which fingerprints could be significant. "You mean you found someone's fingerprints on the nail gun?" I asked.

"That information is on a strict need-to-know basis," O'Reilly snapped. He headed toward the door. "I'll get CSI down here ASAP."

My mother called the office later that morning. I immediately felt a pang of guilt. I hadn't done a single thing toward finding a marketing representative for Taylor's workstation design. When I confessed as much to her, she said, "That's not why I'm calling. But I do have another favor to ask of you."

"By all means. What do you need?"

"Taylor's landlord called me. She wanted to know when I could . . . clean out all of his things so she can rent out the apartment again. I just . . . can't bring myself to—"

She broke off, and I knew she was crying. "I'll do that for you," I promised. "I'll go first thing this evening."

We chatted for a few minutes, then said our good-byes. I'd barely gotten back to work when the pretty little brass bell over our door jingled. I smiled as I waited to greet whoever had opened it. My smile swiftly faded as Rebecca Berringer breezed in. "Oh, good morning, Erin. I was in the neighborhood and thought I'd drop by. Have I missed Steve entirely?"

"'Fraid so. He's in south Crestview till two. Shall I tell him you dropped by?"

"Yes, please do. I was actually hoping to take him out to lunch. I'll just have to do it the conventional way and call him up for a date."

"Apparently so."

She narrowed her eyes at me, then said, "I was so sorry to hear about how your on-air anxiety attack spoiled your television debut."

"How did you hear about that?"

"Oh, I have my—" she ran her fingertips tenderly along the edge of Sullivan's desk "—sources." She gave me a triumphant grin. "I'd offer you some advice, but I've never really been intimidated by large audiences. They say that public speaking is the biggest phobia in America, so you're in good company." She chuckled. "My, my, Erin. First you fainted at the sight of blood, then you nearly fainted in front of a TV audience. And people are always assuming *blondes* like me are the weak ones."

"And what a ridiculous notion *that* is. To assume that hair bleach could wield that kind of power."

She froze. "Oh, my. The kid gloves have come off in a hurry, haven't they?"

"I wasn't aware that either of us was ever wearing them."

"Don't underestimate me, Erin. You had your chances with Steve Sullivan, and you didn't capitalize on them. I've no intention of making the same mistake with mine."

Apparently I'd surpassed my witty-comeback quota. My mind was a complete blank, and I could only watch her sweep triumphantly out the door. My cheeks felt blazing hot and tears of anger stung my eyes. After the door had shut behind her, I said, "Well, la-de-da." That was never going to earn me a place in *Bartlett's Familiar Quotations*.

I used the speed dial to call Sullivan. Before he could as much as say hello, I demanded, "Did you tell Rebecca about my stage fright on Audrey's show?"

"What? No!"

"She *implied* that you did!"

"Maybe you misunderstood her."

"No, I think it's pretty clear that I'm not the one misunderstanding her. I get where she's coming from loud and clear. Which is more than I can say about you!"

"About *me*? What did I do? I *told* you I was seeing her casually to try to keep up with Pate's connection to your brother."

"You're so sure you've got to keep an eye on Pate. But all the while Pate's not acting half as suspicious as *she* is. And you can't see that because you're too busy being attracted to her!"

"Hey! You're the one who's always batting her eyes at Pate!"

"You're jealous of Pate Hamlin?"

"No. But you're jealous of Rebecca Berringer!"

"The woman's a viper! You cannot continue to date

that woman! Not if you want to stay business partners with me! If that makes me sound jealous, then so be it!"

"Now, why would your giving me an it's-her-or-me ultimatum make you sound jealous?" The humor in his voice was humiliating and infuriating. I pressed the disconnect button with as much venom as I could muster, and longed for the good old days when I could slam the phone into its cradle.

I arrived at Taylor's apartment building at quarter after five, carrying a couple of flattened empty boxes under one arm. His apartment had been in a three-story yellow brick rectangular structure. The architect seemed to have gone out of his way to avoid providing nice views of the Rockies or adding any appealing design elements whatsoever. The door to the lobby was open, and a sign indicated "Manager" on one of the dozens of push buttons that buzzed the apartments. There was no name by 1C, Taylor's old apartment.

I rang for the manager. A gruff: "Yeah?" came over the intercom.

The manager's name was J. Slokowski, but from the one-word response, I didn't dare venture a guess if this was a Mr. or Ms. Slokowski. "Hi. I'm Erin Gilbert, Taylor Duncan's sister."

"Oh, yeah. Good. Your mother called. Said you'd be gettin' his stuff. Be right there."

The owner of the gruff voice turned out to be a gruff-looking elderly woman. She was wearing black stretch pants and an overgrown sweater, with the mottled hue and texture of lint. She suffered from a smoker's hack, which she could barely control long enough to open the glass front door for me. As soon as she caught her breath, she said, "You really Duncan's sister? Two a you di'n't look a thing alike."

"He's my half brother."

She nodded, coughed up some phlegm, then shuffled ahead of me down the hall, her slippers clapping against the cheap brown-flecked linoleum with every step. The air reeked of burned popcorn, and two of the four doors we passed had set their TV volume to blare. "He seemed like a decent enough kid. Never gave me any trouble, at least. That's more 'n I can say for half the tenants here. Always bellyaching 'bout their places bein' too hot or too cold. Can't never please 'em."

She unlocked a door. The room held just the barest of essentials—a twin bed, its yellow-white sheets and burnt orange wool blanket left unmade, a four-drawer dresser with its fake wood-grain veneer peeling off and a brick to replace the missing foot, a ladder-back chair, and a pair of dark blue plastic crates for a nightstand. The thought of a brother of mine living like this was so depressing that I had to bite my lip to distract myself. Thank God it was me seeing this place and not Emily.

"All the junk... the stuff in here was his, 'cept the bed and the dresser. Lemme know if you need somethin'."

"Thanks."

She closed the door behind her. I sat down for a moment on the foot of the bed, the ancient bedsprings squeaking beneath my weight. This hovel had been intended as Taylor's temporary quarters. It had been an upgrade from his six months in prison.

What type of a life was it that my brother had led? He'd only been out of high school for two years. He hadn't even gotten the chance to figure out who he was. And yet the autopsy results had proven that he *had* been clean. He'd wanted to get his act together for Emily's sake. He'd deserved the chance to try, damn it all!

I swallowed my sorrow and retrieved his suitcase from under the bed and packed up his clothing, emptying out his dresser. All of his other possessions fit into the milk crates and the two cardboard boxes I'd brought. He had a handful of photographs of his friends and of our mother. Surprisingly, there was one of me right on top of the stack. It was painful to think he'd had that next to his bed in this dreary little room. I had no pictures of him. I packed up his toiletries from the three-quarter bathroom, then was done.

I stacked the now-full containers in the hall, managing to prop open an exit door in the back so that I wouldn't lock myself out. As I returned for the last box, Ms. Slokowski was glaring at me, hands on her hips. "You propped the door open."

"I didn't want to keep having to bother you to buzz me in through the front door."

"Yeah, but the alarm goes off when the door's kept open more'n an inch and more'n a minute. Rings right in my apartment."

"I'm sorry. I didn't realize."

"Must run in the family."

"Pardon?"

"Caught your brother doing that a couple times. He stopped, once I explained about the alarm."

"Had he been loading things into his truck?"

"Naw. When he kept wanting to go in and out 'cuz he was working outside. He did masonry work for the building owners in exchange for rent. He fixed that wall behind you." She pointed with her chin. "Di'n't do a very good job, though. Left a loose brick."

"Oh," I said, trying to feign disinterest. My heart was pounding, however. Could this be another of Taylor's hiding spots?

The moment I'd loaded my last box into my rental car,

I sneaked back over to the brick wall. I quickly found the loose brick that Ms. Slokowski had mentioned and, after checking to ensure that I wasn't being watched, removed it. Two unmarked and ordinary-looking house keys were tucked away in the cracked mortar. I hastily pocketed them and returned the brick to its slot.

I gave the door to the building a quick glance and saw that the keyhole for its lock looked about the right shape and size for one of the keys. Just in case, I tried one of Taylor's keys. To my disappointment, it fit. If the second key fit Taylor's apartment door, my discovery was worthless. I tried the second key in his lock. It turned. Damn it! I'd dearly hoped that one of these keys would be to a storage unit where he'd hidden the evidence he'd said he was going to show me, right before he died.

I looked again at his tiny former abode, wondering if I could have missed a hiding spot. I checked every inch of the bed—nothing—and the dresser drawers—no false bottoms. I looked underneath the dresser, thinking the brick for the missing leg could have been hollowed out, but no such luck. I did my best to return the lopsided drawers to their slots. The ceiling was the popcorn texture that screamed '70s. No chance for a cubbyhole there. The walls were Sheetrock. No loose baseboards. The shower stall had a plastic liner, which was coated in years of soap scum. Nothing. No baggies in the toilet tank.

I left and drove to Emily's home, feeling frustrated and discouraged. I'd let my brother down. As tenuous and fledgling of a relationship as we'd had, it had been *something*. He and Emily were my only remaining blood relatives in the world. The relationship deserved to have been nurtured. Now he was gone, before I'd ever gotten the chance to fully experience having a brother.

chapter 14

We need to acknowledge and celebrate the key events in our lives. They should no more be neglected than you would forget your child's birthday. They show our progress and how we are a part of life's evolution.

—Audrey Munroe

That night, I stared at the flickering oranges and yellows of the warm fire in the elegant marble fireplace. Hildi had curled up against my thigh, and I stroked her soft fur. In the background, a lovely flute and piano concerto was playing on the stereo, and the aroma of our delicious meal lingered in the air.

Despite all the heartwarming trappings around me, a feeling of melancholy clung to me like a burr. I ruminated over what I could do to cheer myself. I bolted upright on the comfy sofa. "We never celebrated my forming a new business with Sullivan!"

Audrey peered at me over the top of her reading glasses. She was knitting a teal blue baby blanket for her three-month-old granddaughter. She was also reading, having placed her novel on a book stand. Audrey always had to be doing two things at once or she felt her time was being underutilized. "Pardon?"

"I've been a bit blue lately because, on top of everything else, I missed Taylor's twentieth birthday. I should have made more of an effort to mark these special occasions. And it hit me, we already messed up with Sullivan and Gilbert."

She blinked at me, then set aside her yarn and needles. "You're right, Erin. That was a terrible oversight. I should have thrown you two a grand-opening party! Well, it's not too late. Your business is still within its first annual season . . . plenty of time for a semi-grand-opening celebration."

"Oh, you don't need to do that," I protested.

She snorted. "If I felt *obligated,* I'd be too resentful to go through with it. As it is, it's my idea and it will be my pleasure." She hopped up and grabbed her Mont Blanc pen and her Tiffany appointment book from a small drawer in the mahogany console. "We'll present this affair as a kickoff party. Two weeks notice is all anyone will need. We can squeeze it in on the Friday after Thanksgiving. Not ideal, but we don't want to let this go any longer. After the first week of December, everyone starts getting ready for the holidays, running around like chickens with their heads cut off. My theory is it's an unconscious show of sympathy for the turkeys they just ate."

"So, according to your theory, we could still hold the party in mid-December, provided we invited only vegetarians."

Audrey was already scribbling notes. She replied, "Yes, but that would force us to serve only meatless appetizers."

"We wouldn't want that."

"I'll find a way to mention your business kickoff on a show segment. And I'll, of course, invite all the high-profile locals. Especially the ones with large homes and money to burn. Honestly! I can't believe I didn't do this already!"

Hildi let out a raspy meow from her seat beside me, either an objection to the sudden flurry of activity or simply wanting to get her two cents in.

"That's okay, Audrey. Really. It's totally wonderful of you to be doing it now. That was never my intention. I was just thinking Steve and I could maybe have a few friends over to the office for some tapas and pot stickers and cocktails."

"Pot stickers?" Audrey clicked her tongue. "You're thinking much too small. We're going to turn this into the after-turkey-day event of the year. An open house to show off your fabulous office, complete with photographs of your biggest triumphs."

"Triumphs? We've been in business for less than two months. And, let's face it, a triumph for us is when we design a home . . . and nobody dies!"

"That's not exactly something to put on your business cards, dear. Let's forget about the photos, then. I'll hire a couple of members from the Crestview Orchestra to play. No matter what, we have to perform some sort of formal ceremony. Do you think Steve would go along with a smudging ritual? For clearing the space of negative energy, I mean?"

I laughed. "*Sullivan?* Shall I get you a ceremonial feather to fan the embers while we're at it?"

She arched an eyebrow.

I said, "That doesn't exactly sound like something that's up Sullivan's alley, no."

"We'll surprise him with it, then. I did a show on open-house rituals last month. Did you know that studies have shown that sage smoke actually changes the polarity of the ions in the air?" She frowned. "Or something to that effect. In any case, there's plenty of science behind these ancient purification rituals."

"But that's the problem right there, Audrey. We'd lose Sullivan along with half our guests at the word 'purification' alone."

"In that case, focus solely on the fact that you're creating a new space for yourself to fill with a new awareness and a new positive direction. I can put myself in charge of the procedure. I'm over sixty and I'm a local celebrity of sorts. People *expect* me to be eccentric. The ritual isn't complicated. You simply light the clump of sage leaves, starting at the doorway, and you work in a clockwise direction, steering the smoke along the tops of door and window frames, and the walls."

"Any mention of Hare Krishna? And do you chant while you're doing this?"

"No, but I'd be happy to make one up just for you."

"Throw in a conga line, and you've got yourself a deal."

She scribbled some final notes, then squinted at me. "Honestly, Erin. Do you mean to tell me that, instead of having any kind of celebration, you moved your office furniture over there, added your name to the sign on Steve's door, and that was *it*?"

"Not entirely. We sent out announcement postcards to both sets of clients and our prospective clients. Then Sullivan and I shared a split of champagne."

She rolled her eyes. "You're self-employed at a highly competitive start-up business, and you nearly missed this huge publicity opportunity."

"Sullivan didn't think of it either," I muttered.

"Of course not. He's a man. Women are the party planners. That's what we get in exchange for our sitting in the passenger seat while the men drive. We provide the event; they provide the chariot to get us there."

"How sexist."

"Maybe so, but you know what they say about the foolishness of trying to fix that which isn't broken."

I thought about her party plans and tried to picture a string quartet and a hundred people jammed into Sullivan's and my small office. "Maybe we should settle on some sort of candle-lighting ritual to signify Sullivan's and my . . . burning passion for our careers."

Audrey mumbled something that sounded disturbingly like: "And for each other."

"What?"

"I was reminding myself to invite each mother—yours and Sullivan's."

"Maybe this whole thing isn't such a good idea,

Audrey. As wonderful as all your ideas sound, this isn't a good time to be throwing a party. Emily will feel like we don't care about Taylor's death at all."

"Erin, this is important. No friend of mine is going to open a new business without a celebration. Not on my watch. Now let's get going on your invitation list. Oh, and call Mr. Sullivan and invite him right away."

"I'll tell him to fire up his chariot," I said with a sigh and grabbed the phone.

chapter 15

The next day, a few minutes after noon, a client called the office and rescheduled her one o'clock appointment; we suddenly found ourselves with a long lunch break. I grabbed my coat and told Sullivan that I'd see him at two.

"You heading home for lunch?" he asked.

"No, I'm going to pay an unscheduled visit to Shannon's."

"But didn't they say they'd be gone all afternoon?"

"Exactly. And David's crew will be on their lunch break right now. This is the perfect chance for me to snoop around for clues into Taylor's murder."

He grabbed his navy blue pea coat. "I'm coming with you."

"Jeez! Someone took the plywood down!" Sullivan was staring at the house as I pulled into the Youngs' driveway.

Indeed, someone had removed the covering over the framed-out window, yet there were no cars or trucks in the driveway. I caught a glimpse of someone with white hair ducking out of sight. "I think Pate's inside."

Sullivan cursed under his breath and bolted out of the car before I'd barely come to a full stop. As I trotted after him, he shouted, "Pate! What the hell are you doing here?"

Pate leaned through the window opening. His cheeks were pink. He looked like the proverbial kid caught with his hand in the cookie jar. "Uh, borrowing some nails."

"Cut the crap!"

He sighed. "I'm undoing a harmless but stupid prank I pulled a couple weeks ago."

"What 'prank'?" I asked. "What are you talking about?"

Sullivan vaulted through the opening for the window to investigate matters for himself. "Let me see that," he demanded. He snatched a brown paper bag from Pate and rifled through its contents. "Nails and screws," he muttered. He shoved the bag back into Pate's chest, who grudgingly accepted it, still looking deeply embarrassed. "You've been swapping their supplies with ones that are wrong for the job!"

" 'Fraid so. Like I said. It was just a dumb prank."

Sullivan uttered a few choice curse words. He turned toward me. "Erin. Call Officer Delgardio. We need to report this to the police."

"There's no need for that," Pate said. "It was no big deal. And I'm trying to fix things now."

"You're trying to cover your tracks, you mean," Sullivan snarled. "So you broke into Shannon's house."

He shook his head. "I'm undoing the damage. Replacing everything I took." He peered over my shoulder. "Where's your van, Erin? Are you driving a rental car all of a sudden?"

I had no intention of answering. "What in God's name were you thinking, Pate? Were you forcing our carpenters to use smaller nails and screws so that the construction would fall apart?"

"No! I was just having a little fun. Playing a stupid practical joke. Switching hex screws for flat-heads . . . that kind of thing. After Taylor's accident, I realized how idiotic my stunt had been. Not to mention badly timed. I've been watching for the chance to remedy things ever since. This was my first opportunity."

"Wait a second!" I exclaimed. "Did you change the size of the nails that Taylor had been using?"

Maybe his death *was* an accident after all. Albeit caused by Pate's "little fun."

"Good Lord, no, Erin! That could have caused a hideous—" He stopped. He held the bag open so I could see. "Look! I only swapped boxes of individual nails, not the strips for nail guns. This has nothing whatsoever to do with your brother's death."

Gravel crunched from the driveway behind me. I glanced back. David Lewis had returned with two members of his crew. He was gaping at us as he parked his truck.

"How are we supposed to believe you?" Sullivan demanded. "We caught you red-handed!"

"What's going on?" David strode across the lawn, his hands fisted.

"Not much," Pate replied. "I'd had a few too many beers one night and messed with your building materials."

"You what?!"

"Erin and Steve here caught me trying to make it right again. Like they say, no good deed goes unpunished."

"You call this a *good deed?*" Sullivan retorted.

Ignoring him, Pate said, "Erin, I'm... sorry. Tell Shannon I'm giving her a check for ten thousand as compensation for my stupidity. Made out to No Big Boxes."

"You're trying to buy a clear conscience?" Steve fired back.

"No, man. I'm just trying to compensate for a stupid but harmless act." He reached into his back pocket and removed a folded sheet of paper. "Here." He held it out to me. "I figured there was a chance I'd get caught in the act, so I made this out already."

I took it from him and opened the paper while he pivoted and walked away. It was the ten-thousand-dollar check, folded inside a note that read:

> I, Pate Hamlin, in compensation for an act of mischief that involved exchanging two boxes of nails and three boxes of screws for dissimilar products, am hereby making a donation to No Big Boxes. In no way is this to be taken as an admission of liability for any problems whatsoever that ensued on the property at 1580 Jay Hawk Road, belonging to Shannon Dupree Young and Michael Young.

I thrust the note at Sullivan and charged after Pate. I was so angry that I could barely see straight. "Wait!" He stopped on the sidewalk across the street, and I ran up to him, ready and willing to attack him physically. "Did you kill my brother?"

"No. Erin, I swear to you on my own life, I did *not* kill your brother. I liked Taylor. I would never kill anyone. And I didn't start the fire, either. Yes, I've been having some fun with Shannon... designing motifs that drive her crazy with all her feng shui nonsense... swapping carpentry supplies... But that's all."

"Feng shui is really *not* nonsense, Mr. Hamlin. There's a reason it's endured for six thousand years."

"Maybe so. But then, so have chopsticks. You don't see Western culture finding enlightenment in *those* old-culture ways, now do you?"

"Comparing feng shui and chopsticks is hardly fair."

"True." He grinned at me. "At least it made you think long enough to stop yelling at me."

"If our positions were reversed, I'd imagine you'd yell, too."

"Hell. I'd do more than yell at you. I'd have wrung your neck." He gazed at my neck for a moment. I felt my cheeks warm. He lowered his voice. "You know who I think is guilty?"

I said nothing, not wanting to allow him to assume that he was off the hook.

"Shannon's pseudo-Asian friend."

"Ang Chung? Why?"

"He had the most to gain. From the fire. And from your brother's death. He's been bilking Shannon and Michael for months with all his phony compasses and charts and yin-yangs. Plus Shannon had a thing for your brother."

"She did?" Taylor had told me about Rebecca Berringer. He'd never mentioned Shannon.

"That's right. I saw them making out through the

window. That one." I looked where he pointed. The window was in the spare bedroom.

If Shannon had been involved with Taylor, it could only have been the shallowest possible of relationships; two more different people were difficult to imagine. Could that have given Michael a motive to murder Taylor? Even though Michael had been fooling around himself?

Pate continued, "Happened a couple of days before Taylor died. Ang Chung was standing in front of my house, drawing some silly map. He had to have seen them, too."

"Even if Ang *did* see the two kissing, why would he have cared? Are you saying he and Shannon were lovers?"

"Uh, no. Rebecca told me that Ang's gay. But Taylor was a threat. He knew Ang was a phony. Taylor was gaining influence over Shannon, so Ang was afraid Taylor'd be taking away the goose that kept laying his golden eggs."

I gave him no reply. I glanced over my shoulder. Steve was glaring at us. I waved the check at Pate. "Thanks for your donation. It's very generous. If contrary to your own interests."

He chuckled. "Ah, my lawyer suggested it. Besides, I already told Shannon I'm knocking another twenty K off my bid on her property. So I don't deserve any Boy Scout badges."

"You're still trying to buy her home?"

He shrugged. "'Course I am. It's good business. Meantime, property values here are sinking every day. She can sell to me now, or for a lot less later."

"You're right, Pate. You're no Boy Scout. Quite the opposite."

"I'm a businessman. And this is business." He said

gently, "But I would never do anything to hurt you or your family, Erin."

"Not unless it was good for your business."

"You misjudge my intentions, Erin." He reached out, and for a moment I thought he was going to take back his check, but he merely touched my hand, then turned and headed toward his house.

Once again, Audrey was pacing anxiously when I got home at the end of the day. "Everything was exactly as I suspected," she announced without preamble. "Chef Michael canceled his appearance tomorrow. Claims he has a head cold, but he didn't even have the decency to fake a case of the sniffles. He's *leaving* my show."

Hildi trotted up to me, and I swept her into my arms. She purred appreciatively. "He was *that* upset over his combo salad tongs/pepper mill?"

"No. As I suspected all along, that nonsensical invention of his was a setup. He already had his irons in another fire. A friend of mine from the studio caught him shooting an ad with Rebecca Berringer. She was announcing the newest addition to her cast. The 'incomparable Chef Michael.' "

"He's switching to Rebecca's show? Seems strange she'd hire him, considering she claims to have recently dumped the guy."

"She's supposedly happy as a clam about it. Apparently, she was so bubbly during the filming of the ad, she was a human Alka-Seltzer. Which is ironic, because she's so nauseating."

"I wonder when he was planning to tell you he was breaking his contract with you."

"The answer is tomorrow morning, although it may come as a surprise to him."

I stifled a "Yikes," thinking that Sullivan and I were meeting with Michael—and Shannon—tomorrow morning. Earlier this evening, Shannon reported Pate's "robbery, break-in, and criminal mischief" to the police, despite his "cheap-ploy donation" to her cause. (Sullivan and I had been working clear across town by then, but Shannon had gotten us up to speed over the phone.) Apparently Pate was filing countercharges against her for attacking him: She'd insisted that she deserved more than ten grand, so he'd offered to name the BaseMart repair garage "Shannon's Feng Shui Fix 'em Good Car Shop."

"You're going to call Michael in the morning?" I asked Audrey hopefully. "Or talk to him at the studio?"

"No, I'm planning on confronting him at his house. With any luck, Erin, you'll be there to back me up."

After breakfast the next morning, while I milked an already cold cup of mint tea, Audrey peered over her newspaper and asked what my schedule for the day was. I gave her a deliberately vague, "Various appointments with clients." My hope was that she'd take off immediately for Michael's house, so their confrontation would be over and done with by the time I arrived.

"And are any of your various client appointments with Michael Young?" she persisted.

"Yes."

"What time?"

"Nine-thirty. Give or take. The Youngs will be coming from their hotel."

"Are you and Steve going together?"

"No, he's meeting me there."

"Wonderful! I'll follow you. I'm not actually all that sure where they live."

She paid no attention when I tried to give her directions. I resorted to telling her directly that I didn't want her business with Michael to coincide with mine—that it would strain my relationship with him. Audrey ignored me. She had long ago mastered the art of selective hearing.

We arrived in our separate vehicles, despite my attempts to lose her at a couple of traffic lights. I asked Audrey if she could please either go first and allow me to wait a couple of minutes before going up to the house, or vice versa. She merely shrugged off the request with a curt "We're both going to the door now. Don't worry. He isn't going to think the worse of you for accompanying me."

"How do you know that? It's going to look like we planned this as a show of strength, both of us arriving at his door to confront him about his contract with your show. Yet he and I are involved in a completely different business relationship."

"I'll be tactful, Erin. Everything will be fine."

No doubt General Custer had made similar assurances to his troops. She all but glued herself to my shoulder as we walked up the path to the house. She gestured for me to knock, and I obliged.

Michael swept open the door, his smile fading when he saw Audrey beside me. "Morning," he said to me, talking loudly over the carpenters' sawing and hammering in the background. He shifted his gaze to Audrey. "This is a surprise."

"I thought I'd bring you some chicken soup for your cold," she announced, extracting a store-brand soup can from her bulgy leather purse and holding it out to him. "You seem to have made a remarkable recovery."

He sighed. Then he spread his arms and said, "You caught me. I didn't really have a cold. I'm switching to

Rebecca's show. It was just business, Audrey. Her show is higher rated than yours."

She dropped the can back into her purse. "It won't be for long, Mr. Young. I plan on using every possible *ethical* method at my disposal to boost my ratings."

"Like what? Short of replacing yourself with a younger hostess, that is."

I winced and took a step back. Audrey merely replied, "You'll be hearing from my lawyers, Mr. Young."

"About *what*? You plan on forcing me to appear on your show till my contract expires, fine. Just be prepared for a surly guest chef who spends all his time demonstrating his combo salad tongs/pepper mill."

Audrey retorted, "I suggest you reread your contract first. Especially the clause about advertising and self-promotion." She turned on a heel and tossed a cheery, "Have a good day," over her shoulder. She brushed past me without saying a word, her head held high. I watched her leave, wishing I could applaud without offending my client.

Steve arrived just as Audrey drove off. He started to wave, then saw Michael and me standing on the porch. He gave us a long look as he turned off his engine, then he went about the business of unloading our presentation materials. I could read his mind as he decided it was best not to ask about Audrey. He gave me a reassuring smile as he strode toward us and greeted Michael with a hearty: "Morning! Lovely day, isn't it? Should I set up the easels in the den?"

That was a spacious room with excellent natural light—a southern exposure—perfect for presentations. The space was where we'd given previous showings of our sample boards and drawings. Although the furnishings were, frankly, unexceptional—a set of mahogany end and coffee tables and your basic beige upholstered sectional—the accessories were divine. I loved their fabulous original artwork, the vivacious throw pillows, and the extraordinary ceramic table lamps and vases.

"I'm not sure. Shannon's not here," Michael said, glancing at his watch. "Still. She got a call at eight from the police regarding her charges against Pate Hamlin. She'd thought it'd only take a few minutes, but . . . Maybe we should reschedule."

"We can do that," Steve agreed pleasantly. He was showing wonderful restraint; our getting their final okay on the new design had dragged on for days now, ever since the fire last week.

Michael looked past us at the road. "No, never mind. Here she comes now."

Shannon was speeding toward us. Her tires squealed as she hit the brakes. She saw the three of us standing in the doorway and marched toward us.

"Is everything all right, dear?" Michael asked timidly.

"Get out!" she screamed at him, gesturing wildly. "You lying, cheating scumbag! Get out! *Now!*"

chapter 16

M*ichael paled. "Shannon. What's the* matter?"

"I know all about that Berringer tramp! How could you?! You broke our wedding vows!"

"Oh, like *you* haven't?" he fired back. "Don't try to tell me you've been faithful to me! I saw you kissing the carpenter."

"I kissed him on the cheek, for heaven's sake! After he'd helped me move a batch of furniture into the guest room. I've never cheated on you! Not once! Not in our entire marriage! Get out of my house!"

"I already *have* moved out, remember? The fire already forced me to move!"

"Then get out of my *hotel room*. Don't ever come back to my house! *Or* my hotel!"

"Fine! I'm gone!" He fished his keys out of his pocket. A moment later he peeled onto the road and soon vanished over the hill.

Shannon stood frozen in place, her eyes shut tight, struggling not to cry. Sullivan and I exchanged glances. "Would you like me to stay with you for a while, Shannon?" I asked quietly.

I touched her arm, but she jerked away from me. "Just clear all these workmen out of here. I want to be alone in my own house for a change!" She stepped through the doorway and screamed, "*Stop working!* Everybody get *out!* You're hereby on vacation for the rest of the week!" The whirr of power tools in the addition from Dave's crew stopped instantly.

I followed her inside. I looked back and saw that Steve was already rounding the house to hustle anyone out back to leave the premises. A trio of carpenters emerged from the addition. "Sorry, ma'am," one muttered as he brushed past us.

Wracking sobs overtook Shannon. She gestured at the door, and I took the cue and followed the men out, quietly shutting the door behind me. I dearly hoped there were no stragglers left inside. Sullivan instructed the new foreman that this job was "halted until further notice." Sullivan said he'd call David and explain the situation. We all made our way to our vehicles. "Meet you back at the office," he muttered.

"I *told* you we should be worried about this job," I murmured.

"Congrats. You were right," he whispered back harshly.

I waited till we were in our separate vehicles to retort

aloud to myself: "You don't have to be such a grouch! It's not like any of this is *my* fault!"

Instantly, I had second thoughts. Maybe things would have been different if I'd been a better, more involved sister.

Shannon called our office mid-morning the next day. With no preamble, she declared, "I need to talk to both of you. As soon as possible." I assured her that we'd "make time in our schedule" and offered to squeeze her in at two o'clock.

"Good," she replied, sounding surprisingly calm. "I'll see you around two, then."

We arrived a few minutes late. Although her eyes were red and puffy, Shannon was upbeat as she let us inside. "Look what I got, guys!" She led us into the den and said, "Feast your eyes on *that*," as she pointed to a samurai sword, housed in a gorgeous ornate sheath. She'd cleared all the furniture from the center of the room. Only the sword was occupying the spacious area, lying on an Oriental area rug. Sullivan and I exchanged glances; he looked every bit as surprised and uncomfortable as I felt. Was she next going to reveal a samurai assassin whom she'd hired to off her husband?

She beamed proudly at the sword and reverentially unsheathed it. "Do you believe how magnificent this is?" she asked us. "It's an authentic Japanese heirloom. It cost me a fortune, but it's going to be worth every penny. It's metal, of course, so it will work to dominate wood, drain earth, and dissolve water. And, since it's Asian, it will be the most powerful piece in the house. I want you to work it into the motif for this room. Right here on this exact spot. Whenever I'm not working, this is where I spend the most time."

Again, Sullivan and I exchanged glances. "You want it in the center of the room?" he asked.

"Yes, I do." She returned the sword to its holder. "I know that's going to be a challenge. You'll have to move the furniture around to make it work. Ang told me this is the start of a horrible new cycle for this house, which is going to last for an entire month. My protecting stars are utterly overwhelmed. I'm desperate! You saw for yourself how bad my luck is right now. My marriage is on the rocks. Erin's brother got killed by a nail. If only I'd gotten this powerful sword sooner, he might still be alive."

"Can't you stay at the hotel till the month's over?"

She shook her head. "The insurance company won't pay to rent me a new studio for a day, let alone a month. I already begged them. We simply can't afford to pick up the costs ourselves. I should say, *I* can't. Since there's no longer a 'we.'"

"Did Ang recommend your buying this sword?" Sullivan asked.

"Of course. He's the one who helped me purchase it."

Sullivan gave me a slight nod, which meant: *You take it from here*. The coward! I cleared my throat. "The thing is, Shannon, even though it's metal and Asian, it's also a weapon. Which you want to bring into your primary place for sitting and relaxing. That's as far from feng shui principles as you can possibly get."

"But Ang suggested it! He acquired the sword!"

"I realize that... but I can't tell you how strongly I disagree with him on this matter, Shannon."

"Then work this out with him later!" She grabbed both my arms firmly, looked me square in the eyes, and pleaded, "You have to make this metal element work for me, Erin! Right now! Otherwise, the consequences are going to be dire. Things are already falling apart. Michael's been having an affair with that slut of a designer who works at you-know-who's. Ang warned that I'm going to get deathly ill if I continue to spend ten hours a day in this house."

That feng shui quack was frightening her with his dire predictions into doing what he wanted. I should have seen this coming. "Okay. Obviously suspending it from the ceiling won't be safe. And we can't just have it mounted on any kind of a pedestal."

"Not a stone one, for sure. Earth elements will diminish its power. And it goes without saying that wood can't be used."

"My first thought is we'll build a wide, shallow enclosure... glass and hammered copper. We'll make it into a low table and put pillows around it to anchor the piece so it won't be stranded by itself or look like a display at a museum."

"I suppose that could work. Especially if you use white pillows. That will increase the strength of my number-two white star." She sighed with relief and explained to Sullivan, "Ang told me that's my strongest protective star."

Sullivan started to say something but stopped himself. He merely nodded. He raked his fingers through his hair in a gesture of frustration; Shannon didn't know him well enough to recognize it as such. He retrieved his measuring tape from his pocket and quickly jotted down the dimensions. With a warm smile, he told her, "We'll draw something up for you as soon as possible."

"Great. In the meantime, this can stay just as is, where it belongs." She knelt and moved the long sword in its sheath slightly, so that it was directly on top of a speck on the rug. "This dot marks the exact center of the room. And that's precisely where I want it. So if—" A tinny version of Beethoven's Fifth Symphony began to play, and Shannon said, "That's my cell phone."

"We'll let ourselves out," I said.

"Thanks," she replied, and then said "Hello?" into her phone.

We left, Sullivan saying to me, "Ang Chung must be stopped. Someway, somehow, we've *got* to get him under control."

I unlocked the rental car. "No kidding. I wonder if there's some kind of a governing board for—"

"Erin?"

I turned.

Shannon was leaning out the door. "Can you come here for just a minute?"

I nodded and murmured to Sullivan, "Watch. Now she'll insist we suspend the sword over the sofa with fishing line so it's hanging there invisibly."

She was saying her good-byes over the phone as I came back inside. "That was Ang calling. He thinks he can do an emergency karma sweep of the home."

"A karma sweep?" I repeated.

"It'll be most effective if we can clean the karma of the frequent visitors to my home at the same time. Ang's cleared his schedule for the remainder of the afternoon, so I just need you two to wait here till he arrives. He thinks it'll be ten or fifteen minutes, tops. Or you can come back anytime before five."

This was too much to take, and I said, "Shannon, we have a really busy schedule this afternoon, and frankly—"

Making placating gestures at me, she interrupted, "I know you think this is silly, but it's my treat, Erin. You'll each have a cleansed personal karma out of the deal, and it'll only take five minutes. Please?"

I weighed my options. All of our remaining appointments were in South Crestview. We could reschedule the first one, but driving there and back would waste forty minutes, minimum. Sullivan and I needed to confer about what we could do about Ang Chung's inane suggestions before our entire remodel was destroyed. "Fine, Shannon. We'll swing by again in twenty minutes or so."

"Oh, thank you!" Shannon hugged me. "My luck is finally going to change. I can sense it!" She sighed. "I am so relieved!"

There was a small coffee shop nearby and Sullivan and I headed straight for it. We both ordered decaf lattes and discussed strategies for handling Ang. We decided to contact the Better Business Bureau to see if we could talk to former clients of his. Some thirty minutes later, we were still batting around ideas as we pulled back into Shannon's driveway.

Sullivan stared at the house. "The door's wide open."

I did a double take. "Oh, God."

Shannon would never have intentionally left her front door that way. We tore out of the van and raced up the porch steps. At the doorway, Sullivan stopped in his tracks and turned to face me.

"Call nine-one-one," he said, gesturing for me to go back. "I'll handle this."

He hadn't blocked my view in time. "Oh, God. Poor Shannon!" I grabbed Sullivan's arm to steady myself.

Shannon was sprawled, lifeless, in a pool of blood. The samurai sword that she'd been so proud to acquire was impaled in her chest.

chapter 17

S*teve called 911 on his cell. I turned away and staggered* to a corner of the porch where Shannon's body was out of my line of sight. I took slow, deep breaths and hoped to avoid repeating my fainting episode.

Ang Chung should have already been here by now. Was this *his* doing? While suspicions were festering in my brain, I spotted Ang's Toyota Celica on the road, speeding toward the house. I headed toward the driveway to keep him away from the crime scene.

He parked and emerged from his car hastily. "Afternoon, Miss Gilbert. I apologize for being late. I was meditating, which is critical when preparing for a karma sweep. I lost track of the time."

I studied his dark eyes, trying to assess his guilt. He *did* seem more agitated than usual. "Did you happen to be with anyone while you were meditating?"

"No. I drove out to a peaceful hilltop nobody else seems to know about. That's where the dragon vein is strongest. Why?"

"You might need an alibi."

He paled. "What for?" He glanced at the house, then turned in the direction of the faint sound of sirens in the distance. "What's happening?"

"Somebody's murdered Shannon."

His jaw went slack. He stared at me, truly shocked, but was that from my news or emotional remnants from his brutal crime? "My God. Shannon's . . . dead?"

"The murder weapon was that fake samurai sword you conned her into buying."

He narrowed his eyes. "I don't care for what you're implying, Miss Gilbert. It sounds a lot like slander."

"It isn't slander when it's the truth, Mr. Chung. Shannon's murder is going to ensure that the police investigate your shady financial dealings with her."

"You don't want to make enemies with me," he snarled.

As the sirens in the background reminded me, he was correct; he was a prime suspect, and I'd just foolishly tipped my hand. I did my best to feign contrition. "No, I don't. I'm sorry. It's the shock talking. It was just so upsetting . . . suddenly finding Shannon's body like this."

He gave me a slight bow, but his laser glare made it clear he was furious. "Understandable. Perhaps *you* should find a quiet place for meditation at your earliest opportunity."

Two squad cars arrived a few moments later. Sullivan joined us on the walkway, saying into his cell phone, "Yeah. They're here now."

To my immense relief, my friend Linda Delgardio emerged from the first vehicle. She gave me a sympathetic smile, but strode to the doorway and glanced inside. "Has anyone checked to see if there are any more victims?"

"I did," Sullivan said. "While I was on the phone with nine-one-one. The house is empty."

"Do either of you know the whereabouts of her husband?"

"No, we don't," I answered. "Shannon and Michael had a fight yesterday. And they'd been living at a hotel."

"Because of the fire?"

"Yes."

The same balding officer who'd investigated my brother's death took charge. Linda spoke to him quietly, then she strode toward me. The senior officer ordered Mansfield, Linda's partner, to take Sullivan's statement, and his own partner to take Ang's. Meanwhile Linda ushered me into her squad car.

"What a disaster all this is," she said under her breath.

"No kidding. At least now Detective O'Reilly can't insist that *this* death was an accident."

She pursed her lips. Linda never criticized her fellow officers to me. "Let's start with how you and Mr. Sullivan discovered the body, and work backward, okay?" She opened her notepad. "Why did you come here today?"

"Ang Chung, that Italian-looking guy over there, was supposed to do a karma sweep on the house... and on Sullivan and me."

"A karma sweep?"

"That's what major feng shui devotees like Shannon do. As a last resort, to purify a structure with really bad karma."

"So Ang Chung was going to be performing the... purification procedure?"

"Yes. I've never heard of a feng shui expert doing a 'karma sweep' on the occupants of the household, let alone on houseguests. But even before Steve Sullivan and I started working closely with Ang, we've both been of the opinion that the guy's a quack."

"So why were you going along with this?"

"To keep our client happy."

"I see."

"We happened to be here an hour ago, right when Ang called Shannon and said that he'd be here to do the sweep. We left for half an hour, came back, and found Shannon dead. Ang should have beaten us here by ten or fifteen minutes, but there was no sign of him. He drove up five minutes later, supposedly for the first time that day."

"But you're thinking he might have come here between your two visits and killed her?"

"Right. I don't trust that guy for a—" I broke off as a beige sedan pulled up beside us. It was O'Reilly. "Damn it! Don't you have any other detectives?"

"Sure, but he's in charge of an active investigation at this residence."

I watched him march toward us. "So Shannon's stabbing is his case by default."

He yanked open Linda's door. "Del. Go see if you can give Meyer a hand. I'll talk to Miss Gilbert myself."

Linda gave my hand a quick squeeze, then got out of the car. O'Reilly slid behind the wheel in her place and slammed the door shut. It felt as though he had instantly sucked all the air from the car. "So, Miss Gilbert. You're at it again."

"Look, Detective O'Reilly, I would rather be in a hospital, being treated for malaria right now! Instead I returned to my client's home half an hour after our first appointment and found her brutally murdered! I've done nothing wrong!"

"Didn't say you had. Just noting that you've got uncannily lousy luck when it comes to your clients' life expectancy. Good thing I'm single. I'd never let my spouse hire you to pick out our curtains."

"Imagine my disappointment," I fired back. Given half the chance, I'd recommend that he put heavy, velvet curtains in his kitchen, which would soak up the cooking odors and make him miserable.

"So you said you came out to this residence more than once today?"

"That's right. I explained all that to Linda just two seconds ago."

He narrowed his eyes. "We're going to go through your whole story again. Humor me."

With little choice in the matter, I took a calming breath of the now stale air, then obliged. He held up his hand when I said that Shannon had been trying "to intensify the feng shui elements in her living space." He asked, "So you're saying *that* entailed putting a machete in the family room?"

I spread my arms, though the gesture was hampered by our cramped quarters. "That's what Shannon said she wanted. She told me it was Ang Chung's advice."

"Why? Was that legit feng sway?"

"Feng *shui*. I wouldn't say that anything Ang advises his clients to do is necessarily 'legit.' The sword has a particularly strong metal element . . . especially because, according to Ang, at least, it was an ancient item from the Orient, where feng shui originated. But I've never heard of a consultant recommending a lethal weapon like this."

"I'll need to talk to him again," he muttered, making a notation in his pad.

"Good. I think he killed my brother, too."

He held my gaze. "Got to admit, with your brother's tox screens having been clean and now this, you might've been right about his cause of death."

"I *am* right. And I *might* be right about who did it."

O'Reilly took the extra frustrating step of driving Sullivan and me to the police station and taking our full statements *again* there. By the time an officer finally drove us back to fetch my car, the sun had set. Our afternoon's schedule had, of course, been decimated, and as we headed to our office, I told Sullivan, "There's no way I'll be able to jump right back into my job tomorrow morning. Audrey's undoubtedly going to keep me up half the night, talking about Shannon's death."

"Why don't you take tomorrow off?" he said grudgingly. "I'll handle your appointments."

That was my cue to decline his offer and soldier on, but I really did need a brief hiatus. "Great. Thanks. So I'll see you first thing Monday, then."

The next morning, while Audrey went to work taping another show in Denver, I lounged around in my dusty-rose microfiber bathrobe and wallowed in guilt. Sullivan had gone through every bit as much trauma as I had yesterday. Even so, I couldn't face chatting with clients and reps, so I did nothing to remedy the situation.

By mid-morning, it hit me that, although I wasn't up for doing my work, I was up for sleuthing. The search for my brother's killer had been made both more urgent and more specific by Shannon's death; the culprit was clearly someone with a motive to kill them both. Sullivan could have been right all along: I'd been avoiding considering Pate as the prime suspect. Maybe Pate's ruthless determination to buy Shannon's property *was* at the heart of all this. That possibility made me determined to do some research at a place where I'd never gone before: a BaseMart store.

For months now, Pate and the other owners of the store chain had been trying to strong-arm Crestview officials into offering major financial incentives in exchange for all the sales-tax revenue. With Audrey's and Shannon's help, however, the city politicians had been made aware that the company routinely relocated their stores into the *county* as soon as those subsidies ended, long before the towns broke even from sales-tax revenue. The nearest BaseMart was therefore twenty miles away, just outside the borderline of *that* store's patsy-played city.

My mind was in such a whirl that I was caught by surprise when BaseMart loomed on the horizon. The parking lot was huge—and depressingly crowded. "No Big Boxes" had been aptly named. The store was an enormous boxy-looking structure, as though the architect's mandate was Cheap and Ugly. I crossed the lot. The nippy air combined with smoky gray sky had the feel of an imminent snowstorm. The glass front doors were plastered with yellow, orange, and red ads about their "low, low, LOW prices." I mused about bickering with a salesclerk that sure, these prices are low, maybe even low, low, but definitely *not* low, low, LOW.

I didn't bother to grab a cart, and had to say "No, thanks" when the senior citizen in the BaseMart purple vest tried to foist one on me. I wove my way through the aisles at random. As I'd expected, the store itself was a massive warehouse with row after row of stuff, every kind of merchandise, from applesauce to photocopiers. The ceiling was unadorned girders and fluorescent light fixtures which cast an ugly yellow glow on everything. I just hoped the roof would hold in the event of a big snowstorm.

Out of the same kind of perverse curiosity that made me stare at car accidents, I eventually located the furniture department. Their icky merchandise would fall apart within a year of regular usage.

I stopped dead at the sight of a workstation. It was identical in concept to Taylor's prototype! I took a closer look. The materials were cheap stand-ins for what Taylor had used. The store had a stack of five boxes behind the sample workstation, which was on top of a high shelf. The strategic placement must have been to prevent customers from actually sitting on its built-in chair or adjusting the settings, which could cause it to collapse. Instead, the customer would have to buy the kit and assemble it at home—where it would no doubt promptly collapse.

I examined the nearest box to find out the name of the company that had produced the workstation kit. The only name listed was "Pied Piper," the name on many of their products, obviously BaseMart's own brand name. Pate's last name was Hamlin. Could this be his in-joke, naming his brands after the Pied Piper of Hamelin of folklore?

My thoughts flashed back to Emily describing how someone had soured Taylor on the viability of his invention, just before he went into the spiral that landed him back in jail. I tore out of the store.

Was Pate such a bastard that he had deliberately deflated my brother's dreams and expectations? Only to profit from the idea himself?

I parked on the opposite side of the street from Shannon's house and ignored the commotion there; her home had been cordoned off and, some sixteen hours after the crime, still hosted at least a half dozen police vehicles. I pounded on Pate's door, too angry to press the doorbell. I instantly tensed when Tracy Osgood, Pate's supposedly estranged wife, opened the door. "You're here again," I cried. "What's going on?"

"It's another coincidence, believe it or not. I dropped by last night to discuss divorce proceedings, and the police kept me here, interviewing me. It got so late, I wound up sleeping in the guest room."

"Is Pate home?"

"I think so."

"What unfortunate timing for you to have been visiting this neighborhood just now," I said, testing.

"You can say that again! Poor Shannon!"

"So you and Pate were here . . . together when she was killed?"

She grabbed my elbow and said in hushed tones, "I didn't get here till after supper time. And by then the—"

"Tracy?" Pate's deep voice emanated from inside. "Who are you talk—" He broke off when he spotted me. "Erin. I'm terribly sorry about your client's death. Shannon and I may not have been able to get along, but I hope they catch the coward who did this to her and string him up by his . . . thumbs."

"Thanks, but I'm here on a different matter, which I hope for your sake is unrelated. I wanted to talk to you about a product you're selling at your store. A workstation."

He chuckled. "You want a *discount*? Hell, I'm happy to give you any furniture product we carry."

"No. This is about your selling my brother's design for the All-Position Workstation. Did you steal—"

He held up his palm to cut me off. "Erin, maybe we should step into my office." He glanced at Tracy, still lingering by the door.

"This isn't a social call, Mr. Hamlin. I need a simple yes or no before I go to the police. Did you steal Taylor Duncan's design when your Pied Piper products made the All-Position Workstation?"

He crossed his arms. "No, I did not. And, by the way, the thing's not exactly flying off the shelves. We just have it in a couple of local stores to test the waters. It's tanking, big-time."

"How did you get hold of my brother's design?"

"It *wasn't* his. I acquired it... legally, of course. David Lewis holds the patent, under his name and his alone. He approached me about that product last year, showed me the manufacturing specs and all the paperwork—including authentic patents—and got me interested enough to follow him to his house and see it demonstrated."

That made no sense. Taylor had said that he'd met David for the first time just a couple of weeks before he was killed... and that David had given him the foreman's job to set him up for a fall. Considering Taylor's criminal record, I couldn't leap to his defense; maybe Taylor had been lying about who came up with the workstation design.

A sudden gust of wind blew my hair into my eyes and ruffled Pate's. Tracy's, however, must have been sprayed into place. I took a moment to collect myself, then asked, "What did the prototype look like?"

"Rustic but functional. Made mostly out of old exercise equipment." He shrugged.

That was Taylor's work, all right. Had David actually taken Pate to *Emily*'s house? "Where does David live?"

"A town house in South Crestview."

Emily's house was a two-bedroom house east of town. Taylor or David must have constructed a second prototype. "How much money did David make on the deal?"

"I paid Lewis ten grand for an exclusive agreement, with bonuses and percentages if the thing got hot."

"Did you know anything at all about Taylor Duncan's having come up with the design a couple of years ago? And building his own prototype to test it?"

"No, I didn't. And clearly you're going to have to take up the matter with David."

I nodded. "Thank you for your time."

He grinned at me and cast a quick sideways glance at Tracy. "Would you like to turn this into a social call *now*? My soon-to-be-ex-wife was just about to leave, but I'd be happy to take you on a tour of my home."

This was a first—declining an offer to see the rooms in a house that I'd found fascinating from the outside. "No, thanks. I need to go see David Lewis immediately."

Tracy stepped forward, "I'll walk you to your car, Erin."

As soon as Pate was out of earshot, she said, "Erin, I know how this must look to you . . . my answering the door at Pate's like that. Again. But I was just here trying to get our divorce papers signed. And . . . once I heard about Shannon, I wanted to see if he had an alibi."

"*Did* he?"

"No."

"And where were you?"

Her jaw dropped. "I was organizing a charity function in Denver all day."

"These days it's impossible to know who to trust."

"No kidding," she murmured sadly and turned away.

I got into my rental car and called David Lewis's cell. He answered with his ubiquitous "Yeah?" and I said that I had something important to discuss with him right away. He said to come to his office—a ramshackle trailer southwest of downtown.

When I arrived, David seemed to be in a foul mood,

which made two of us. He didn't have his usual quota of sawdust in his hair, I noted. "Is this about Shannon?" he asked as I took a seat on the folding chair in his drafty office. "All I can say is, God help the piece of crap who killed her. And I hope he or she meets Him soon."

"I'm surprised you feel so strongly about her death. She didn't seem to treat you very well."

He glared at the wall behind me. "She was demanding to work for, thanks to that asshole, Ang Chung, but she was a good person. She sure as hell didn't deserve to get killed."

"No, she didn't." *And neither did my brother*. "That's not why I'm here, though." I filled him in on how my mother had shown me the prototype for Taylor's workstation that he'd been developing for at least two years. "Imagine my surprise when I discovered the product on the shelves at BaseMart. Pate says that you showed him a patent with your name on it."

"Right. Because it's my invention." David maintained his scowl. "Far be it from me to challenge your memories of your brother and all, but the simple truth is he must have been feeding you and your mother a line of bull."

"Oh?"

"*I* designed that station. Me. Acting alone. I was trying to cut costs wherever possible, and your brother was young and inexperienced, but talented. I hired him to redraw my blueprints and build me a prototype, based on my design."

That had to have been done clear back before Taylor's final stint in jail. "When was this?"

"About two years ago. I don't remember off the top of my head. But I can go back and look at my notes for the design."

"You told me you didn't *know* Taylor when he came

looking for a carpenter's job. But that you needed a foreman and gave him a shot."

"I *didn't* know him—merely met him a couple of times for a month or two. It was way back when he was still in high school, or a recent grad, maybe. Kind of like temporary summer labor."

I was highly skeptical but said, "I see."

"So is there anything else?"

"I'd really like to see all the legal agreements between Pate Hamlin and yourself. Along with the patent. That should go a long way in determining who's the legitimate owner of the concept."

"No problem. I'll have my secretary locate them. She'll make copies for you."

"Thanks."

He squinted at me. "You do realize that . . . Taylor was something of a blowhard, don't you? This is hardly going to be the first time he tried to steal credit for someone else's work. I mean, we are talking about a two-time convict and a druggie."

"Which is why the documentation is so important. It will clear the whole thing up right away."

"Right. Sure. Good."

I glanced at his desktop and, even though I was reading upside down, the name Taylor Duncan jumped out at me. I tilted my head and scanned the page. "Is this an insurance claim?" I blurted out.

David's eyes widened, then he frowned and said firmly, "Yeah. He was my foreman. I always take out insurance policies on my foremen."

"So are you getting paid for my brother's death?"

"No, nothing like that. It was just a policy insuring me against liability. In case he did something stupid and the client sued. You can imagine how crucial that was for me in Taylor's case."

"And yet now we're all probably out of a job."

He looked at me in surprise. "I doubt that. Michael's going to need to have us finish up. He can't get any kind of good price on his house while it's still under construction."

"So he's selling the house? He told you that?"

"Er, no. I'm just assuming he will."

I nodded and left, now convinced that Michael and David were in cahoots. I hoped I would be able to find out just what that partnership entailed.

chapter 18

Never be afraid to change your surroundings. We need the chance to experiment and to try new things to keep ourselves free and young in heart and mind.

—Audrey Munroe

"I'm thinking of doing something dramatic with this room," Audrey announced. We were sitting in the den, and she'd had a faraway look in her eye for a while now, which usually meant trouble.

"You're moving the furniture around again?"

She continued to gaze pensively around the room. "What would you think of installing an oxygen bar in here? We'd put in three or four of those tubes that allow you to inhale some lovely scented oxygen. Eucalyptus or lavender would be especially nice, after a long, hard day, don't you think? Along with several of those antique Arabian water pipes?" I was too stunned to answer. At length, she prompted, "Erin?"

"Oh, sorry. I was just thinking that this must be how the interior designer for Graceland felt when Elvis suggested putting the green shag carpeting on the ceiling in the jungle room."

"That would be a no to my suggestion, I take it?"

"That would be an omigod *hell* no, Audrey. An oxygen bar *and* a batch of hookahs?"

"Hookahs." She chuckled. "That sounds like how Tracy, with her Texas accent, would say 'hookers.' "

"And a bevy of call girls would be every bit as elegant an addition to this room as hookahs. At least *they* might be able to teach us a thing or two we don't already know."

"Speak for yourself, honey," she said, affecting a Mae West voice.

Embarrassed, I didn't reply.

"But it'd be fun for a while," Audrey prompted.

"The water pipes and the scented oxygen? Or the hookers?" I teased.

"Do you think we could rent a portable oxygen bar for a party?" she asked, not to be deterred.

"So long as you've got the money, you can rent anything. Which is not to say that you *should.* Doesn't it seem at all dangerous to you to put pure-oxygen dispensers in the same room where you want people to be smoking? Not to mention counterproductive?"

"Maybe so," she mused. "Let's forget the hookahs and just concentrate on the oxygen."

I massaged my suddenly aching temples.

"Erin, a headache can be a symptom of oxygen deprivation, you know. And here in Colorado, we're already a mile above sea level. We probably suffer from that all of the time and don't even realize it."

"What's going on, Audrey? Are you going through some kind of midlife crisis that's taking you back to your wild days in the sixties? Feeling nostalgic for Woodstock?"

"Those were good times for me. But I was hardly into drugs and free love. I was dancing in the New York City Ballet then."

I studied her expression. Something was up. "Please promise this isn't a trick."

"A trick?"

Uh-oh. Her cheeks pinked up, and her tone had a too-innocent quality to it. "You've already looked into renting hookahs and an oxygen bar!" I cried. "You're planning on featuring them at the Sullivan and Gilbert kickoff party!"

"It was just one possibility. . . . Over the years I've found that adding an unusual twist to one's parties makes them stand out in people's minds. That's especially advantageous when you're planning a party to promote a business venture."

"So . . . your mind went directly to oxygen bars?"

"No, it took a circuitous route. Remember how we talked about doing that housewarming ritual for your office with the smudge stick? Well, I set fire to the sage in the kitchen as a test, and it had a surprisingly disagreeable odor. That got me to thinking that maybe I could experiment with different spices. Which, in turn, led me to hookahs and oxygen bars."

"You're sure that was just *sage* you were inhaling? You didn't hide marijuana in the spice rack at some point, did you?"

"Of course not. Although that would make for an interesting lifestyles tip during one of my *Domestic Bliss* programs. . . . '*Now here's a little tip for all you teenagers in the audience who are trying to hide your stash from your parents.*' "

We both laughed. "At least you'd be hitting a chord among the younger audience marketing segment that your producer claims is so critical."

"True." With a sparkle in her eye, she added, "All of this reminds me, Erin. As much as I love that ceiling medallion you installed, I'm thinking a thick shag carpeting up there would be even nicer."

"Oh, stop," I groaned.

"It's high time shag carpeting made a comeback—"

"That would be wonderful. And maybe I'll finally be able to dust off my hot pants and leggings."

"Well, my dear, let's make a deal. You put those on, I'll don my leather miniskirt and halter top, and you and I will go out on the town."

"And we'll look like hookahs," I muttered.

chapter 19

Our pleasant banter was interrupted by an abrupt bang. It sounded like a gunshot. Almost simultaneously, there was the clinking noise of shattering glass above our heads.

"What was that?" I cried, leaping to my feet.

"Probably an engine backfiring." But Audrey had paled. She obviously wasn't buying her explanation any more than I was.

"It sounded like an upstairs window broke."

She rose and headed toward the foyer.

"Audrey, wait! You're not thinking of opening the front door, are you?"

She froze, then said, "No, that would be reckless. I was

just going to go upstairs and see if our windows are intact."

"I'll go." I headed for the staircase. "I'm sure it's nothing."

I went straight upstairs to my bedroom and threw open the door. The breeze that riffled my silver, raw silk curtains and lace sheers was an immediate giveaway. So was the shattered glass.

Someone had shot a bullet through my bedroom window.

"I understand how serious this is." Officer Mansfield, Linda's partner, was trying in vain to placate Audrey. He'd even made a flip remark about "minimal damage." Neither Linda nor I was making any attempt at jumping to his aid.

"Oh, good," Audrey replied with false gusto. "Just so long as I'm sure that you understand how upsetting it'll be if one or both of us is shot dead the next time we look out a window, we can all sleep soundly tonight."

Mansfield frowned. "We'll send patrol cars out to circle the area, ma'am."

"Rather than circling the area, why not have one park across the street? Are you really so overextended in Crestview that you can't spare even one squad car and an officer?"

"With all due respect, ma'am, you said yourself that the lights were out upstairs and the room was unoccupied at the time. It was probably just a prank. And no one got hurt. All it did was break a window—"

From the corner of my eye, I saw Linda flinch, mirroring my own reaction. "The window isn't the problem!" Audrey snapped. "It's the deadly projectile that passed through it! I would strongly suggest the Crestview police take all reasonable precautions to prevent another one—one that might find a human target!"

Mansfield tugged at his shirt collar. He towered over Audrey physically, but was looking a tad intimidated. "Of course, ma'am. I'm sorry. I'll do what I can to honor your request for increased patrols."

"We're hoping that the casing we retrieved will have a fingerprint, Ms. Munroe," Linda interposed, before Audrey could pounce on his "I'll do what I can..."

"Yeah," Mansfield added earnestly. "And we'll do our best to catch the shooter."

"And how good is your best?" Audrey challenged, staring up at him. "What are the chances of your making an arrest?"

He cast a nervous glance at Linda before he answered. "That would depend on lots of factors. Witnesses... evidence from other similar crimes... urgency... and, er, so on."

Audrey donned her patented I'm-losing-my-patience smile. "Then I'd better let you get back to work at catching the shooter, Officer. In the meantime, Erin and I will work to improve our limbo skills whenever we pass in front of a window."

He tipped his cap and mumbled, "Evening, ma'am," and scooted out the door. Linda bobbed her head and started to follow him. I had a strong urge to leave with them, knowing I'd be in for a major lecture from Audrey about how I needed to curb my tendency to involve myself in murder investigations.

"I'll keep you posted, as best I can," Linda said, when she reached the door.

"Great. Thank you. Have you gotten any solid leads on the killer?"

"Not really. Though Shannon's husband looks awfully

suspicious. He just raised the price of her art pieces by a factor of ten."

"He did?"

Linda nodded. "A little fishy, huh? A grieving man immediately thinks to raise the prices on his artist wife's works. And they'd separated the day before she died. How's that for coincidence?"

"Michael's always looking out for himself, first and foremost," Audrey declared. "To appear on the competition's show, he's breaking our contract. Although that's another suspect you should consider taking a strong look at."

"Rebecca Berringer? We'll see if they both have alibis for tonight's shooting."

Audrey beamed at her. "That's an excellent idea. One that might actually get us somewhere."

Linda left, and I sighed. "It's been a long night," I told Audrey. "I'm going to go clean up the broken glass and then—"

"Erin, we need to talk."

"What about?" But I knew what she was going to say. My heart sank.

"We need to figure out what it is about you that makes you keep bashing heads with killers. If you don't put a stop to all this amateur sleuthing of yours immediately, I'm going to host an intervention."

Desperate for a diversion, I took a sharp right and wandered toward the den. "So—an oxygen bar, you were saying?"

The phone rang in our office on Monday morning. Michael's voice was so strained with emotion that I scarcely recognized it. Sullivan had scooted his chair close to mine as we went over some plans for a living room makeover. He immediately asked me, "Michael?"

and I nodded. He surprised me by giving my arm a reassuring squeeze before returning to his own desk. Even more surprising was the electric feeling that surged through me when he touched me.

I murmured a few cajoling words here and there as Michael rattled on and on, repeatedly asking who could possibly have done such a thing and why, vowing to avenge his wife's death, wallowing in his guilt about his affair, and explaining that, sure, he and Shannon had had serious problems, but that "this was the last thing I wanted. . . ." All the while, I was struggling to gauge his credibility. He *sounded* like a truly shocked, heartbroken man who'd lost his wife. "Every couple of hours, I forget that she's gone. I'll start to ask her about something, and then I remember. It's like I have to keep reliving the shock of her death, several times a day," he told me.

"I can't begin to imagine how painful that is. . . ."

"You can more than most, though. You just lost your brother."

I gave no response, still too uncertain of his innocence to want to consider him as a comrade in grief, far too unsure of his guilt to want to treat him like a murder suspect.

"But I've been bending your ear too long," Michael went on. "I called to tell you that the insurance company called me an hour ago. The roof and attic passed inspection. I can move back home." He made a harsh noise in the back of his throat. "Ironic, isn't it? Not to mention cruel. No way would Shannon have forgiven me this fast. I'd still be at the hotel."

"It'll be good to get out of the hotel, I'm sure."

"I suppose," he agreed with a sigh.

Sullivan was listening in. "Ask if we should come over," he said quietly.

"Maybe we should drop by," I told Michael. "Sullivan

and I could give you a hand getting resettled...and discuss how you want us to proceed with the new design."

"Terrific idea, Erin. I want to sell. I can't live there again. Not knowing it's where my—" He broke off. In a choked voice he said, hastily, "Sorry. I gotta go," and hung up.

The morning flew by. Sullivan and I had a packed schedule, thanks to all of the appointments we'd been forced to postpone. When we arrived at Michael's house at noon, his car was parked in the open garage.

"Bet he's going to sell every last one of Shannon's pieces at scalper prices, then buy himself a ritzy condo downtown," Sullivan remarked quietly.

"He'd said he wanted to open a new restaurant," I remarked as we made our way to the door. As I rang the bell, I had to battle flashback images of finding my brother's and Shannon's bodies just on the other side of this door. I certainly couldn't blame Michael one iota for wanting to sell the place.

When Michael appeared, his skin was so pale and his eyes had such dark circles under them that he looked like a ghost. "Come on in," he murmured. "Grab seats... someplace. I don't know. I can't even think of where to sit. Every room reminds me that she was—"

"Let's just go sit at your kitchen table," I suggested. As a chef, he would undoubtedly be the most comfortable in his kitchen. "Can I make you some tea, maybe?"

"No, no. I'm fine." He ran his palm over his bald pate. "I can't stay here. You have to help me get the house into marketable condition. As fast as possible. I just can't bear it..."

"No problem," Sullivan assured him, though his

shoulders tightened visibly. "At the very least, we'll need to get your front room completed. And the porch."

A workman, with the visor of his Rockies baseball cap hiding his features, stepped through the back door into the kitchen, then froze. He pivoted as though he'd forgotten something. My warning flags were instantly flying, but the men had seen the guy, too, and yet they prattled on without concern. I was either being more alert than they were, or more paranoid. Probably both. I relaxed enough to add my two cents to our list of must-do items for Michael's goal of getting this property ready to list.

In the corner of my vision, I spotted the skulking workman wearing the baseball cap. He'd now entered through the front.

Michael grumbled, "I just wish we hadn't poured the cement for the courtyard. That was all Ang Chung's nonsense—squaring off the house. Adding the gazebo." His expression hardened. "I fired his ass. I don't have any proof, but I think he's the one who killed my wife. Maybe she finally caught on to how he was scamming her. But even if he's innocent of murder, we've got to undo his lamebrain projects now."

"Let's take a look out back and see what we can do." Sullivan and Michael promptly headed outside. Suspecting that the furtive carpenter was listening, I joined them, but then excused myself and doubled back.

I tiptoed down the hallway. The door to Shannon's studio was closed. Carefully and silently, I turned the knob and peeked inside.

The carpenter in the cap was rifling through Shannon's file cabinet. I recognized him at once. "Ang!"

He jumped back in surprise, then stared several inches above my head. "Your astral projections are seriously out of alignment once again, Miss Gilbert."

"What are you doing?"

He donned an expression of innocence incarnate. "I'm simply following the dragon."

"And you think that energy lines are in Shannon's files?"

"Yes, as a matter of fact. I was looking for the old geomantric charts that I'd given her."

"Yeah, right," I said through clenched teeth. "While you're dressed like a workman and avoiding everyone."

"You needn't be so suspicious of my every little movement, Miss Gilbert. Shannon has been a huge advocate of mine. I'm the last person who would benefit from her death." Ang gave me a wry smile. "Whereas, the word is that you have quite a track record for getting involved in homicides in this town. I hope *you're* not abusing your relationship with the police department in order to escape detection yourself."

"You're accusing *me?*"

"Shannon Dupree did *not* kill your brother, you know."

"I've never suspected her for a moment. She was speaking at a luncheon when he died."

He narrowed his eyes. "And it never occurred to you that the hotel was only a couple of miles away? So she could have easily slipped away for fifteen or twenty minutes . . . long enough for her to return home, unmissed?" He let that nasty suspicion sink in for a moment, then asked, "Aren't you afraid that the killer is gunning for you next, Miss Gilbert?"

"Are you afraid the killer's gunning for *you*?" I shot back.

"I can take care of myself."

"What are you really looking for in Shannon's file cabinet?" I demanded.

"Something that could be embarrassing for me if the police were to discover it. But not so much that I'd take another person's life," he added solemnly.

Michael appeared at the doorway. His jaw dropped. "What the hell are you doing in my house!" he snarled at Ang.

"I'm looking for something that belongs to me."

"Nothing in my house belongs to you! Get out! I'm reporting this to the police!"

"If you'll excuse me." After giving me a sneer, Ang brushed past Michael and strode out the door with his head held high.

At the end of my long day, my neck and shoulder muscles were aching as I made my way home. I needed to draw myself a nice hot bath and forget about everything for a while. I looked up at my bedroom window. Audrey had already had the damaged pane replaced. My spirits sagged. Two people had been killed. Why? To know which window was mine, the killer must have followed me to my house at some point. Was I the next target?

I unlocked the front door and stepped into the foyer, shutting the door behind me. I heard a slight noise. "Audrey?"

No answer. No doubt it was Hildi. Oddly, the French doors to the parlor were open. We almost always kept them closed.

I opened the closet, but hesitated before shedding my coat. Something didn't feel quite right. I tiptoed over to the French doors. "Hildi? Come here, kitty."

Hildi peered at me from around the corner. She trotted toward me, then she stopped. She let out a loud meow.

Before I could move, a hideous pain resounded in the back of my head. Instinctively, I put my hands out. The floor seemed to be rising to meet my face.

chapter 20

The pain in my head was horrid. Hildi sat two inches from my nose. Maybe I was hallucinating.... Then I remembered where I was and what had happened: I'd been knocked unconscious.

My vision swam as I struggled to my feet, ignoring Hildi. The door was open behind me. The intruder had to have run out that way. I could only have been unconscious for a couple of seconds; the air wasn't even cold from the open door. I kicked it shut and staggered over to the sidelight. Through the beveled glass, I couldn't see anyone running or starting up their car. My purse was on the floor. I sat down beside it, retrieved my cell phone, and dialed 911.

Linda Delgardio and her partner arrived in less than ten minutes.

"You told the dispatcher not to send an ambulance?" Linda asked.

"I'm fine. I already called Audrey; she'll be home any second. She can drive me to the hospital if necessary."

"Did you get knocked out?"

"No," I lied. I didn't intend to sit in the emergency room for half of the night. "At least, I don't think so. I got knocked to the floor, and I shut my eyes for a moment. But I heard the storm door slam behind whoever did this."

I'd gotten a bag of frozen green beans out of the refrigerator. It was now icing the lump on my head.

"Is there any chance you're wrong about that?" Linda persisted. "About the intruder leaving through the front door, I mean?"

"No, I'm positive that I heard . . ." I paused and reconsidered. "I guess there's always the chance that I dreamed that part. When I first started to get up, I had a moment of confusion, where I thought I'd gotten up and run to the door to try to catch whoever conked me, then that I lay down on the exact spot where I'd fallen, and opened my eyes. *That* had to have been a dream."

"Yeah. Which you experienced when you were knocked out," Linda said with a scowl. "Be sure you have Audrey take you to the hospital. Head injuries aren't anything to dismiss."

Or I could have Audrey watch me for signs of a concussion, or worse, tonight. I knew that Linda knew I wasn't going to the hospital if I had anything to say about the matter.

Mansfield strode toward the French doors. "I'm going to check the house for signs of the intruder."

"Okay, take me through what happened again," Linda demanded of me in her investigator's voice. "You unlocked the front door and stepped inside. Did you look around at all?"

"No, I entered and shut the door behind me."

"So someone could have been standing behind the coatrack, and you might not have seen him or her?"

I glanced at the offending coatrack. It was a monstrous item that Audrey had purchased at a garage sale. Maybe I should pounce on this opportunity and suggest to Linda that they take it with them as evidence. "It's possible, yes. That's the direction I think the intruder rushed at me from."

"Here's how he got in," Mansfield called. "The back door's been jimmied."

"Call for CSI to come out," Linda called back. "Maybe we'll get lucky for once and be able to lift some fingerprints."

I was reconsidering my statement about the coatrack. "On second thought, Linda, all I really know is I didn't hear anybody come through the door. So whoever did it was hiding in the foyer."

"The intruder could have been hiding in the closet, then." She glanced at my clothing. "And you still haven't taken off your coat?"

"No. I'm cold." Not wanting to get carted off to the hospital, I added hastily, "But not because I'm hurt, only because I've been holding frozen vegetables against the lump on my head."

"Was the closet door open when you came home?"

"No, I started to take my coat off, but changed my mind. Then I thought I heard a noise—a small thump, which could have just been the cat." I paused as a Gilbert and Sullivan lyric—"Silent be, it was the cat"—raced unbidden through my addled brain. "At that point, I went over to the doors and called for Audrey, then Hildi."

"Could the noise have come from behind you?"

"It felt like it came from over there somewhere." I waved in the general direction of the den. "But maybe the intruder banged against the back of the closet. And I merely assumed the sound came from the other room."

Linda pursed her lips. She put on plastic gloves and began examining the double-wide closet. She seemed reluctant to change the spacing on any of the coats and held them in place as she ran the beam from her flashlight over each one. She focused her attention on my London Fog raincoat. "Is this yours?" she asked.

"Yeah. It's been too cold to wear it the last few days."

She patted down my coat, then reached into the pocket. "Is *this* yours?"

Dumbfounded, I stared at Linda's discovery. "Oh, my God! How did a *gun* get into my raincoat pocket?"

Her partner rushed into the foyer and gaped at the gun in Linda's hand. She frowned at him. He said, "I searched the main level and basement. No signs of the prowler."

She nodded and gave a slight glance at the staircase.

"I'll go check the upstairs," he said.

Linda returned her attention to me. "I'll bet someone was framing you and broke in strictly in order to put this firearm in your coat."

"But... framing me for *what*? Taylor was killed with a nail gun. And Shannon was stabbed with her sword."

She hesitated. "Friday night when your window was shot out? There'd been a related burglary in town, earlier. A forty-four Magnum was stolen."

I watched as Linda slipped the weapon into an evidence bag, which she labeled. "And *that*'s a forty-four Magnum?"

She didn't answer.

"Whose house was it stolen from?"

Mansfield returned. He must have "searched" the

upstairs at a dead run. Linda told me, "I'm not at liberty to say. Sorry." She gave me a sad smile. "I'll take this into ballistics for testing. I have a feeling it's going to match the slug and casing for the bullet that was fired through your window."

"So somebody broke into a house and stole a handgun? Then shot a bullet through my window Friday and broke into my house tonight, just to hide the gun in my pocket? That makes no sense."

Audrey had made a noisy entrance through the back door, and now she swept toward us. Her camel wool coat was unbuttoned and her face was flushed. Mansfield straightened his shoulders. "Evening, ma'am."

She focused her laser glare on him. "This is *unacceptable*! If not downright *appalling*! I told you to keep a keen eye on my house, and this happens, three nights later!"

"Sorry, ma'am."

She curled her lip at him, then turned her attention to me. "Why would someone do this to you? Did you interrupt a burglary?"

"I don't think so. The person who hit me stuck a handgun in my raincoat pocket. Apparently it's the same type of gun that fired the bullet Friday night. Linda thinks someone's trying to frame me."

"For shooting out your own window? That'd be idiotic."

"It's possible whoever did this is trying to make it look as if *Erin* was trying to shift suspicion away from *herself*," Linda explained. "If Erin hadn't come home right when she did, the original plan probably would have been to plant the weapon and then place an anonymous call to us, reporting a prowler in your house."

Audrey let Linda's words sink in, then looked at me. "You have no idea who attacked you?"

I started to shake my head, which was a mistake. It

hurt. "No, it was dark. And he or she was behind me the whole time. I think I might have been clocked with a flashlight, though. So if we see someone using a dented flashlight, we can arrest him on the spot."

Audrey put her hands on her hips. "I don't see how you can be so cavalier about all of this, Erin. You could have been killed. Or *I* could have been, if I'd been the one to walk through that door."

"No chance of that. You always use the back door." My knees were wobbly. I needed to lie down.

She gave me a withering look, and I held up a hand in apology. "Point taken," I muttered hastily. I started to edge my way through the French doors, craving the chance to sprawl on the beloved sage sofa and restore my strength. "I *was* lucky . . . in that I wasn't hurt any worse."

Audrey shed her coat and started to reach for a hanger. "Stop," Linda said. "A pair of crime scene investigators will be here shortly to test for fingerprints."

"Oh. Of course." Audrey folded the coat over her arm.

Linda gestured to her partner. "While we're waiting, Officer Mansfield and I will walk you through the house, just to double-check that nothing's missing or out of place."

Audrey nodded grimly.

"I'm going to sit down for a minute," I muttered, and made a beeline for the sofa. Hildi was already perched on a cushion and meowed at me.

Audrey followed me into the parlor and draped her coat across the wingback chair. "You persist in sticking your nose into murder investigations, Erin. It's like an obsession with you! One of these days you're going to get yourself killed!"

"Audrey . . . I'm an interior designer, not a mob boss or a drug dealer. I don't pose a threat to anybody."

"Tell that to whoever mugged you."

The next morning, Sullivan was on his best behavior. For once, I'd been timely and remembered to tell him about my bad experience, so as to spare myself from having to hear his we're-partners-and-blah-blah lecture. He was downright charming as we worked to complete our plans for a bedroom remodel in the foothills. He was unwilling to argue with me on anything, quickly acquiescing to my every suggestion. It was a little creepy, frankly. Till that moment, I hadn't realized how beneficial it was to have such an exacting, snarky sounding board and devil's advocate.

After a while, I caught him staring at me instead of at the fabric samples I was holding up for comparison. "My head's still reasonably round," I snapped at him. "Or were you waiting to see if horns would pop out?"

"Pardon?"

"I had a big lump for a few hours last night, but that mostly went away. It's a little tender to the touch still, is all."

He frowned. "Wouldn't it have been smarter for you to take some time off today? I can hold down the fort, you know. Did you have X rays taken? A CAT scan?"

"My head is perfectly fine. There isn't a thing wrong with meatballs. Constant kadoodles for being so wahwah bedoink."

Although I managed to keep a straight face while spouting gibberish, I cracked up when his eyes widened in horror. "Just kidding."

"Real funny, Gilbert. It's no wonder somebody smacked you upside the head."

Still laughing, I said, "True. Thanks for worrying about me, though." He was fighting back a smile. "And please stop being so nice to me. It helps my creativity when—"

I broke off as the door opened. Pate Hamlin was wearing a tailored jacket over a rumpled white shirt and blue jeans. "I was in the area. Thought I'd better discuss things with Erin." He gave me a small smile. "About her getting mugged, I mean."

"How did you hear about that?" I asked, startled.

"The police paid me a visit last night."

Sullivan rose and stepped toward our pseudo living room by the gorgeous palladium window, saying, "I think we'd better *all* have a little discussion. Pronto."

The words struck me as so much macho posturing, but Pate didn't take the bait; he merely sat down on one of the slipper chairs. Sullivan eased reluctantly into the leather chair beside him. I had no choice but to move to the love seat across from the men. "I had a break-in at my house last week," Pate said.

I studied his face. *Now* I knew who owned the handgun that Linda found in my pocket last night. Had his gun truly been stolen, or had Pate staged this break-in himself? "I'm sorry to hear that. I wonder if it was the same person who broke into Audrey's."

"That's what I need answers about," Pate replied, glowering at me.

"What do you mean?" I asked, confused.

"The police investigated when my office at home was ransacked. All of the fingerprints they found there were easily explained. Except for one set of prints." He held my gaze. "Yours."

"*Mine?* I've never as much as set foot in your office."

"And yet *your* fingerprints were on a hanging file folder. Which had been emptied."

"Pate." I leaned forward to emphasize the sincerity of my words. "That's simply not possible."

"Unless it *wasn't* really your folder, but one of Erin's," Sullivan interjected.

It took me a moment to make the connections. "Oh, of course! That's the only logical explanation!"

"I'm not tracking any of this," Pate said irritably.

"Last week," I began, "somebody stole a standard-issue, khaki-colored hanging folder out of my desk. It would have been covered in my fingerprints. Easy enough to swap tabs with yours... and make it look like I'd been handling that one file in your desk."

"Exactly," Sullivan said. "But why would you think Erin had any interest in going through the records in your desk?"

Pate tented his fingers. "The folder contained reports about an organization that's near and dear to her heart."

"No Big Boxes?" I guessed.

"Yes. And my file delineated the improprieties that Shannon and/or Audrey Munroe were responsible for."

"Improprieties? No way!" The accusation was so preposterous it was all I could do to stay seated. "Audrey's the most ethical person on the planet."

"Maybe she was kept unaware. It appeared that Shannon Young had been pocketing the donations to that committee. The records that I was compiling and planned to present to the authorities were swiped right out of my office. And the folder had your fingerprints on it."

Maybe it was the result of my minor concussion, but I had a moment of disjointedness. Our conversation struck me as absurd—the three of us sitting in this warm, cozy setting and discussing serious treachery. "Again, Pate," I said, exchanging glances with Sullivan, "I don't buy that about Shannon, either."

Pate gave a barely perceptible shrug. "My inside information would seem to say otherwise."

"And by insider, you mean your *wife*? The one you'd hired to run dirty tricks on the organization, spy on everything, and report back to you?"

"No, Erin. Tracy had nothing to do with it. The woman hates my guts. She'd sooner spit on me than keep me from drowning. And, before you go letting your imagination run even wilder, I did *not* concoct a phony burglary and then shoot a bullet through your window."

Sullivan glared at me. "Someone shot at you through your window? Why didn't you tell me?"

I sighed in exasperation. "Do you want me to start wearing a minicam atop a helmet just to keep you informed?"

"Maybe. Sure would've helped last night. You'd have spared yourself a head injury!"

"For your information, nobody 'shot at me.' I was downstairs at the time. Entirely different floor."

"Judging from the questions the police were asking me last night, the shooter used *my* forty-four Magnum," Pate interjected—a welcome interruption to our bickering. "Which had been stolen out of my desk in my office, along with the file."

"Somebody is trying hard to frame us," I told him. "There isn't—"

"Erin, we've got to leave for that appointment," Sullivan interrupted. He was right, although he could have waited till I'd finished my sentence.

Pate rose. "I should be going." I stood up, too, and he touched my arm gently. "On a much happier note, I meant to ask, Erin. My divorce will be finalized this Friday, and—"

Sullivan piped in, "I thought you and your wife were still arguing about which of you gets the house in Crestview."

"Tracy changed her mind. She agreed to a cash

buyout. She knows I'll win out in the long run and develop my property as I see fit."

Sullivan made a noise of disgust. "That house won't be worth owning by the time you're through wrecking the neighborhood."

"Anyway, Erin," Pate said, ignoring Sullivan, "I just wondered if you were free to help me celebrate over dinner. Friday night? At the Overlook."

My eyes widened. One minute the man was all but accusing me of breaking into his office, the next he was inviting me to the fanciest restaurant in town? How bizarre! My first instinct was to decline, but seeing Sullivan glare at me was tempting me to do otherwise. "Um, let me check my schedule."

"We have that bid on the job in Longmont Friday evening," Sullivan interjected.

"The reservation isn't till eight-thirty. I like to eat late."

"Typical yuppie," Sullivan muttered.

His rudeness sealed the deal for me. "Dinner sounds nice, Pate. Thank you. I'll be looking forward to it."

"Me, too. Pick you up around eight?"

"Fine."

He asked for my number and address, saying he'd remember and didn't need to write them down. Then he left.

As Pate closed the door behind him, Sullivan spat out: "He doesn't need to write down your address because he *already knows* where you live. He fired a bullet through your window and attacked you there! That was probably his real motive for dropping by just now... to find out if you were hospitalized or comatose. You need to cancel out on this dinner!"

"No! You're just making it sound dangerous because you're jealous. I'm merely researching a suspect over dinner. The same way you researched Rebecca over lunch."

"At least *Rebecca* wasn't asking me to celebrate her divorce with her." He grabbed his coat and charged outside, forcing me to trail after him.

I locked the door behind us, calling over my shoulder, "That's true. *She* was merely *causing* a divorce between our clients! Immediately prior to one of them winding up dead!"

He waited for me by his van. His face looked red hot. In the nippy air, it was easy to imagine steam rising from his head. "You're looking for trouble, Erin. Check that. You don't have to look for trouble. It strolls into our office all on its own." He hopped into the driver's seat and slammed his door.

We left. While I was ruminating on the fact that Sullivan's comment was too lame to warrant a response, my cell phone rang. It was Detective O'Reilly. He had "information for me" and wanted me to come down to the station house to "discuss" it. I checked my schedule and told him I could get there around three that afternoon.

At a few minutes past three, an officer escorted me to an interrogation room, then said he'd let the detective know I was there. I muttered, "Thanks," but was miffed. Regardless of whatever "information" O'Reilly had ostensibly beckoned me here to discuss, an interrogation room was the last place I wanted to be. O'Reilly must have known how reluctant I'd be to stay put, because he appeared at the doorway while I was still standing at the table, weighing whether I should sit or walk out.

"Afternoon, Miss Gilbert. Have a seat."

"I'd rather not stay that long."

He pulled out the cheap chair at the head of the

fake-wood laminate table and squinted up at me. "You in that big a hurry? If so, we can do this another time."

"The only reason you've put me in this horrid little room is so you can record our conversation. There's no reason for that. I'm not a suspect!"

"We like to record our interviews with witnesses, too. Helps us sort things out sometimes. You're free to leave, if you want. Though it'll help us solve your brother's death if you'll just give us a couple minutes of your time. Up to you."

I rolled my eyes, hating to be played like this, but I took a seat, opting to sit next to him instead of across the table, hoping that would at least throw him off his game.

"Like I said," O'Reilly began, "we've got some new evidence."

"By evidence, do you mean the fingerprints on the empty folder at Pate's house?"

"How'd you know about that?"

"Pate came to see me this morning."

"He shouldn't have done that."

"Well, in any case, Steve Sullivan and I have a theory about what happened. Remember the stolen folder? We're thinking it was swapped with Pate's. And, since I've never been in Pate's home office, you folks must have noticed that there were no fingerprints of mine anyplace *else* in the room. So a pilfered folder from my office is the only explanation. Other than that I was a complete moron and wore gloves as I was entering, searching, and leaving the room, but took them off while I was handling the one folder."

"That inconsistency occurred to us as well." He narrowed his eyes. "Which is why I didn't want anyone to spill the beans too early about Mr. Hamlin's break-in."

"'Spill the beans?' In other words, you still think *I* broke into his office?"

"You could have worn gloves and planted your empty folder there yourself, then switched tabs on it, just so you could claim you were being framed."

"Give me a break!"

"Hey. That's just as likely as *your* theory."

"Oh, please! For the record, I did *not* break into Pate Hamlin's house, and I most definitely did *not* murder anybody."

"You're acting pretty defensive, Miss Gilbert."

"That's because *you* are acting as though you suspect me. I was with Steve Sullivan both times . . . when Taylor Duncan was killed, and when Shannon Young was killed."

"You have an alibi for *most* of the time. But according to my notes, you were the last one to see Ms. Young alive."

"Sullivan was there too!"

"Not according to your statement," he countered promptly. "You said you went back inside alone. *Then* you and Mr. Sullivan left together."

"But . . . Shannon's and my whole conversation lasted less than a minute."

"Right. And that minute is what concerns me."

"Why?" I cried. "What possible motive would I have to kill my own client?"

"Avenging your brother's death."

"By stabbing Shannon? That's ridiculous!"

"You knew that her fingerprints were found on the nail gun."

"They *were*?"

"You confronted her, and she confessed the murder to you. Vengeance for your brother's life is a pretty good motive, by my way of thinking."

"Except she *didn't* confess. And *I* didn't suspect her, then or now. I didn't know about Shannon's fingerprints, but even if I did, she could have simply handled the nail gun before she left for the luncheon the day Taylor died. By *my* 'way of thinking,' the same person killed both of them. Furthermore, I *know* I'm innocent. Yet *you* keep insisting Taylor's death was an accident."

"We're still considering an accidental death as one possible scenario."

"Which I'm sure was exactly what the killer wanted everyone to think. And if he or she *could* have made it look like Shannon tripped and fell onto the sword, you'd have considered *that* a possibility as well."

O'Reilly laced his fingers and peered at me in silence. Finally, he asked, "Is there a reason for your hostility toward the police?"

"Frankly, it's not directed at the police in general, but to you personally, Detective O'Reilly. You're implying that I had a hand in my client's murder. Call me a hothead, but that doesn't lead me to harbor warm and fuzzy feelings toward you."

"I'm just doing my job, Miss Gilbert."

"And I'd really like to get back to *mine*."

"Fine. I'll get right to the point, then. It was reported that you spoke up at the council meeting in support of No Big Boxes. Did you know that Shannon was allegedly pilfering funds from the organization?"

"Pate told me that just this morning. But it's a batch of baloney."

"We found records and cashed checks for donations in her personal file cabinet."

Maybe those *were the records stolen from Pate's file*! *As one more attempt to shift police attention onto me!*

O'Reilly continued. "Which gives you yet another motive for murdering the woman. Wouldn't you agree, Miss Gilbert?"

"No! For one thing, Shannon Young had an alibi for

Taylor's murder. She was speaking at a luncheon. And, for another thing, Shannon could have been selling her pieces herself, occasionally. I'm sure her customers paid her in checks and cash all the time. She could have easily had deposits that were unaccounted for. That money could have gotten mixed up with donations for No Big Boxes from time to time. In any case, she was highly successful. She wouldn't have been stealing petty cash from the campaign."

"I'm talking about five thousand dollars that's gone missing and seems to have shown up in Shannon's bank account. Hardly petty cash. Plus, the Royala Hotel where she was speaking is just two miles from her house. And there's a fifty-minute gap where nobody at the luncheon remembers seeing her."

Precisely the scenario that Ang Chung had painted for me. Was he getting fed information by the police to use against me? No, this time I *was* being paranoid. "Am I under arrest, Detective?"

"No."

I left without another word. O'Reilly made no move to stop me. I got into the car and sat there, struggling to breathe and to keep from vomiting. My God! I was actually a murder suspect! O'Reilly had scared me so badly I could barely move.

What should I do now? No way could I go back to work. I counted to ten, then to thirty, and took calming breaths. Then I called Sullivan. I told him my head was starting to ache after all. He said he'd cover for me. I drove straight home, needing to shore my spirits; I craved comfort furniture the way other people ate comfort food.

I went for the whole treatment—a cup of Grandma's Tummy Mint tea, the sage sofa in the parlor, my lavender angora afghan, and an engrossing paperback. I tried unsuccessfully to coax Hildi to my lap. She did at least deign to occupy a seat in the same room—Audrey's wing chair. I'd only just gotten settled when the doorbell rang. It was Emily.

"Hi, come on in," I said, truly happy to see her, although she looked ill; her face was pale and her features drawn.

"Thanks. I should have called first, I know, but..."

"You don't need to have a formal invitation before you can drop by. It's just that I'm gone a lot, so I'm glad you caught me in." I ushered her into the parlor. "Is everything all right?"

She sighed and lowered herself onto the far end of the sofa, and I reclaimed my seat. "I haven't been sleeping well," she confessed.

"That's understandable."

She pursed her lips and nodded. "Erin, I finally got myself together enough to go through the boxes from Taylor's apartment. Did you look at any of his papers?"

"I glanced at one or two of them, but that's all. Why?"

"I found this." She pulled some sheets of paper out of her purse and unfolded them. It looked like a packet of four or five pages, stapled together. She held it out to me, and I rose and took it from her. "It's a signed contract. Taylor really *did* have a written agreement with David Lewis, giving him all ownership rights to his workstation design."

"Oh, my gosh." I dropped back into my seat and flipped to the last page. I stared at the two signatures on the bottom—David's and Taylor's—and at the date that each man had printed. "This was just the day before Taylor died! Does the signature look like Taylor's?"

She gave me a grim nod. "It's his handwriting. I'm sure of it."

"Strange timing," I muttered and started reading the terms of the contract.

"It's all pretty clear-cut," Emily said in a sad voice. "Taylor agreed to receive two thousand dollars for the idea itself. He'd get bonuses as well . . . but only if a ton of the units were sold."

"Oh, jeez. That's pathetic! He sold his big idea for peanuts."

"Yeah. And to his *boss*." Emily added bitterly.

I was holding the contract with clenched fists. "This is just . . ." I let my voice fade as I took stock of Emily's expression. She was clearly both livid and heartbroken about her son having been duped. It would be best for me to wait till I'd talked to David yet again before telling her that Pate claimed to have paid him ten grand last year for "his" idea.

Could Taylor have learned about David's deception and gotten into a fight to the death with him? And maybe Shannon had uncovered David's murderous role, so he killed her too.

"Emily, back before his final stint in jail, did Taylor ever mention the name David Lewis to you?"

"No. They'd just met for the first time when Taylor interviewed for the job. Not even two weeks before he was killed."

"Are you sure about that?"

"Positive."

I nodded, then skimmed through the rest of the document, looking for a reference to Pate. I found none. "Is Pate Hamlin's name in this contract? Or BaseMart?"

"No. And I've read every word."

"What about Pied Piper? That's the brand name for the BaseMart product line."

"No. The contract is a personal agreement between Taylor and David. It says David's buying all rights to the All-Position Workstation. That's all. No one else is involved. Why?"

I looked at the date again and sighed. "The thing is, Taylor's design is already being marketed at BaseMart stores." Emily's eyes widened. "BaseMart must've had the design in the works for at least a year now."

"But . . . that could only be possible if somebody stole the idea back when Taylor was first building the prototype. Before he was put in jail."

"Are you *sure* he got a patent . . . in his name?"

Emily furrowed her brow. "I *assumed* so. He was all excited about the initial feedback. But then we had that falling-out, and he went to jail, and I never actually saw the physical documentation for his patent."

I gestured at the contract. "Can I keep this for a while?"

"Of course. Are you going to take it to the police?"

"Yes." Soon. "And I'm going to get to the bottom of it myself, as well."

She mustered a weak smile. "Thank you, Erin. Thank God I have at least one person on my side. And on Taylor's."

David Lewis was hunched over some blueprints on his desk when I arrived. We exchanged a few words of chitchat, then I asked, "Where are those patents for the workstation you said you'd show me?"

"I'll have my secretary fax you the information about the contract with Pate in another day or two," he snapped. "What's the rush? It won't bring him back to life."

"I am well aware of that. Tell you what . . . you can just have her send everything straight to the Crestview police. We'll let them untangle the whole thing."

"Jesus God! Give it a rest, Erin! I didn't do anything wrong!"

"That's impossible for me to believe." I reached for my cell phone.

"Who are you calling?"

"The police."

"Wait. There's . . . no need to get them involved. Okay. I'll . . . tell you the whole story."

"Go ahead, David, but I'm warning you, I'm convinced this is a matter for the police, and my patience is at an end." I dropped into a chair.

He hesitated, then released a gusty sigh of resignation. "About a year ago, Duncan comes stumbling into my office, high as a kite. He claims he wants a job, but he's obviously doing everything he can to sabotage the interview. This was right at the end of the day, a Friday, and I'd just been given a six-pack for winning a little bet. I figure, what the hell. I offer him a beer, and we wind up shooting the breeze. He tells me about this design for a computer workstation he's putting together in his basement. I didn't think the guy should be driving, so I do the responsible thing and give him a ride home. All the way to Lafayette. He shows me his model, gives me the blueprints, asks if I want to be partners."

David spread his arms energetically, trying, too late, to be appealing. "Thing is, it's not half bad, you know? I'm thinking, with a little work and revision, who knows? Maybe this idea could be worth a couple grand. So I figure, I'll help the guy out, maybe find out how to go about getting a product out on the market. He gives me a copy of his blueprints. I give him my business card, tell him to stop by my office next week some time." He snorted. "I never hear from the guy again. Meantime, I've been working with this connection . . . well, with Pate Hamlin, as you know, and things are happening. I knew Taylor's name and where he lived, but that's all. So, three or four months later, I went back to his place. Nobody's home. I left my business card again, but he never called. Then, a couple weeks ago, he strolls into my office for the second time. The guy obviously has no recollection of our ever having met. . . ."

I was seething. I believed his story this time, but it was also painfully easy to read between the lines. All he had to do was glance inside Emily's mailbox and he'd have learned her last name. "E. Blaire" was listed in the phone book, along with her address. With a minimal effort, he could have located Taylor. He hadn't *wanted* to find him. "So you stole his design."

"Not true. I'd made so many changes by then that it was *my* design."

I rose and rounded my chair—a pathetic piece of furniture, a flimsy, mud-colored, metal folding chair, which this pathetic man felt was adequate for potential clients. I gripped its backrest, wishing I were the sort of person who could bash him over the head with it. Just as *he* very well might have done to *me* the other night. "We're going to have to let the courts decide that."

"Get real!" He threw up his hands as if I were guilty of exasperating *him*. "I've made all of two thousand dollars on the design! Pate says he'll be lucky to break even. We gave it a shot, but it didn't sell."

I wasn't about to reveal that Pate had told me he'd paid five times that amount, and that I had a copy of David's and Taylor's contract, signed well after David had already fraudulently sold the design. The man was a swindler and we both knew it. "Maybe an icky BaseMart store was the wrong market for my brother's design."

"Before you get all high and mighty on me, remember that *I* was the one who gave your no-account brother a good job, when nobody would hire the guy to clean their gutters. He made more working for me, and doing a lousy job, too, by the way, than I did on his input for the design."

"Let me tell you something, Mr. Lewis. My mother told me that somebody denigrated his idea and his prototype, and that it broke his spirit. She was talking about *you*. You deliberately lied to him about his invention's viability, so you could get it from him for a pittance. *Then* my brother died, with a nail in his head, at the work site where *you* hired him to work!" *I was taking the contract straight to the police.*

David's face was now crimson. He spat out, "I'm sorry about that, but I didn't kill him. Our computer desk design has *nothing* to do with his death."

I started to lift the folding chair, still longing to hurl it at his face. I set it back down. Resorting to physical violence was stupid. I pivoted and said over my shoulder, "My advice for you is to get a lawyer."

chapter 21

"*You've been distracted all evening,*" Audrey remarked as I picked at my beef stew that night.

My argument with David Lewis was still too raw, so I decided to spare us both from relating that sad story. "Detective O'Reilly told me today that there were financial records in Shannon's files that made it look like Shannon had stolen five thousand dollars worth of No Big Boxes donations. But *Tracy* was doing your bookkeeping, right?"

"After taking over for Shannon. Who was impossibly disorganized when it came to any kind of paperwork. But there is absolutely no *way* Shannon would have embezzled funds. She'd have lost something like fifty times that amount if BaseMart succeeded in building by her house. She donated ten K herself!"

"At some point could she have decided she wanted a partial refund?"

Audrey shook her head. "She made the donation months ago, when BaseMart was trying to move into city limits. If she wanted to take half of it back, she'd have discussed it with me first. And I'd have made up the difference."

Maybe she'd been too embarrassed to do so, I thought, but kept the remark to myself. Instead, I told her about Pate's handgun being the one that wound up in my coat pocket, and my certainty that my empty file folder had been planted in his office. "My hunch is that Pate's records were planted in Shannon's cabinet and doctored to make it look like she was embezzling funds."

"Why?"

"To frame *me* for her murder."

"The police think *you* would kill Shannon because you found out she'd supposedly embezzled a measly five thousand dollars? Out of a campaign you were barely even part of?"

"Well, more importantly because Shannon's fingerprints were on Taylor's nail gun. Which I'm thinking got there when she happened to pick it up at some point."

"What nonsense! Considering you as a suspect is preposterous! Wasn't Steve with you the whole time?"

"For all but a minute or so." I sighed, not able to muster any righteous indignation at the moment. "Is it possible that *Tracy* was acting as an amateur double agent? That she was working for Pate all along, and not for No Big Boxes?"

"You think Tracy Osgood was planting incriminating evidence against you? You two have barely met!"

"I know." *But if she thought I was after her husband,*

she could have despised me even so. "It's just something I'd like to rule out."

"I doubt Tracy was sabotaging us. I sincerely think she's been working hard to undermine Pate. Though I guess it *is* possible, considering she deliberately didn't tell us about their relationship." Audrey dabbed at her lips with her cloth napkin and scooted back her chair. "I know how we might be able to find out. When it was clear that Shannon wasn't the right person to be in charge of the books, I asked her to give the records to me. I had a copy made for me before I handed everything over to Tracy."

"That could be a big help."

She rifled through her desk for quite a while, but eventually she returned, clutching an inch-thick stack of papers. "I'll bet this will vindicate Shannon. If anything was changed in the records that the police now have, maybe it'll help them find the culprit."

"I'll get them to Linda. Thanks."

She held them out to me, but didn't relinquish her grasp. "Erin, I know you want to help your clients. And I know that you want to help your mother to get some closure in your brother's death. That's all very admirable. Just don't act like an undercover officer. Please."

"All I'm doing is keeping my eyes and ears open."

"That's fine." She finally let me take the No Big Boxes reports from her. "But don't do anything stupid, like dating that awful Pate Hamlin. Please."

My jaw dropped. "Audrey! Did Steve Sullivan put you up to saying that?"

"Don't be silly. Of course not. I was watching the way Mr. Hamlin was looking at you at the city council meeting last week. It was quite obvious that he's attracted to you." She frowned. "You're not seriously thinking of dating him, are you?"

Not wanting to lie or tell her the truth, I stalled. "Why would you even suggest such a thing?"

"He seems like your type. The brooding, handsome, self-possessed kind. And judging by your reaction just now, you obviously *have* been thinking about dating him. Somebody shot out your window. And conked you over the head. Not to mention that you're being framed for murder. Don't you think you've got enough on your plate as it is? Do you *have* to add dating a prime suspect to your to-do list?"

She was right. What was I thinking? That my going to dinner with him would encourage him to confess? I had to get out of this date. Here I was suspecting either him or his wife of perhaps murdering my brother and my client. And how did I even know he was being truthful about his divorce being finalized? Plus, he was currently Audrey's adversary.

At the earliest opportunity, I sneaked upstairs and called him. Unfortunately, he answered; it would have been easier to leave a message. Before he had the chance to put his salesmanship skills to work on me, I said, "I'm having second thoughts about our date. I think it'd be best if I declined, at least until everything gets resolved with Shannon's murder."

"Her death is tragic, but we still need to eat. Why should that stop us from going to dinner?"

"It feels like a big conflict of interest, if nothing else. I'm working for Michael, after all, and the two of you still have unresolved issues . . . and the police still have an unsolved murder investigation going on."

"You think *I* murdered Shannon?"

"Pate. You're asking me if I think you *murdered* someone. Do you *seriously* want to argue that this is the right time for us to go on a first date?"

"You have a point." There was a pause. "Then again,"

he added with a chuckle, "we'll never be at a loss for conversation topics during dinner."

I fought not to laugh. The last thing I wanted was to discover that the man had a good sense of humor. That invariably led me to disaster. "I'm sure you'll find other ways to celebrate your freedom."

"Yes, I'm sure I will, too."

There was a pause. I was tempted to tell him about my argument with David and ask if I could see a copy of their contract. O'Reilly had told me to keep the matter quiet when I'd given him the contract Emily had discovered among Taylor's papers, however.

Pate said, "As long as we're on the phone anyway, there's a second matter to discuss. You need to talk to your client."

He could only mean Michael, but I asked, "Which one?"

"Michael Young. He's installed a miniature gallows on his front yard. I'm being hung in effigy."

That was appallingly juvenile of Michael, but I wasn't about to criticize my client to a third party. "Did you talk to him about it?"

"Of course. I asked him nicely to take it down. He insists that Shannon had created it. He claims that since it's on his property, he has a right to display his dead wife's artwork. I'd like to get this resolved peacefully before we both have to call our lawyers. Michael's trying to goad me into destroying it so he can level criminal charges."

I was sure that was his motive as well, but again held my tongue out of client loyalty.

"I'll talk to him, but I doubt I'll have a lot of sway in what he wants to have on his lawn."

"I can try asking Rebecca, too. She might be able to talk Ang Chung into telling him to take it down."

The remark startled and confused me. “Why would you want Ang to get involved with this?”

Pate hesitated. “Come to think of it, that’s a good question. He wielded plenty of influence with Shannon. I suppose Michael can’t stand the guy.”

“And why would Rebecca carry weight with Ang?”

“No reason. I was just talking through my hat. Sorry you’re canceling out on dinner. Maybe some other time.”

The following morning, thanks in no small part to me, Sullivan and Gilbert Designs would now be massively behind schedule unless we handled as many appointments separately as possible. Even so, I headed out to Michael’s neighborhood to see how bad his new lawn ornament really was.

It was very bad—about four feet high, ugly, and artless. I didn’t for an instant believe that Shannon had created it, unless she’d had a psychotic break. Pate’s “likeness” was a Raggedy Andy doll with a head shot of Pate trimmed from a newspaper and glued over the doll’s face. The supporting structure was built from two-by-fours and looked like a real gallows, with a length of twine serving as the rope.

Roberto—a thirtyish, competent member of David’s crew—happened to be unloading supplies from his pickup when I emerged from my rental car, and I asked him if he knew if Michael had built the thing himself.

“Nah. That guy doesn’t know which end of a hammer to use. He brought us the doll just before our lunch break yesterday and gave each of us a twenty. Asked us to slap the thing together for him. Said he wanted to install it himself, though.” He pointed at the gallows with his chin. “Pretty lame, huh?”

I held my tongue but couldn’t refrain from nodding.

Michael came outside while Roberto returned to work. "Did Pate call you about my art piece?" he asked.

"Yes. He's assuming you're trying to provoke him into destroying it."

"Could be. It's not like I'm out of line here. Either he or Ang killed my wife. *One* of them deserves to be hung till they're dead!" He glared at Pate's house for a moment, then smirked at me. "Or maybe I'm just into . . . what do you call that kind of tacky stuff that looks like someone's kids did it? Primitive art?"

"Michael, aren't you cutting off your nose to spite your face here?"

"What do you mean?"

"Didn't you want to put your house on the market as soon as possible? How impressed are prospective buyers going to be by the likeness of your closest neighbor being hung in effigy on their new lawn?"

His eyes widened. "You have a point. That won't be good. Frankly, I thought the contraption would disappear overnight. I'll for sure take it down before the For Sale sign goes up."

"You shouldn't wait that long. You're lucky you haven't drawn photographers from the *Sentinel* out here so far. Buyers are *already* going to be aware that two people have died in this house. Now you're publicly airing your ongoing squabbles with your neighbor. Buyers want homes where they're going to *like* their neighbors, not want to hang them in effigy. Not to mention that you'll be hammering home the fact that your neighborhood's getting ruined by Pate's development plans."

More color drained from Michael's face. "Oh, God. I didn't think of that. The press was already here. I'll call the *Crestview Sentinel* now and threaten to sue if they run the photographs. Can you get rid of that thing in the meantime? Please?" He dashed back inside his house.

Easier said than done, as it turned out. I untied Raggedy-Andy-cum-Pate, but the gallows were well constructed. The post had been sunk deep into the ground, and a supportive base prevented me from simply jiggling it back and forth till it came loose. I hoped I wouldn't have to pull Roberto away from his work. While I struggled with the ugly contraption, I heard a car pull into Pate's driveway. I turned. Rebecca Berringer. Gag me.

She gave me a smug grin as she emerged from her car. Her stiletto heels were soon clicking on the concrete as she approached. "Well, Erin. I see you're now expanding your business to include *exterior* design. Can't say that I think much of your taste, however."

"I'm helping Michael remove this, as you undoubtedly already realized."

"Good decision. It just didn't have the overall panache that your *partner*, at least, achieves with his designs."

Too irked to hold my tongue, I snapped, "I haven't heard Steve mention your name lately. I take it things haven't worked out between you two."

"Oh, on the contrary, we're just choosing not to jinx our relationship by advertising it. We have a date on Friday night, as a matter of fact. At the Overlook."

Damn it! What the hell was Sullivan thinking? My cheeks were burning. I turned my back on Rebecca, pretending to be absorbed in removing the pseudo gallows once more. "Have a nice time," I said over my shoulder.

"At the Overlook? That's a given. Yummy food... yummy companion."

My anger at Rebecca and Sullivan gave me new strength. I yanked the hideous thing up and out of the ground. Just then, Rebecca said, "Oh. Here he comes now!"

Startled, I turned and indeed spotted Sullivan's van heading this way. I let the gallows crash onto the lawn while he parked. Rebecca immediately yammered to him about how much she was looking forward to their date. I kept my back turned the whole time, pretending to be transfixed by kicking dirt into the hole. At length, she cooed, "See you soon," and I heard a kissing sound just prior to her clacking footfalls as she made her way back toward Pate's home.

"Hey, Gilbert."

Don't mention his date! I silently commanded myself as I turned and forced a smile.

"Hi, Sullivan. I didn't realize you'd be stopping by here."

"Likewise. Actually, I wasn't planning on coming out, but a reporter called our office. Wanted to know if we had any comment on what our client had put in his front lawn. Thought I'd better see what was going on."

"That's why I'm here, too. Pate told me about it."

"Ah. So you rushed right out and took it down. That must've pleased Pate to no end. Having you at his beck and call."

I clenched my fists. "If you were planning on spying on us at the Overlook Friday night, you'll be disappointed. I canceled."

"You were going to the Overlook?"

I rolled my eyes. "As if you didn't already know that."

"Huh. That must be how Rebecca suddenly wound up with dinner reservations there on the busiest night of the week. He must have let her take them when you canceled. Must have figured he didn't want to keep them if you weren't joining him."

I had no response. "So you and Rebecca are still dating?"

He ignored my question and opened his van door. "Now that I know you've got this under control, I'd better get going to the Kahns' house."

"And I'm going to stop by Crestview Windows and get some prices on their bays."

Sullivan drove off. I watched as a biker in a black leather jacket headed down the hill, his engine noisy. To my surprise, he pulled up right beside me. He cut his loud engine and asked, "Is Antonio Scollotti here?"

"No, I'm sorry. I don't know anyone by that name. The owner of the house is home, though . . . Michael Young?"

"Nah, Antonio might be working here. Doing that feng shui stuff for the wife."

Antonio? "A man named Ang Chung used to do feng shui consultations here. Is that who you mean?"

"Yeah, that's gotta be him." He laughed and shook his head. "So he's calling himself by a Chinese name now? Should've guessed as much. He's one crazy dude."

"How do you know Antonio, if you don't mind my asking?"

"We were cell mates. At the Crestview County Jail. S'pose that freaks you out, though . . . talking to an ex-con and all." He gave me a lopsided grin.

"No, my brother spent some time in jail."

"Oh, yeah? He doin' okay now?"

I shook my head. "He died recently."

"Oh, hey, lady. Taylor Duncan was your brother?"

"Yes. Did you know him?"

"Antonio told me he was working here, too, as a carpenter. He was in the Crestview jail the same time we were."

chapter 22

Taylor and Ang—Antonio, rather—knew each other from when they were in *jail*?"

He frowned. "Ain't like we were all pals or nothing, but yeah."

"Neither of them mentioned their having met before."

"Jail ain't like high school, lady. Not a lot of good times, you know?"

"Sure, but..." I was about to say that I was surprised Taylor hadn't at least told me that Ang was working here under a false identity; Taylor must not have wanted to delve into any topic that would have prolonged our discussion about his jail time. In any case, the fact that Ang had a criminal past made Ang/Antonio all that stronger a suspect. "Have you checked to see if Antonio is in his office?"

"Yeah. He wasn't there. Or in his pad."

"What's his home address?"

His expression turned icy. "Seems to have slipped my mind. Sorry." He started up his noisy engine and took off.

Damn it! I hadn't even learned the man's name.

Later that day, I skipped lunch and took a client to the Denver Design Center to look at area rugs and draperies. The spectacular silk items we'd selected would complete her master bedroom makeover in fabulous style. Sullivan called my cell phone just after I'd dropped her off at her home. "Our schedule's gotten out of hand. Where are you right now?" he asked.

"Northeast Crestview," I replied. "I just finished with the Smiths for today and was about to head to the office to meet with the reps from that tile company."

"I'll handle that solo. Can you swing over to Pate Hamlin's instead, since you're already in the general area?"

That was an odd request. "I guess so. Why? What does Pate want?"

"Dunno. Never talked to him. Rebecca arranged this. Said it'd just take ten minutes or so. I was supposed to be there five minutes ago, but I'm still clear across town. You're fifteen minutes closer than I am."

"Will do," I said, grinning. Rebecca was going to be severely disappointed at having me show up in Sullivan's place.

The drive took me ten minutes, which meant I was fifteen minutes late for Sullivan's ten-minute consult. I rang Pate's doorbell, then turned to gaze across the street. From this vantage point I could fully appreciate how much better Michael's house was looking. The police cordoning was gone. The roof had been replaced, and the damage from the bulldozer had been repaired. Maybe its feng shui curse had, at long last, lifted. Just in time for him to put the property on the market.

The footfalls on the other side of the door sounded decidedly feminine—like stilettos. Rebecca Berringer answered. She had apparently spruced herself up for this appointment and was now dressed to the nines. Her face fell. The reaction made my smile all the wider.

With obvious reluctance, Rebecca opened the glass outer door for me. "Hi, Erin. Rumor has it that you're nearly done across the street."

"As rumors go, that's not exactly A-list material, but yes, we're making progress."

She pursed her lips and nodded. "So. Where's Steve?"

"He's still downtown. He got hung up at a client's house."

"*He's* the one we wanted to talk to."

"And yet *I'm* the one who's here."

"Well. This will be awkward, then. But quick. Could you please tell him that Pate is considering hiring him as my co-designer?" She grabbed the doorknob as though primed to shut the door in my face.

"You can't be serious, Rebecca."

"Oh, I am, Erin. Very serious."

"But Pate isn't even *keeping* this house, is he? Isn't he going to raze it for BaseMart or his condo development?"

"Not for another couple of years. And he wants to live in luxury in the meantime."

"But . . . why would you suddenly need a partner? You can't handle the work here?"

She ratcheted up her already haughty expression by arching an eyebrow. "That's called success, my dear."

It was all I could do to keep myself from slapping her silly.

"You see, Erin, I was discussing with my client the fact that my show is such a huge success that I'm forever finding myself needing to be in two places at the same time. All the public appearances and so forth. Sharing my workload is the perfect solution, and Steve is virtually the only designer I could entrust my clients with."

She was wearing a lovely cream-colored linen suit. If only I had a cup of coffee that I could accidentally spill on her! "Too bad that he's already got a business partner, Rebecca, so there's no way he'd ever agree to such a thing."

She chuckled. "When the price is right, all sorts of complicated business strategies suddenly become feasible." She glanced behind her shoulder into Pate's home. "Such as, for example, 'Sullivan and Gilbert' becoming 'Sullivan and Berringer.'"

"Seriously? You think you can just buy me out?"

"Not necessarily. More likely, I'll just buy Sullivan away from you. That way you'll get to revert to your little 'Designs by Gilbert' business."

"I wouldn't be so cocky about that stupid notion if I were you, Rebecca. It's going to take a hell of a lot more than one client to make Steve and me dissolve our partnership!"

"We'll see about that, Erin. Just pass along the message, if you will? Thanks, dear." She shut Pate's door.

Livid, I drove straight to the office. Sullivan was already there, wrapping up the meeting with the tile sales representative. He was gracious enough to recap some of the highlights of his presentation for me before leaving. I pretended to be fascinated.

"How'd things go at Pate's?" Sullivan asked me afterward.

"He wasn't there. Or if he was, Rebecca was playing bodyguard and never gave me access. She claims that she and Pate want to hire you to partner with her on finishing up his house."

He chuckled. "What's the punch line here, Gilbert? She thinks we're suddenly going to become Sullivan, Gilbert, and Berringer?"

"No, just Sullivan and Berringer."

"Come on, Gilbert. Be serious."

I spread my arms. "Those are her words, not mine. She claims she's such a red-hot commodity with her TV show and too-numerous-to-count clients she needs a helper, and that you're the only one she trusts. Again, that's a direct quote."

"Maybe she's just messing with your head... trying to tick you off. No way would she actually believe I'd go for it."

"Which is what I told her. *She*, however, was confident you'd kowtow, once she threw enough money at you."

"Huh." He rocked on his heels. "So how much money are we talking about here?"

"Sullivan!" I swatted his arm.

"Hey. I'm a designer slut. What can I say?" He grinned from ear to ear.

Audrey was puttering around in the kitchen when I arrived that evening. She told me that she too had only recently gotten home—that everyone had been putting in extra hours at the TV station. We threw together a quick dinner: spinach salad, French bread, and pasta with some leftover chicken. Delicious! We joked about how wonderful it was that we were both "Domestic Goddesses." Then we carried our glasses of Chardonnay into the parlor and chatted about silly things like the latest reality shows on TV. The doorbell rang, and Audrey went to the door.

"Hello, Tracy," Audrey said. "Would you like to come in?" I could tell by the sound of her voice that she was as surprised by a visit from Tracy Osgood as I was.

"Just for a moment, if I may. Thank you."

Tracy entered, giving me a sheepish smile.

"Hi, Tracy," I said. "Can I get you something to drink?"

"No, thank you. I just came to tell y'all how very sorry I am about Shannon's death."

"Thanks," I replied, waiting for the other shoe to drop. There was no way she'd come here in person just to offer her condolences for the loss of Audrey's co-chair and my difficult client.

"Frankly, I didn't know Shannon all that well, but I certainly admired her and will miss her," Audrey said. "Have a seat, Tracy." She gestured at the Sheridan chair adjacent to her own favorite seat—a gold damask wing chair with a regal, thronelike appearance. "I assume you have other business with us."

Tracy perched on the seat and gave a tight-lipped nod. She seemed as edgy as a mouse who'd stumbled into a cat's den. "Yes, I do. I also wanted to apologize to y'all for not being up-front about Pate being my ex-husband."

"Yes, you should have told us about that from the start."

"Why *didn't* you?" I asked.

"I was too embarrassed. Here y'all were trying to save the town's integrity. Whereas I just wanted to force Pate to stick the store someplace else . . . so that our divorce settlement would be more lucrative for me."

"Which is why you didn't appear on the scene till the

city of Crestview had already voted to ban BaseMart within city limits," Audrey surmised.

"'Fraid so. I'm the typical NIMBY—not in my backyard."

"Where did Pate get the information for his No Big Boxes file?" I asked.

She looked at me with shocked, wounded eyes, as though I'd slapped her. "I have no earthly idea, Erin. I don't know what he had in that file, let alone how he got his information. I had nothing to do with it."

"But you obviously knew he *had* such a file."

"Yes. Because Pate called me when he first realized someone had broken into his desk. He thought *I'd* stolen it. But do you mean to tell me you think *I* was spying on y'all? That I was *pretending* to be against BaseMart, just to infiltrate your campaign?"

I shrugged. "The documents from Pate's office apparently turned up in Shannon's file cabinet. And were doctored to make it look as though she'd been stealing from the organization."

"I swear to y'all, I had nothing to do with any of that. Those books were a bit... disorganized when I got them from Shannon, but all the money was there and properly accounted for. And I can't imagine why anyone would go to the trouble of fiddling with the books."

Audrey explained: "To throw a monkey wrench into No Big Boxes, and to make it look like somebody believed that Shannon was stealing from the campaign coffers and therefore killed her."

"The only person I can imagine framing somebody for her murder like that is Pate himself. Erin, I know he's been asking you out. And, believe you me, that man can charm the socks off a kitty cat. But he's so competitive that he loses his head. He'd sell his mama's house right out from under her to get ahead."

Was this an accurate assessment? Or merely a bitter divorcée talking?

Perhaps sensing my skepticism, Tracy frowned and stood. "There's one other thing. I only found out the other day that the carpenter that got killed was your brother?"

"Yes. Taylor Duncan was my half brother."

"As my rotten luck would have it, that Saturday was the one other time this entire month that I've been over to see Pate. Right around lunchtime? And... I saw him leaving Shannon's house."

I tensed. "Did you ask him about it?"

"He claimed that he was over there to talk to her and her husband, but that nobody answered the door."

"That's possible."

"Except I saw him *shutting* the door. And... wiping his fingerprints off the knob."

Audrey and I exchanged glances. That was probably when Pate had gone over to the house to swap out their building supplies, as he'd already admitted doing. But, even if so, why would he take the precaution of removing his fingerprints? "You suspect Pate killed Taylor?" I asked Tracy.

"I hope I'm wrong. I really do."

"What did the police say when you told them?"

"They thanked me for the information." She offered Audrey a wan smile and a quick apology "for barging in on you," and abruptly turned to leave.

She'd raised my suspicions, and I said, "I'll walk you to your car," and followed her without giving her a chance to decline. "So, you told the police you'd seen Pate wiping off the doorknob, Tracy?" I pressed.

"Well, no, not exactly."

"He might have wiped away the killer's fingerprints," I exclaimed. "Did you tell Pate you saw him?"

She shook her head. "He has a bad temper."

"*I'll* tell the police, then, Tracy," I cried. "Somebody has to! You can't conceal evidence like this!"

"Fine. But I'll deny every word of this to the police when they ask me about it!"

"So why did you tell *me*? Why tell anyone?"

She pursed her lips and used her electronic key lock to open a forest-green Subaru Outback. "I wanted you to know exactly what you were dealing with, Erin. Pate's attracted to you. But he's also still steaming over how effective your speech to the town council was. If he realizes he isn't going to get to first base with you, he'll do a one-eighty. He's going to destroy your business, and then he's going to destroy your life. And, Erin, he has the money and power to do it. There's nothing you can do to stop him."

"If that's true, what good does your warning do for me? I might as well give up and run."

"Exactly, Erin."

She continued to hold my gaze with an earnest expression. It all struck me as so absurd, I had to laugh. She was just trying to make me leave town! The woman might simply be one of those I-don't-want-him-but-you-can't-have-him types. "Once again, Tracy, thanks for stopping by."

"I'm dead serious, Erin. It's time for you to cover your losses and wave the white flag. Now. Before it's too late."

She drove away without saying good-bye. I mulled over the situation as I returned to the house. I explained to Audrey that I needed to make a couple of phone calls and went to my room. I dialed my friend Linda and reached her at the police station.

We chatted for a minute, then I asked, "Could I please treat you like my own private police officer for a few minutes and run some things by you?"

"What kind of things?"

"Oh, suspicious behavior and fishy timing from some people involved with both my brother and Shannon."

She sighed. "In other words, you want me to be your go-between with O'Reilly."

"That's the blunt way of putting it. Though I can throw in 'please' a half-dozen times."

"I've got too much going on right now. Would first thing tomorrow morning be okay? Seven A.M.?"

I gulped a bit at the early hour, but said, "Sure thing." We finalized our arrangements, then I sat down and wrote up a list of the goings-on with the circle of people at my deceased client's house.

A few minutes after seven the next morning, Linda and I sat at The Corner Coffee Shop, a new place within walking distance of my house. Its location was wonderfully convenient for me, but I'd have patronized this place even if it had been clear across town. I'd designed it myself during my last official job as proprietor of Designs by Gilbert. The café owner had wanted to get away from the uniform look of the chain coffee shops, so we'd gone with unique, homey tables and chairs. I'd procured them from garage sales and secondhand shops, and I'd refinished them. The place made me smile. It was like walking into your favorite elderly relative's house. Everything felt comfy and well loved.

Linda and I were sitting at a circular two-top, and she was studying my notes about the virtual rip-off of Taylor's workstation design. We'd already discussed Tracy's claims of seeing Pate wipe off the doorknob at Shannon's house. At length, Linda said, "An awful lot of the circumstantial clues and motives point not just to David Lewis, but to Pate."

"I know. I just...have a hard time thinking Pate's guilty. He just...I don't know. I can't explain it. He's mega-wealthy. I can't see him firing a nail gun at Taylor or stabbing Shannon with a sword."

"He's a gentleman, so you can't see him getting down and dirty and violent?"

"The logic sounds silly when you spell it out like that."

She peered at me. "Pate's great looking and seems really engaging. Just like Steve Sullivan. Therefore you *assume* he has the same basic decency as Steve."

I massaged my forehead, not wanting to believe her theory. "Things also point back at Michael. Despite what Emily thinks, the murders might have nothing whatsoever to do with Taylor's invention and instead be the classic case of a husband who wants his freedom but also wants the inheritance. Or Taylor discovered David had ripped him off, and David killed him and then Shannon, to cover up his crime. Then there's Ang Chung, a.k.a. Antonio Scollotti. Did you know that Ang Chung was an alias and that he recently got out of jail?"

"He legally changed his name. And, yes, I did know about his stint for burglary. And that he'd met your brother while they were both incarcerated."

"Ang's a burglar? So he used to break into people's homes? Did he use the same M.O. as in my office break-in and Pate's? Remember how I found his button in Shannon's attic?"

"That's not a strong enough connection to allow us to issue an arrest warrant." She gave her watch a glance. "I've gotta run. Thanks for the info. I'll pass it along to O'Reilly."

Shortly after Linda had vacated her chair, the shop owner stopped by my table to join me, bringing me a cup of a new coffee flavor she was wild about. It was delicious. Unfortunately. I'm a caffeine lightweight and would be flying high all day, but I couldn't say no to a freebie. We chatted about how much she loved my design—always a wonderful, cheerful subject—so I stayed for several minutes.

While I was walking home, a red Corvette pulled into a space in front of my house. Pate Hamlin. He spotted me heading toward him as he emerged and waited for me. He sipped coffee from a green and white disposable cup and leaned against his sports car, looking like an advertisement for Corvette, or at least Starbucks.

In the light of Linda's professional opinion about the man I tried to size him up as a killer. Could he be a ruthless murderer underneath a genteel veneer? Or had he really been so worried about getting caught pulling a prank that he wiped off his fingerprints? "You should try the coffee at The Corner Coffee Shop sometime," I said to him.

"I have. Nice place. But Starbucks is right on my way to my office building. Cutting straight to the chase, my ex called last night to rub it in a bit. She says she spoke with you yesterday and, in her words, 'warned you' about me."

"She says she saw you leaving Shannon's around the time my brother was killed."

He nodded. "It's true. She caught me in the act of sneaking over there to play a little mischief."

"Mischief? Which was so incriminating you wiped your fingerprints off the knob?"

"No, Erin." He shook his head for further emphasis. "Tracy got it all wrong. I'd been trying to paint over the red dragon on her door. I wanted to make it look like a black bat. Figured that'd freak Shannon out. Then it hit me what an idiot jerk I was being, so I stopped and scrubbed off my black paint." He spread his arms. "That's the truth, embarrassing though it may be."

Did he really come out here this morning simply to

correct a bad impression that his soon-to-be-ex-wife had given me? Or was he trying to mop up the damage from having been spotted leaving the murder scene? In any case, I was disgusted. He was either my brother's murderer, or a callous jackass who'd played sophomoric gags on my client, before someone else took her life. "I'm surprised you felt you had that kind of time."

"Pardon?"

"Was owning Shannon's property really that important to you?"

"What can I say? I wanted it. She was in my way. The whole thing got to be a game with me. But I did get a grip and tried hard to make nice."

"A game? Jeez! Your stores drive small business owners out of business! You destroy whole towns! Ruin people's lives!" I paused from my tirade, distracted. In the corner of my eye, I spotted Hildi. She must have used her cat door to come out here. She was now across the street.

My surprise turned to horror as she started to prance toward us. A car was zooming up Maplewood Hill, going at least twice the posted speed.

I screamed. This felt like a hideous nightmare! Hildi was going to be hit by a car right in front of me!

Pate threw his Starbucks coffee cup at the windshield. The driver swerved and slammed on his brakes. I covered my eyes for an instant, praying for all I was worth. I heard a meow. An instant later, Hildi raced toward me. At that blessed sight, it felt as though my heart started working once more.

Pate and the driver cursed at each other, as Hildi ran straight into my arms. I hugged her while the men exchanged obscene gestures and the driver sped away.

"You saved Hildi's life. Thank you."

He gave a small smile as he caught his breath. "That's me. Wreck a town. Save a cat. All in a day's work."

He got into his car and drove off. Still too thunderstruck at the close call to move, I continued to hug Hildi long after his car was out of sight.

Just as I'd finally regained my senses, Steve Sullivan drove around the corner. Baffled, I stared at him. He rolled down the passenger side window. "You ready?"

"For what?"

Audrey came trotting down the walkway toward us, waving her arms at Sullivan. "Oh, good, Erin. You're finally here."

"What's going on?" I asked.

Staring at Audrey, Sullivan began, "Aren't we—"

"I decided not to tell her, Steve," Audrey interrupted. "Fortunately for me, she got home in the nick of time."

"Tell me *what*?" I continued to cling to Hildi, but now *I* was the one who needed protection. "What do you mean by the nick of time?"

"Sorry, Erin, but this is an old trick I learned back when I had to take my sons to the doctor for their inoculations."

Hildi leapt from my arms as Audrey was talking and dashed into the house through the cat door.

"As long as I didn't give my boys any warning, they weren't nearly so traumatized. Did you want to sit in the front or the back?"

"What are you talking about?"

She climbed into Sullivan's passenger seat. "You two are appearing on my show."

chapter 23

When you're unsure of how to proceed with a project, it's often beneficial to bounce ideas off someone with very different taste from yours. That way, you can discover an eclectic balance that you might never have thought of all on your own.

—Audrey Munroe

The butterflies in my stomach were doing death spirals. In no way was Steve Sullivan's presence beside me on stage reassuring. The fact that Audrey had refused to clue us in as to the subject matter for our presentations had made me feel faint with fright.

"What we're going to do on today's show is called 'Dueling Designers,' " Audrey announced to her audience. "If you've spotted our latest commercials, you already know that we decided it'd be even more fun if we went live with our broadcast."

I nearly swallowed my tongue at this last bit of news. *Live television?* How long had she been planning this behind my back? She gave me a wink and continued blithely, "We have the sublimely talented designers who own the prestigious Gilbert and Sullivan Designs, and—"

"That's *Sullivan* and Gilbert Designs," Steve corrected. He gave a sexy smile to the camera. "Wouldn't want your audience to get confused when they don't find us listed under 'G' in the phone book. We're located up in Crestview."

"Actually, I listed us as Gilbert and Sullivan Designs too in the white pages to circumvent that problem," I interjected.

"You did?"

"Yep. It'll be that way in the new directory. And on the Internet."

"She's Gilbert, and he's Sullivan," Audrey said. "As no doubt everyone in the audience has already gathered."

Her adoring audience laughed as if she'd just delivered the all-time funniest punch line.

"The two of them are wonderful at harmonizing living spaces. Just like the harmonies of the original Gilbert and Sullivan."

I resisted an urge to roll my eyes.

"What we're going to do now is reveal our special 'Dueling Designers' set." The curtains opened across the large stage, and I stared in surprise. Audrey explained, "As you can see, we've got two identical spaces here, with a wall in between them. In the front of the stage are two piles of identical living room furnishings and accoutrements for Gilbert and Sullivan to choose from. Either of those piles could easily furnish a room three times the size of their allotted space. Working with a pair of professional moving men, their task will be to develop the nicest room in the next ten minutes. We'll then use our sound meters to determine by your applause which design is our favorite."

"I didn't realize we were going to be doing reality TV, Audrey," I said with false cheer.

"What's the matter, Gilbert?" Steve asked, leaning toward me. "Chicken?"

"Not at all, Sullivan. But this has really caught me completely off guard."

Sullivan *tsk*ed comically to the audience and shook his head. "Like I suspected, she's afraid to take me on in a direct competition."

"Untrue. I just hate to be unprepared. I pride myself on being able to understand my clients' wants and needs. That requires preparation."

Audrey announced to the viewers, "Maybe Erin's personality works a bit like Tinkerbell's. Perhaps if we all give her a little bit of encouragement, she'll—"

The audience immediately began to cheer for me. A woman's voice cried: "We believe in you, Erin!"

I had to laugh. I raised my palms in mock surrender and cried, "Okay, okay, I'll do it. But I *do* have to point out that interior design really isn't your typical speed competition."

In a theatrical aside, Sullivan held up his hand to shield his mouth from me and said, "Note that she's already building excuses to massage her ego in case you all vote for me."

"You're going down, loser," I said. "The audience is already behind me, aren't you?" A big cheer went up. "Hear that, Sullivan? I'd be worried, if I were you."

He mimicked quaking with fright, then straightened and said, "I want to win this fair and square, Gilbert." Once again in a stage whisper, he held up a hand and said to the audience, "I'll take my loudest fan to lunch after the show." He winked and gave a thumbs-up to the audience for emphasis.

The audience was laughing and having a grand time. I heard more than one person egging me on by shouting: "You go, girl!"

Audrey said to the camera, "Our designers are now going to charge forth into their timed challenge. We have to break for a commercial, but we'll be right back to see how they're doing. Don't go away, now!"

My moving men were an attractive twenty-something-year-old named Carlos and a hunky-looking thirty-or-so named Jimmy. They had also gotten into the spirit of the competition, and I was happy to see were nearly as handsome and as big show-offs as Sullivan.

I promptly turned into a whirling dervish. I started the same way I would when designing any living room, and selected the sofa first. There were three choices: a tuxedo-style mohair, a floral pattern damask, and a deep red sectional. Because of the nature of this competition, I only had to concern myself with visuals, not with comfort, so I went with the mohair and centered it alongside the longest wall—the one that separated Sullivan's and my rooms.

I soon realized that, as Audrey had hinted, there were three choices for every typical living room item. The area rug was a no-brainer—the three rugs had obviously been selected so that each went with just one of the three sofas, so I opted for the checked pattern, which looked elegant and refined with the mohair sofa. There were six selections for pictures, and again, the color schemes made that selection easy. The modernistic oil painting with its brilliant reds and sunflower yellows really popped above the sofa. I hesitated on the coffee table; any one of the three would look nice. Audrey, meanwhile, had taken her traveling microphone into the audience and was quietly giving the brand names of our selections.

The audience was really into the spirit of the competition, cheering us on, and I played up my indecision over the table and let them choose that item for me. Sullivan must have been doing the same thing for some of his selections, as he was getting raucous shouts on some of his selections and boos over another until, I presumed, he switched. It was awfully tempting to peer around the corner at that point, but I resisted.

Audrey periodically called out how much time was left. For some reason, the audience was in a state of hilarity when we had three minutes left. Sullivan must have been mugging for them big-time.

I hurriedly picked out all the finishing touches—the periwinkle cashmere throw for the sofa, the vase for the end table, a dried flower arrangement in the corner, the sculpture for the bookcase, the blown glass figurines for the end tables, the fresh-cut tulips on the coffee table—

"Time's up," Audrey announced. "I'm going to ask our illustrious colleagues to stay on their side of the partition. When we come back, we'll take our vote."

The two or three minutes that we were waiting for the commercials to end seemed inordinately long, and I tried to coax Carlos or Jimmy into peeking for me. They jovially declined and left for backstage, after I gave them not at all unpleasant hugs. That was certainly one of the side benefits of this task that Sullivan could not have enjoyed as much as I did.

In conclusion, Audrey said brightly, "Let's have our designers join me front stage once again, and we'll view the results together." I anxiously trotted out to join her, as did Sullivan.

We both doubled over with laughter. Our main choices were virtually identical to, and mirror opposites of each other. The only difference was that, with his typical more austere eye, Sullivan had opted for the minimalist extras—a thin narrow crystal vase centered on the coffee table and holding a single lily, a single bowl atop the bookcase, a diagonally placed hardcover on one end table, just a lamp on the other.

We joked with Audrey that "great minds think alike," and she remarked that it was no wonder we'd teamed up. She added in jest, "You two must never argue a bit!"

" 'No, never,' " Sullivan sang. He winked at me, said: " 'Well . . .' " and I joined him in dramatically singing the famous G&S lyric: " 'Hardly ever!' "

When the laughter died down, Audrey had us discuss our differing approaches to the finishing touches for the room, then she took an applause vote, with mine first. The "applause meter" had me as a clear winner, until Sullivan announced, "Wait. There's one important last finishing touch to my room that I haven't shown the audience yet." He then unbuttoned the top two buttons on his shirt and strolled into his space, striking a *GQ* pose on the sofa. "*Now* you can vote." The catcalls alone from the women topped out the meter.

Audrey, however, said, "I'm declaring this competition a tie. Thank you both for coming on my show. Will you two agree to come back and do this again?"

"Absolutely," we said in unison.

"Once again, in perfect harmony," Audrey mused. "So, give Sullivan and Gilbert Designs a call. Or, if you prefer, Gilbert and Sullivan Designs."

She signed off. As she escorted us from the stage, she said, "See, Erin? I knew all you needed to get past your stage fright was to get your competitive juices flowing." She hugged me, and I silently conceded that she was right.

chapter 24

"I *knew it! The show is a ratings hit!*" Audrey exclaimed as she waltzed into the kitchen that evening. "We're going to rebroadcast it, due to popular demand!"

"That's great, Audrey."

Grinning, she wagged a finger at me. "I intend to hold you to your word that you and Steve will return. This could be a monthly feature."

"Let's take it one show at a time. For now, I just want the chance to feel good about its being over. And to forgive you for springing it on me like that."

"I'll accept your answer for the time being. And I do apologize. But I'm going to have to find some guests to fill in until I can get a replacement chef." In conspiratorial tones, she added, "As it turns out, Michael's old restaurant went under because he was sued for a hepatitis outbreak."

"When was this?"

"Five years ago."

"I take it you didn't know about this when you first started using him on the show."

"No, I sure didn't. The TV station's lawyers are the ones who told me just the other day. Michael had managed to hush it up by throwing money at the poor patrons whose meals had made them sick. But he was recently denied a license for a new restaurant. He's appealing that decision, of course, and he'll soon manage to buy his way through the process."

"No wonder he jacked up the price on Shannon's paintings. He needed the capital."

She nodded. "Despite all the exposure he gleaned from me as a chef on my show. Something which you're about to experience for yourself, by the way. You'll get a lot of calls from new clients now. You'll have to turn them away in droves."

"That'll be something to look forward to, then." I paused. "How many people does it take to form a drove, do you suppose?"

The phone rang in the two short rings that meant it was a call for Sullivan and Gilbert.

"More than a passel and less than a throng," she replied. "And I'll wager which one of us has to cook dinner tonight that the caller is going to be part of your drove."

"You're on," I said, confidently snatching up the handset. "Hello?"

"Is this Erin Gilbert?" a slightly breathless woman asked.

"Yes, it—"

"Ohmigosh! I feel like I'm talking to a celebrity! I saw you on TV today, and I knew at once that I absolutely *must* hire you. My husband and I are sick and tired of our wrecked rec room." While I listened to her chatter on about the woeful state of the game room, Audrey handed me an apron.

The next morning, Rebecca was waiting for me as I left my home. She was leaning against her Ferrari, which she'd parked just behind my car on Maplewood. I maintained a steady pace and tried not to betray how surprised I was to see her. She was wearing a plum-colored skirt suit—Armani, if I wasn't mistaken.

"Congratulations, Erin," she said snidely. She stood up as I approached, her spiked-heel sling-backs giving her the extra couple of inches she needed to match my height. "You've managed to turn Steve against me."

I brushed past her and unlocked my car. "Have I?"

"He jilted me."

"Good for him." I tossed my purse and briefcase in the backseat. "I hope you didn't think I'd feel guilty."

She crossed her arms and sneered at me. "I'm not so naïve as all that, no. But business being business, I'm prepared to make you an offer. I saw your show yesterday. My immediate observation was that you and I could be even better 'dueling designers' than you and Sullivan were. We have more antipathy toward each other, and it's going to crackle on the screen."

"In other words, Sullivan already turned you down flat."

She arched an eyebrow. "I already told you that much. That's what I meant when I said he'd jilted me." She touched her lips, then chuckled. "Oh, dear. You must've thought I meant romantically. I should've been more clear. So sorry, but I'm not about to surrender him to you that easily."

She'd set me up with her wording. I gritted my teeth and rounded my car. "I'm in a hurry, Rebecca."

"I'll make this quick, then. Whatever Audrey's paying you for guest appearances, I'll triple."

"Hmm. She's paying me nothing. So, although three times zero is a truly tempting offer, I think I'll pass." I got behind the wheel.

"Five hundred dollars per show. That's my top offer."

"Bye, Rebecca." She was standing in the way of my car door, blocking me from shutting it. I started the engine anyway.

"You should reconsider, Erin. A little piece of advice? Never let your pride get in the way of your profit."

"As a matter of fact, I have some advice for you, too: Try to get an original idea instead of stealing everything from Audrey." I pulled forward and shut the door, leaving her standing on the street, glaring at me.

At the office, Sullivan and I completed our scaled-down plans for Michael's house. Michael had axed the geometric-patterned cedar deck in favor of the standard-fare gray composite board deck. All construction on the gazebo had been halted, along with the partially covered terrace that would have completed the feng-shui-square shape of the house. He'd also opted for vinyl flooring instead of the wide-plank maple in the original front room—a big mistake, but he was adamant.

We drove to Michael's house to meet with David Lewis and go over everything. He and I had managed to avoid each other since our encounter in his office. We found him in the backyard, supervising the deconstruction of the terrace. He was in high spirits, which wouldn't last long if I had any say-so. A couple of days ago, Sullivan and I had discussed what to do about him and agreed that, unfortunately, because David's shady contract with Taylor had nothing to do with David's work for us, we could not fire him solely for that one abuse.

Sullivan had us gather in the nearly completed front room, where David looked over the blueprints. "Yeah. This won't be a problem at all," he assured us. "In fact, since it's mostly just taking away the things we've yet to do, we'll be done with the whole project inside of three weeks. Long before the holidays."

"Yeah?" Sullivan asked skeptically.

"Definitely," he replied with a big grin. "Now that we've repaired the damage done from the fire and the bulldozer, it's all good. The place is finally coming together. The new foreman is a major improvement. He works at least twice as fast as . . ." He let his voice fade as he studied my furious expression. "Sorry, Erin. I forgot. I didn't mean—"

"That's okay," I replied through a tight jaw. This was the last straw! Why hadn't the police arrested the creep? At the very least, he was guilty of business fraud! "I'm just glad to see that the basic construction is finally complete and up to code."

"Yeah, well, no problem," he countered, choosing to ignore my tone. "I'll be making the last walk-through with you tomorrow. So any last details you need me to take care of, I'll handle right away."

"Speaking of *details*," I began, "you left some important ones out of our previous discussions on my brother's workstation design."

He froze. "What do you mean?"

"The fact that you bought the rights to it the day before he died. Why are you trying to cover that up?"

He looked at Sullivan as if expecting him to intervene. Sullivan growled, "Answer her question."

"I explained all that."

"No, you didn't. You neglected to mention that you had a signed contract with him. Did you even pay him the two grand?"

"I gave him a check. It was never deposited, according to my bank records."

"And yet you seem to have a clear conscience about the whole thing."

He glared at me. "I didn't murder Taylor Duncan to stop him from cashing my check. And, yeah, I *do* have a clear conscience. Because I did the right thing! I gave the guy a job, and I gave him a couple thousand dollars of my own money when I didn't have to."

"That's a load of crap. Pate told me precisely how much he paid you for the rights to produce and sell your product. You gave Taylor just one fifth of your profit from stealing his idea!"

"Hey! I didn't 'steal' anything! Like I said, I did all the real work." He started to hurriedly collect his things. In his haste, his cell phone fell unnoticed from his jacket pocket. I surreptitiously kicked it behind me and blocked it from his view. Sullivan was watching me, but said nothing. "I've got to go. Let me know if you want to take me to court, and I can hire a lawyer."

"A good start to avoiding that would be to donate that two thousand dollars in Taylor's name to Habitat for Humanity," I stated firmly.

"Will do. See ya."

"Right. We'll see you tomorrow," Sullivan said with a dismissive nod. "Have the receipt from Habitat ready to give to Erin."

David slammed the door as he left. "I don't trust that guy," I muttered to Sullivan.

"Me, neither. I made a mistake hiring him. From here on out, we're working with your crew."

"Better late than never," I couldn't stop myself from grumbling as I scarped up David's phone.

"So. Why did you snatch up the man's cell phone?"

"I want to check his phone logs." I pressed the scan buttons. "Aha! He talked to Rebecca Berringer twice yesterday!"

"It's still possible that it was Taylor's screwups after all that kept causing—"

I jumped a little as the theme song from *The Simpsons* played from David's phone. The caller—whose name was shown on the screen—was Rebecca. I tossed the phone to Sullivan. "It's Rebecca. Pretend to be Dave. Just say 'Yeah' or 'nah' to everything, then hang up."

"But—"

"Just do it! We might uncover something!"

He answered with a "Yeah?" holding the phone away from his face so we could both hear.

"David. Did you get my EFT deposit?"

"Yeah."

"Good. So we're all square now, right?"

"Yeah."

"Wonderful. Like you said, we've been dodging bullets, but we've got to stop pushing our luck. That Gilbert bitch has been sniffing around like she's some sort of Sherlock Holmes."

"Yeah," Sullivan muttered with a derisive snort that made me want to swat him.

She chuckled. "You obviously can't really talk right now. Is the nosy bitch right there?"

"Yeah."

"Figures. We really beat her at her own game, though. I got bonuses equal to yours for all your information. Not to mention all the slowdowns. Thanks for your good work."

"Yeah," he said and hung up.

At once, I felt triumphant at verifying what I'd suspected all along and yet livid at what we'd learned. "Jeez! I was right all along! David has been taking bribes for sabotaging the job, and Rebecca's getting them, too!"

"Which means Pate's the one making the payoffs. So *I* was right about *Pate* all along," Sullivan declared. "I'll bet he was behind all of it—your brother's so-called accident, the fire, Shannon's murder, and the runaway bulldozer."

"I guess it's possible."

"It's more than possible. It's *likely.* Or have you let yourself get conned, too?"

"Maybe I have. I don't know. It's just that..." I sighed. "I just can't quite picture Pate as a murderer."

"You don't *have* to picture it. The police can get this all squared away. We'll both testify as to what Rebecca said, and she'll be trapped into giving Pate up."

"I'll call Linda right now." I weighed David's cell phone in my hand, trying to tell myself to do just what I'd said. Yet there was a second course of action that had a certain appeal. Out the window, I caught sight of Rebecca leaving Pate's house. That sealed it for me. "After I make one little return call on this phone, that is."

"Wait, Erin," Sullivan protested.

I went ahead and dialed. After the second ring, Rebecca said brightly, "Hi! I take it you must have finally shaken loose from Erin."

"Not exactly, Rebecca." I stepped out the front door and waved at her. Steve came out and stood beside me, his hands in his pockets.

She stood still for a moment, then snarled into the phone, "What are you doing with David's cell phone?"

"He dropped it. That was Steve you were speaking to just now. And I heard every word."

She hung up and marched toward us. She focused on Steve and flashed a brilliant smile. "Let me explain, darling," she cooed.

"Don't call me that."

She visibly steeled herself. "You're not canceling out on our dinner plans tonight, are you?"

"Yes."

She pursed her lips. "This isn't how it looks, you know. I was merely doing my job."

"By paying off our contractor to sabotage our remodel? By taking a cut of the action yourself?" I cried.

"That is not what was happening!" Rebecca hesitated, that ratty little mind of hers obviously working at full tilt. "Pate and I weren't paying David to sabotage the work. We merely paid him to give us copies of your designs. In advance of when you constructed them. That way I could counteract with our own design at Pate's house."

"Bull!" Steve said. "Pate's not into feng shui. He would never pay major bucks to 'counteract' Shannon's home design."

Rebecca gave him a sad gaze, then averted her eyes. To me, she said, "It's true that he wasn't a big supporter at first, but he came around over the last few months."

"Pate was bribing David!" I said. "He was sabotaging the work here! Your phone conversation proved as much!"

"You call that proof? I just *told* you what the money was for. David will back me up."

"Oh, I'm sure he will," I retorted. "Because you no doubt agreed on a story if you got caught."

She gave a snooty toss of her hair. "If you think you've got a case against us, go ahead and call the police, Erin. In the meantime, you can both just quit reading me the riot act. All I was doing was some much-needed preemptive feng shui."

"Preemptive? You and Pate started the whole thing!" I insisted, determined to kill two birds with one stone and give Sullivan a taste of how bitchy she could be toward me whenever he wasn't standing right there.

"All I ever did that was marginally hostile was to suggest the pointed slant to Pate's porch roof. Whereas *Shannon* would practically hurl dead chickens on Pate's lawn in order to send negative forces Pate's way." She was talking utter nonsense now. "Steve, I simply wanted to do the best by my client by preventing *your* client from redirecting poison arrows at him. If I were you, I'd give some thought to how this is going to play in the press." She gave me a triumphant smile. "Quite obviously, *I* was the successful designer. I passed the key litmus test, while you two failed miserably."

"What litmus test?" I snapped.

"*My* client is still alive. Whereas *yours* was murdered. Talk about the ultimate feng shui failure!" She whirled on a pointy heel and strode to her car.

chapter 25

"I might as well go ahead and call Linda," I said to Sullivan as we watched Rebecca drive away. "Even though the two of them have obviously already concocted a cover story."

"Yeah."

Steve looked frustrated. I hesitated, eyeing Pate's door. "Maybe Pate would tell us the truth about what they'd paid David to do if we asked him straight out."

"And maybe pigs'll fly, if you give 'em a hard enough push."

The sight of a pickup speeding down the hill toward us distracted us. "Looks like David realized he'd dropped his cell phone and is coming back for it," I said.

He left the engine running as he got out of his truck and approached. Donning an "aw, shucks" demeanor he said, "Hi, guys. Did either of you happen to spot my..."

Sullivan snatched the phone from my grasp and held it aloft. "Bad luck for you, David. We fielded a call from your partner. Rebecca Berringer just verified everything we suspected about you all along."

"What do you mean?" he asked, now acting surprised and hurt. "You must have misunderstood something."

"Spare me," I snapped. "You already played that card, and it didn't work the first time."

Sullivan said firmly, "Clear out. Now."

David gaped at him. "You're *firing* me?"

"You got it, Skipper. You're not allowed to set foot on this property again. Or on any Gilbert and Sullivan clients' property."

"Hey, dude! Give me a break! All I ever did was keep Rebecca and Pate up to speed on what was happening with Shannon's remodel. That's it!"

"And the *real* reason you hired my brother and made him foreman was because you assumed he'd louse up!"

He shrugged, his cheeks reddening. He shifted his gaze to Sullivan. "Please, man. I know you're ticked at me. But you gotta see it from my side. Rebecca and I are old friends. And my kid's been sick. I've been having a hard time keeping up with his medical expenses. Most of the time, I wasn't even giving out accurate information. I just made stuff up. *They* were the ones I was scamming, not you guys. They were so eager to get an edge on Sullivan and Gilbert, they fell for it, hook, line and sinker."

I said, "Just because you were ripping them off, too, doesn't make things cool between us. You were sabotaging the job here. You turned my brother into your fall guy. *After* you made money off his idea for the workstation. You're going to be damned lucky if we don't sue you!"

He held up his palms, his features tight with anger. "Hey, lady. You can believe what you want. But your brother was a moron. I didn't need to sabotage anything. He kept lousing things up all on his own."

My anger was getting the best of me. I couldn't hold my tongue. "He was getting too much evidence about the scams you were pulling on everyone. So you killed him! Shannon must have found that out, so you killed her, too!"

David took a step back, holding up his palms. He looked at Sullivan. "Your partner's lost her mind. I didn't kill anybody."

Sullivan dropped David's phone into his pocket. "We'll let the police put all this together. I'm giving *them* your phone, so they can check its list of previous calls."

"Keep my damned phone," David growled. "*I*, for one, have work to do today."

"Yeah? That's lucky," Sullivan retorted. "You won't have it for long, once word of your accepting bribes gets around."

David gave us the finger as he got back into his still-idling truck and drove off, tires squealing.

Sullivan sighed. "We need to talk to everyone on his crew. Give 'em the option of staying on here and working directly for us."

I caught sight of Roberto standing in the shadows of a cottonwood at the side of the property, listening. I pointed at him with my chin. "Their boss having been fired might not come as a complete shock."

Sullivan went into the backyard to talk to the workmen, and I took a seat on the stoop and called Linda. I recounted all of our conversations with David Lewis and with Rebecca Berringer. Linda was quiet and listened without commentary, but her "uh-huhs" and "go ons" were growing more and more grumpy as I went along. After I'd finished, she snapped, "You're not running DNA tests or anything, are you? I'd hate for us in the CPD to waste our time, duplicating your efforts."

"Sorry, Linda. I'm not good at waiting quietly in the wings."

"You need to get better at it, fast, kiddo! First you removed evidence from the attic, and now you got your partner to pose as someone else. How do you think that'll play out during a trial? Rebecca can simply say that she knew it was Sullivan all along and was just yanking his chain!"

"I never had any illusions that it'd be solid evidence in a court of law. I simply figured it'd be helpful for the police to know that two of the suspects—Rebecca Berringer and David Lewis—were involved in a scam at the expense of the two murder victims."

"And the people of Crestview, Colorado, are greatly appreciative for all your help. Now quit it!"

"Okay. I'll . . . wait in the wings from now on."

She sighed. "Yeah. Sure you will. I'll talk to O'Reilly about posting surveillance on you, as soon as possible."

"That isn't necessary, Linda."

"If you keep up with this Junior Detective crap, it sure as hell is! It might just save your life!" She said a snarky "bye" and hung up.

Before I had the chance to feel duly contrite, Ang Chung's car pulled into the driveway. I rose and watched his carefully measured steps as he neared. "Ang, what are you doing here?"

"Michael called me. He said he's reconsidered and wishes to rehire me."

That made no sense. "Steve? Can you come to the

porch for a sec?" I called. To Ang, I explained, "Steve and I were just about to leave. And Michael isn't here."

"He will be momentarily. I just spoke to him."

Steve appeared, along with David's crew members, all of whom were packing it in for the day. As they got into their vehicles and left, Ang gave Sullivan the same explanation for his presence as he'd given me. Sure enough, we heard an engine and spotted Michael's car on the hill.

Michael emerged from his car and marched toward us. "Oh, good. You two are still here." Presumably, he meant Sullivan and me.

"Good afternoon, Michael," Ang said brightly.

Michael ignored him. He was carrying some rolled-up papers and a book under his arm, its title hidden. He brushed past us and let us inside, saying, "I wanted to show you all something." He ushered us into the kitchen and opened his book on the table. "Look at this. This is a book on feng shui I got out of the Crestview library." He began to spread out the papers next to the book. "And *these* are the charts that Ang supposedly customized, just for us."

We followed Michael's instructions. Or rather, Sullivan and I did. Ang lingered back.

"As you can see," Michael continued seconds later, "the floor plans for the two houses are totally different, yet every single thing the author labels on the charts for *that* house is echoed exactly on *our* charts. That *should* be impossible, according to feng shui, considering the house layouts were so different to begin with. Furthermore, when you read the next several pages, you discover that the author's descriptions and cures for the house's problems are word-for-word identical to ours." While glaring at Ang, he continued, "Ang *copied* the written report that Shannon paid thousands to have him create for us."

Sullivan and I studied the published drawing and compared it to Ang's "*ba-gua* chart." Michael demanded of Ang: "You're going to return every penny we paid you!"

Ang turned and started to walk away.

"Stop right there! You owe me a small fortune!"

"No. You brought me here under the false pretense of hiring me!"

"You wouldn't have come if I told you that I was planning on exposing you!"

"Expose me for *what*?"

Michael gaped at Ang, then cried, "You plagiarized my home's charts! You charged me a fortune for them! I've got the evidence right here!"

Maintaining a serene attitude, Ang replied, "It was a remarkable coincidence that the two houses' controlling factors were so similar."

"You're a crook and a fraud!" Michael shouted at him.

"And *you're* a fraud of a cook." Ang sneered. "Shannon told me all about you, about the hepatitis B outbreak at your restaurant that forced you to close your doors. And about the recipes that you stole from other *real* chefs."

"That's a lie!"

"You're a little man," Ang said, his expression growing fierce. "One of those little hand puppets that they trot out in front of the audience . . . the marionette that dances for the applause while the puppet master is the one who has all the real genius. You and I both know who that was. It was always Shannon who was the real brains behind your showmanship."

"Shut up! Get out of my house! I only wish I hadn't fired you already so I could fire you again. But I will anyway. You're fired!"

"You were jealous of your wife. You hated her! She was nothing to you but a free ride!"

"You're speaking about yourself, and you know it! That's true for you, not me!"

Without another word, Ang swept out the door.

Michael grunted in frustration. "That bastard! Those lies about me!"

"I *did* hear something about the hepatitis outbreak," I replied.

"That *wasn't* my fault. But I'm the one who paid the price. Meantime, he got caught in his big lie. I'll bet every 'chart' he's done ever since he set up shop in Crestview has been copied straight out of this book!"

"Maybe so."

"*Definitely* so. He's just flinging lies and accusations at me because he can't deny his own deceit."

Steve was still studying the charts, as if oblivious to the drama surrounding him. I nudged him, and he said quietly, "Erin? There is one major departure from the author's map and the one that Ang did for this house."

"What's that?"

He tapped Ang's drawing of the family room. "The samurai sword."

I looked at the room and its notations. There was no need for metal whatsoever in the fifth position of the room. In the author's work that Ang had plagiarized, the spot should have held wood, which we would have easily handled with a coffee table.

"Let me see that," Michael cried and all but shoved me aside to look at the charts. "You're right," he said at length. "I'm pointing this out to the police right away. There was never any feng shui justification for her buying that sword. The weapon that was used to kill my wife was a complete contrivance on Ang's part. It was all premeditated. That monster killed my wife in cold blood!"

Sullivan and I left. We fell silent during the drive back to the office. After a few minutes, I remembered to fill in Sullivan on my conversation with Linda Delgardio. Afterward, I remarked, "Michael's making money hand over fist from his artist wife's works now that she's gone."

"That doesn't necessarily make him a suspect, though," Sullivan countered. "It's not like we can expect him to keep everything hidden away. I mean, he's having hard luck financially, what with Pate putting the squeeze on him."

"True, but some of Ang's accusations... or Antonio's, rather, which is his real name... hit a nerve with me. I'll bet Michael was harboring a lot of resentment over Shannon's refusal to sell way back when they could have gotten full market value for her house. So he's got a combination of motives."

Sullivan said, "Although when it came to Shannon, either Michael or Ang would have been killing the goose that was laying his golden eggs."

"The difference is that *Michael* was able to sell those golden eggs at an inflated price, once his wife was dead."

chapter **26**

Though *hyperaware of my silent phone that evening,* I didn't hear anything from Linda or anyone else on the police force. I had a feeling that they weren't rushing out to arrest anyone based on my meager information. I'd been home for about an hour when our doorbell rang. I went to it and saw Pate standing on the stoop. He wore an exceptionally dashing black wool coat, with the collar turned up in the back. He gave me a charming smile and asked, "I'm sorry I didn't call first. Am I interrupting your dinner?"

"No, not at all." I glanced behind me. "Would you like to come in?"

"I can only stay for a minute. I just wanted to let you know I've decided to shove off."

"You're leaving town?" I silently chastised myself for the stupid question. What else could he possibly mean by "shove off"?

He searched my eyes. "Not immediately, but in the next month or two. Before the end of the year."

"Where are you going?"

"Eastern Kansas. I got a great deal on some land. In a town that appreciates one-stop shopping."

"So you're buying a house there, too?"

"Of course. Near the future site."

"So what happens to your property *here*?"

He shrugged. "The county seems to think it should be turned into homes in keeping with its surrounding neighborhoods. I talked to a developer, and he assured me that an extra two thousand dollars in top-of-the-line molding will let us jack up the price of each home by another hundred K. At those prices, everybody wins. I'll build fewer homes, but will make the same profit. 'Course, my partners in BaseMart aren't exactly thrilled to be dropping the store, but Crestview's already surrounded by a half-dozen BaseMarts, less than an hour away. We're already getting the town's business, whether all you yuppies admit it or not."

"Michael must be ecstatic, at least. This news will probably double the value of his house."

Pate chuckled. "Yeah, but it'll be too late. I bought his house this morning. At the time, the press was all over my wall-to-wall condos, so his property value was bottoming out. He panicked." His smile broadened. "Can't wait to see his reaction, once the word gets out that I'm building a prestigious housing development instead."

"I'd imagine he'll be less than pleased." I fought back a smile, unwilling to admit that I felt my client was getting exactly what he deserved. Then again, Tracy was getting quite the shaft. Now Pate's house would keep its full market value, but she, too, had settled early. I hesitated, trying to think of how to phrase my loaded question. "Did you pay Rebecca and David to sabotage our work at Shannon's house?"

He gave me a sly wink. "Let's just let that be water under the bridge."

"Considering that my brother and my client *died* in that so-called water, I'm not especially inclined to let it go."

Instantly, he grew somber. "I would never condone the use of violence, Erin. I certainly wouldn't pay for anyone to act as my hired thug. I can take a lie-detector test if that would assure the police of my innocence." He sighed. "So. I've obviously overstayed my welcome. Already. I wish you only the best."

"Thank you. I wish you . . . would go into a different line of work."

He smirked, shook his head, and left. It was lucky for me that we'd canceled his celebratory dinner. The man was a pure salesman, with the silver tongue to go along with his hair. For all I knew, he could pass a lie-detector test even while claiming he was a Martian.

The next morning was a Saturday, but because we hadn't worked the last two weekends in a row, we'd already agreed to put in a full day. We met at our office at nine. Sullivan promptly mentioned that he hadn't heard anything about new leads in the murder investigation. "Did Linda give you any news?"

"Not a word. We haven't spoken since my phone call yesterday afternoon."

"I wonder if she interrogated Pate."

"I doubt it. He's leaving town by the end of December, by the way. He's trying to keep it quiet, but he's building prestigious houses on his property instead of a store or condos."

"How'd you hear 'bout that?"

"He stopped by to say good-bye last night."

"Did he." He made the words more of an accusation than a question.

"Yes. We talked for all of two minutes, then he left."

"So you let him inside your house? Right after we discussed how he was in on everything. What's going on, Gilbert? Did he compliment your designs or something?"

"No! Why did you think that?"

He shrugged. "You seem to get suckered in pretty fast that way... as if the shortcut to your heart is praising your work."

"That is *so* not true! Give me one example of when I let somebody win me over just by tossing some praise my way!"

He grinned. "You're right, come to think of it. I must have been thinking of myself. So, what deep and meaningful discussion did the two of you have that led to your change of heart?"

"Like I said. We barely talked. But I'll never forget how he rescued Hildi from getting run over by a car the other morning. Right before you arrived to drive me to the show."

Sullivan snorted. "Oh, well then, my God! If he saves a cat from getting crunched, he can't possibly have been a killer. Everyone knows that killers never have pets, right?"

I clicked my tongue. "This is why you and I should never talk, Sullivan. We should just do our designs together and only speak to our clients... maybe pass notes to each other, or use sign language when we're alone together. The fact of the matter is, you compulsively put me down."

"*I* put *you* down? Have you ever listened to your own statements toward me? You're the one who—"

Mercifully, the door opened at that moment. An instant later, I was taking back my gratitude at the interruption; Rebecca Berringer waltzed into our office. "Steve!" she cried, as if they were long-separated lovers. "Thank *goodness* you're here!"

"Rebecca. Come to spin more yarns about your dealings with our former contractor?" Sullivan's surly response to seeing her did wonders to lighten my spirits.

"No. I'm being stalked!"

"You can use our phone to call the police," I suggested, far too used to her theatrics to be concerned. "Unless they're the ones stalking you. By the way, Pate told me that he's moving to Kansas. Is that going to damage your business irreparably?" I asked hopefully.

She cocked an eyebrow. "I'm a survivor, Erin. Rest assured. It was all getting to be too consuming, what with two full-time careers—on TV and in design." She crossed her arms and regarded me coolly. "I hope you and Steve don't let your flash-in-the-pan success on *Domestic Bliss* get to your heads. You'll never come close to the chemistry you had on your TV premiere. You can only be new and fresh to the public once, and you've had your shot. You're already yesterday's news."

"It's big of you to sound so happy for us, Rebecca," Sullivan said.

Rebecca's cheeks turned rose-petal red. She must have gotten so riled at me that she momentarily forgot Sullivan was still in the room. She touched her face and said, "You two sure crank up your heat high enough!" In a husky voice, she told Sullivan, "I'm getting all hot."

I glanced at the thermostat. "It's set at sixty-eight," I retorted. I wondered if she was feeling the heat from the police investigation. If so, she might be willing to blab about her client. "Tracy was sure upset at Pate for vowing to develop that land behind his house," I prompted. "Has Pate heard from her lately?"

Rebecca merely smiled at me. Drat! She was taking the high road for once! What lousy timing!

"Pate and Tracy had nothing to do with the murders. If I were you, though, I'd look closer to home. Michael needs money, and now he's making beaucoup bucks by cashing in on his wife's dramatic death."

"*You* were having an affair with the man!" I cried.

"Once I began to see who he really was, I couldn't break things off fast enough." She added under her breath, "Not that *he* can accept that."

"Michael's still pursuing you?" I asked, surprised.

"He's the one stalking me right now!"

"You actually saw him following you?" Sullivan asked.

"Yes! It's gotten so bad, I'm afraid to go anyplace on my own."

"Yet you came here by yourself," I intoned, not inclined to feel sympathy toward her. "And you never hesitated to snatch him from Audrey so that he would appear on your show."

"I know, but I *shouldn't* have. That was just business. But being afraid to be alone is just dreadful." She grabbed Sullivan's hand and looked at him with pleading eyes. "Do you think you could walk me to my car? I was window-shopping downtown for some clients this morning. Now my car's a full ten blocks away!"

I rose and grumbled, "Maybe I should turn the thermostat down a notch after all."

As I changed the setting to sixty-seven, a memory hit me: Taylor had a thermostat in his shabby room. It was on the lone exterior wall, right next to the window. Why would any builder have placed a thermostat in the least efficient place imaginable?

Steve was saying: "Erin and I have a lot of work to do, Rebecca. If he's really following you, let's get a police escort for you. That'll discourage him pretty quick . . . show him you mean business."

"No, no. I really don't want to get the police involved. They have enough on their hands, trying to solve two murders."

"Actually, Steve, maybe you *should* walk her to her car. I have to run out to Harlem for a few minutes anyway." (A day or two after collecting my brother's things, I'd described the apartment to Sullivan, and he'd quickly identified the building as "Harlem"—its nickname among longtime locals.) I glanced at my watch. "I'll meet you back here in twenty minutes."

"Why are you going to Taylor's? Hasn't his room already been rented out again?"

"Probably. But I want to ask his former landlady something." I brushed past Rebecca and grabbed my coat. "Be right back." With the strong feeling that I was about to know once and for all who killed my brother, I rushed out the door.

chapter 27

My thoughts in a whirl, I raced to Taylor's apartment building and parked in back. I dug through my toolbox and stuck a screwdriver in my jacket pocket in case the faceplate for the thermostat had to be unscrewed. I trotted to the front door and buzzed the manager. No answer. I pressed the button for Taylor's old apartment. Again, no answer.

"Damn it!" I leaned on the manager's button, to no avail.

I headed back toward the parking lot, deeply annoyed. If there was any one thing I'd known for certain about my half brother, it was that he had a compulsion for building elaborate hiding spaces. It would have been just like him to install a hollowed-out thermostat as a small hiding place.

After all, this apartment complex was hardly the Ritz. I was intending to ask the building manager if the tenants even *had* individual heat controls. She'd mentioned that they were always complaining about the temperature. And the placement for the would-be controls—beside a window on an external wall—was utterly bogus. If the manager verified my suspicions, I'd planned to beg and plead with her to let me into his old apartment.

Just as I stormed around the corner of the brick building, I stopped in my tracks. Taylor's spare keys! I still had the ones he'd hidden behind the loose brick!

I dug up the two keys from the bottom of my purse. Hurriedly, I unlocked the door. I was trespassing, so I wanted to make as quick and quiet an exit as possible. I eased the door shut without letting the noisy latch fully engage.

Nobody was in the hallway at the moment. Good. I didn't have to explain my presence. In fact, this whole hall was dead silent. Strange that there were so few people up and about on a Saturday morning. Maybe the entire apartment building had been condemned.

I tapped on Taylor's old apartment door. No answer. Holding my breath all the while, I used his key and opened his door, praying that I wasn't going to barge into somebody's home.

The room was still empty, everything precisely as I'd left it. Management must have had a hard time finding anyone so down on his luck as to have been desperate enough to rent this place in the middle of the month.

I made a bead for the thermostat. I pulled off the plastic faceplate, which merely snapped off, and looked inside. A cell phone!

Taylor had called me on a cell phone from the

Youngs' house before he died. Detective O'Reilly had said they'd found a phone in his pocket. What was so special about *this* one that Taylor had hidden it?

My memory flashed to a conversation with Emily from last month. She'd mentioned that she'd bought a state-of-the-art cell phone to give Taylor whenever he got out of jail, but was thinking about returning it, because she'd found out he already had a fairly new one that he planned to reactivate.

I examined the phone. This one had the ability to record a video segment.

My God! Everything fell mentally into place for me.

Taylor had said he had evidence that could show me "what's really going on." This apartment was right on the way to my office from Shannon's house. With his penchant for hiding spots, Taylor had hidden the phone here, safe and sound, counting on dropping by to collect it on his way downtown to show it to me. Except the killer got to him first, so he never had the chance.

With trembling hands, I turned on the phone. I pressed the buttons to see if Taylor had stored any video clips. There was indeed a saved video. I cued it up.

The frozen opening frame showed Michael, his back to the camera. He was in his kitchen. One edge of the image was blocked by a wall, as though Taylor had positioned the camera at a corner. I could imagine him staying out of sight behind a wall, holding out just the camera.

I pressed the start button. Michael was talking quietly into the cordless phone. I couldn't quite make out the words.

A moment later, he turned. He was crying. Both cheeks were wet. Now that I could read his lips, I could tell he was saying, "You can't leave me, Rebecca! I'm telling you, Shannon's out of my life. She's as good as dead." He paused. "Rebecca?" He pressed a button on the handset and then slammed it down on the granite counter in disgust. He grumbled to himself, "She thinks I'm kidding."

"Taylor?" Shannon's voice called in the video.

Michael looked up and right into the camera lens, his jaw agape, just as the camera jerked away. An instant later, the picture faded to black.

My heart was pounding. Though I racked my brain for alternative explanations, this could only be the evidence that Taylor had meant to show me. When he'd said that he had "pictures" that were going to clue me in as to what was "really going on," he'd meant video pictures. As well as those photographs of Michael and Rebecca I'd found in Emily's garage.

Michael had looked up and caught Taylor in the act of making this recording.

I checked the time stamp. It was Friday evening, a few minutes after six P.M., the eve of Taylor's murder.

Michael must have killed him to stop him from revealing his insidious plan to kill his wife. Taylor had pushed his luck too far by going there on Saturday. He'd probably hoped to gather yet more evidence. Maybe he'd reasoned that this little recording wasn't rock-solid proof that Michael was plotting to murder Shannon. And Taylor must have been right, because surely Rebecca would have told the police about this conversation right away, yet they hadn't made an arrest. Or maybe Taylor had tried to blackmail Michael with this evidence, and that greedy act had cost him his life.

I tried to replay the clip, curious to see if I could make out Michael's first words on the recording.

A noise behind me made me jump. I whirled around. My heart leapt to my throat. Michael was standing in the doorway, staring at me.

"Michael! How did you get here?"

"I followed you. Again. See, I also followed you earlier to find out where Taylor lived. That time when you cleared out all his stuff. I figured the gig was up way back then. But nothing happened. Then the way you . . . took off from your office just now. You were practically pulling wheelies. I realized Rebecca must have told you something I'd said about Shannon, so you were coming out here again. I knew then that he'd hidden the cell phone here, after all."

I tried to act naïve and forced a smile. "Yes, he did. But the phone belonged to Taylor. Why? Were you afraid he'd stolen it from you or something?"

He laughed. "Erin. Don't mistake me for a fool."

"I . . . don't know what you're talking about."

"You don't? Then why are you so scared of me?"

"I was just startled. That's all. I didn't hear you come in."

"You were too mesmerized by that damned video clip that your idiot half brother shot."

Still clinging to my hopeless act, I replied, "I guess so." I tried to chuckle. "That was quite a convincing routine you put on for him. You really had me going there for a minute. Must be all that experience on camera. It sounded at first like you were completely serious."

"Yeah, yeah. Nice try, Erin." He stepped inside the tiny apartment and closed the door behind him. "This is where we do the song and dance about my phone conversation being taken out of context and me being innocent. I don't have the stomach for it. And one look at your face makes it very clear you'd know I was lying. You're as stubborn as Shannon. The fire, the bulldozer—" he scoffed, "she still wouldn't give up and sell! And you just kept befriending the bitch, making the place nicer, wasting our money. She knew about my dire finances, but she ignored me! I *had* to sell while the freaking thing was still worth something! But there was no stopping you. Not even when I tried to frame you. Just now you were seconds away from calling the police on me."

"No, I wasn't. Why would I bother? The recording doesn't prove anything."

"Oh, gee, Erin. That's too bad," he taunted. "So, you still don't know who killed your brother? And my wife?"

"I'm afraid not."

He held out his hand. "Let me see it."

"No, it's . . . the last thing I have of Taylor's. I need to hang on to it." I stuck the cell phone in my pocket.

He took another step toward me. I took a step back. I bumped into the wall behind me. There was no place for me to go.

chapter 28

Michael had an empty look in his eyes, as if they weren't fully focused. Although he was staring right at me, he didn't seem to actually see me. I'd first witnessed a shadow of that detached emptiness when he'd gotten so angry at Audrey, in what turned out to be his final show with her.

"I kept trying to scare you off, Erin," Michael said in a low, eerily calm voice. "But you wouldn't listen. Now you've gone and made it impossible for me to let you live. Just like your brother did. Snooping around in other people's affairs must run in your family."

"I'm *not* snooping on you. I was just trying to find my brother's things. To collect them. You know. Keepsakes?"

I was so frightened I was babbling, but couldn't stop. "To remember him by. To remember Taylor with. Now that he died. In an accident."

He waited till I stopped talking. "It's not like I wanted to do it, Erin. I liked Taylor. And I didn't want to kill Shannon, either. She was impossible to live with. It got so bad, just being in the same room with her made my skin crawl." Despite his intense words, his tone was eerily detached. "But I tried my best... kept up the daily routine as best I could. While, all along, *she* never gave a moment's thought to anyone but herself. She'd been so miserly with her earnings. We were supposed to be life partners, for God's sake. But if she'd had her way, I wouldn't have gotten a dime from her. I'd lost all of *my* money, through no fault of my own."

"You mean because the hepatitis outbreak shut down your restaurant?"

"That's right. It was the prep chef. *His* fault. Spread his germs around. Like I'm supposed to do blood tests on my employees? Yet *I* wind up paying through the nose! Besides, I'm in love with Rebecca. She'd never have married me if she found out how broke I was."

Reaching as deep as I could for camaraderie, I mustered a sympathetic look. "I understand. Shannon was keeping you from being happy. And so was Taylor."

He blinked. He gave no reply. He was still inhumanly calm.

In this whole apartment complex, *somebody* had to be nearby! I strained my ears, desperately hoping I would hear some background noise or voice, anything to let me know that someone was within earshot so I could cry out and have a chance at getting help. Nothing. Except for Michael and me, the building seemed to be utterly deserted.

"He ruined everything," Michael muttered. "Shot my plans all to hell."

"Who did?"

He pointed at my pocket, where I'd stashed Taylor's cell phone, I grabbed it. I needed to dial 911 when he wasn't looking. "I *thought* I saw him recording me on his cell phone. But Taylor played dumb... showed me his phone. He could only take still pictures with the thing. Next morning, I set him up, pretended to leave and doubled back. Heard him arrange to meet with you. That's when I knew he had *two* cell phones. I just... hadn't figured anyone so down and out would have two cell phones. But he did. Probably stole 'em from someplace."

Michael shrugged. "The kid left me no choice. If I'd let him live, I'd be in jail. Same way now. You've also left me no choice."

"No, Michael." My thoughts were racing. Empathizing with him hadn't worked. Would he listen to logic? "There's no point in killing me. You'd only make things worse for yourself. It's too late. The police are closing in on you. I already called them. It was the first thing I did when I found the phone. Your best chance is to run now. Before they get here."

He stared at me. He looked strong and fit. There was no way I could hope to overpower him. I had to dial the police without looking. That was my only hope. I coughed and tried to pretend that I was struggling for air to divert his attention away from my hand.

"You're trying to dial them now."

"No, I'm not." I brazenly pulled the cell phone out and hit "send."

Damn it! I'd dialed 811!

He charged at me. I screamed. We went flying backward. The phone skittered across the linoleum floor. My head hit the wall with a thud. "Help!" I screamed at the top of my lungs.

He grabbed me around my neck and started choking me. His grip was incredibly strong. I couldn't breathe. The pain was so intense my vision was going black. I tried to knee him, but I'd been squished against the wall and the floor. I felt as weak as a rag doll.

I was going to die at his hand! Just like Taylor. Just like Shannon. Knowing I had to grab a weapon, I groped blindly for the screwdriver in my jacket pocket with one hand. That only increased the force of his death grip on my neck.

I grasped the handle of my screwdriver and stabbed at his face. He screamed and released me. I'd driven the tool through his cheek and into his mouth.

In the second or two that I'd bought myself, I gasped for precious air, keeping a grip on my only weapon. With my free hand, I grabbed hold of the stretcher on the wood chair and tried to scramble to my feet. I only made it to my knees. Michael grabbed my hair.

"You bitch!" His breath was hot and ragged against my cheek.

"Help! Somebody! Call nine-one-one!" I yelled. My voice box must have been damaged when he choked me; I had no volume.

"The place is deserted," Michael said. "You can scream all you want. Nobody will come."

Still grabbing a fistful of hair, he pulled me over backward. I released the chair. I tried to stab at his arm behind me with the screwdriver.

He grunted, clawed at me, and started to pry the screwdriver out of my grasp. He was stronger than I was. It felt as if my fingers were breaking. I thrashed my free arm along the floor over my head. The brick that Taylor had been using for the missing leg on his dresser was there someplace.

I got hold of the brick just as Michael wrenched the screwdriver away from me.

I turned and swung the brick at his face, connecting with a solid thud. He groaned in pain. His nose started spewing blood. "You little bitch!"

He tried to stab me with the screwdriver. I blocked the blow with the brick. Swinging at him wildly as though I held a baseball bat, I fended him off and got to my feet.

He stood up before I could get away. I kicked his kneecap. He cried out and bent over in pain. I hit him on the back of the head. He went down in a heap.

I was facing the window and caught sight of a splotch of brilliant yellow in the distance. A woman was crossing the parking lot. Without thinking, I hurled the brick through the glass. She stopped and gaped at me.

"Call the police!" I shouted to her. "A man's trying to kill me. I knocked him out with the brick."

Michael was moaning, already regaining consciousness. I was torn, uncertain of whether or not I could reach my car before he could get to me. I yanked off my leather belt and cinched his wrists behind his back.

Had the pedestrian called the police? Taking no chances, I located Taylor's cell phone and called them myself. Barely able to speak above a whisper, I gave the address and my name. "Michael Young killed two people and tried to kill me. His arms are tied, for now."

The dispatcher told me that the police were on their way. She asked what the situation was, but Michael was now struggling to get his hands free. I shut the phone and jabbed it sideways against his back, bluffing, "Don't move. Or I'll shoot."

The police sirens were nearing, but I was on the verge of losing it. Michael had to know I didn't really have a gun. He was desperate, and he was so much stronger than I was.

"You're lying!" Michael growled.

There was a thud that sounded like a hall door banging open. An even louder thud resounded, and an instant later, Sullivan barged inside. At the sight of my strong ally, Michael gave up the struggle. He dropped back down with a moan of defeat.

Sullivan took a look at Michael, then helped me to my feet. He gave me a hug that lasted just a second or two, then put himself squarely between Michael and me, saying, "Rebecca told me some threats Michael had made about Shannon, so I... My God, Erin. Stop trying to get yourself killed! I'm begging you."

I looked at Steve. This was finally over! And yet, Taylor had died in vain, trying to help Shannon. I struggled to keep my breath calm and my emotions at bay. Echoing one of my brother's frequent figures of speech, I muttered past the lump in my throat: "No problemo."

As a former ballerina, I've found that, as long as you've already mastered your own steps, it's easy and fun to dance around the occasional obstacle that is invariably thrown in your path.

—Audrey Munroe

The day of the arrest, I'd come home feeling heartbroken and depressed. Later, I begged Audrey to cancel the cocktail party she was throwing in our honor. She'd insisted that we wait at least a week to reevaluate how I felt. By then, my psyche and my minor physical wounds had started to recuperate, and we all agreed to go ahead with everything as planned.

The afternoon of the party, I was feeling like myself again, and was looking forward to the enchanting evening that I knew Audrey was so very capable of putting together. The catering company Audrey had hired was located in Denver, and she'd offered up our kitchen as a staging area.

My workday ended at five P.M., and I rushed straight home. Tantalized by the aromas that greeted me the instant I opened the French doors to the parlor, I made a beeline into the kitchen to get a peek at the food. To my surprise, Audrey was there by herself, although I caught a glimpse of the caterer's van parked in front of her one-car garage. She was pouring chocolate chips into a sandwich bag. In front of her was a huge tray of fortune cookies. She smiled at me as I approached.

"Audrey? Why are you cooking?" I did a double take out the window. "And why are the caterers on break outside? You told me *they* were handling all the food prep tonight."

"They are. I'm simply seeing to some last-minute changes."

"Changes?" I looked at the array in front of her. "These are fortune cookies. What's going on? Did you change menus entirely? Aren't we serving *Mediterranean* hors d'oeuvres and desserts?"

"Yes, but the caterer made a mistake. We got these instead of the *kourabiedes.*"

Still baffled, I hesitated for a moment, having to mentally page through the menu that Audrey and I had selected for the Sullivan and Gilbert kickoff party. "So they got brandy sugar cookies confused with fortune cookies? Isn't that a major leap . . . from one continent to the next?"

"Yes, but we're going with the flow." She grinned and winked at me. "*And* I'm getting a big discount from the caterers as compensation for our flexibility."

Suspicious, I studied her petite features. Audrey was

known more for her perfectionism than for her flexibility. "And you don't object to serving fortune cookies along with our cherry-almond focaccia, our crepes, our lemon-pistachio biscotti. . . ."

"Oh, heavens, Erin. It's not as if we're going to throw all the cookies together onto a single tray and have our guests serve themselves, buffet style. We'd be thumbing our noses at the Chinese tradition and spoiling the fortune cookie's very spirit!"

Sensing a story in the offing, I slipped onto a barstool in front of her, as she stood in front of me at her gorgeous black granite countertop. "The spirit of fortune cookies?"

"Absolutely. We did a Dom Bliss segment on that very subject. Fascinating history, really."

"Do tell."

"During the 1300s or so, China was occupied by the Mongols. Eventually, there was an uprising in Peking to oust the invaders. So, of course, the Chinese had to find a way to organize themselves without alerting the Mongols. The rebels knew that Mongolians typically didn't like the taste of the Chinese moon cakes. One clever revolutionary disguised himself as a Taoist priest and entered Peking, handing out moon cakes. Inside each one, he and his cohorts had hidden instructions that helped coordinate their uprising."

While talking, Audrey had sealed the plastic bag containing semisweet chocolate drops. She now placed it in the microwave and pressed a couple of buttons.

"So fortune cookies originated from a revolutionary overthrow in China? And the American Revolution started with dumping tea into Boston Harbor." I watched as Hildi pranced toward the legs of my chair. I patted my lap in invitation, but she just flicked her tail at me and walked away. "I wonder if there's a psychological link there . . . tea and cookies."

"You're interrupting."

"Sorry."

"Centuries later, the Chinese laborers building the American railways in California celebrated their all-important moon festival every year. But they were dirt poor. All that they had to exchange were biscuits, instead of moon cakes, with happy messages inside. Thus the fortune cookie was born."

"Hooray! And so tonight we've been inspired to serve the little treats, instead of Greek-style butter cookies. Although the brandy in the latter might have left our guests feeling happy, too."

"Rest assured, Erin. We'll have plenty of brandy available at the bar. Grab another of those heavy-duty plastic bags and give me a hand."

I rose and joked, "We're filling our fortune cookies with melted chocolate? Won't that make the fortunes difficult to read?"

Audrey rolled her eyes. "We're going to drizzle chocolate over the cookies to dress them up a bit." She grabbed her bag of now-melted chocolate, snipped off a small corner with scissors, and gently squeezed the bag, making perfect figure-eight loops on the cookies.

"Looks delicious," I said.

"Indeed. The caterers will present one cookie to each guest at the end of the evening. Just like the traditional exchange of a happy message to one's guests when parting company."

I quickly filled my sandwich bag and started the microwave on a Defrost setting and watched Audrey work. "What about guests who leave early tonight?"

"The servers will have been instructed to coordinate the cookies with the cloak room. As the guests ask for their coats, the waiter will appear with their cookie."

The microwave dinged, and I retrieved the chocolate. "Or we could simplify the departure process and surreptitiously drop a cookie in one pocket of each coat."

"Except then nobody will know the cookies are there, and they'll get crushed. In effect, we'd be giving our guests a pocketful of chocolate-covered crumbs."

"Well, as they say, that's—"

"The way the cookie crumbles," she completed for me. She snatched my bag of melted chocolate out of my hands. "Never mind helping me with the chocolate, Erin. Go get dressed for the party. Then I'll coordinate *my* outfit accordingly." She grinned and winked at me. "Can't have me upstaging the hostess, after all."

chapter 30

The *"Sullivan and Gilbert Kickoff Party" was a rous*ing success. We'd gained well over a dozen solid leads for future jobs and, more importantly, our guests were all in high spirits by the time they left. Knowing that we'd given our guests such a pleasant experience made me feel as though I were walking on air. Well, that and the fact that I felt fantastic. Audrey had convinced me to pull out all the stops in terms of my wardrobe. I'd worn a shimmering mango sleeveless gown and silver stilettos. Perhaps she'd given Sullivan the same advice, because he was wearing a black tuxedo.

I spent a disproportionate amount of my time chatting with Sullivan's parents. Although this was the first time we'd met, they were easy to talk to. His mother was hilarious, sharing many stories of "little Stevie's" antics as the only boy in a family with four sisters. They had been among the last guests to leave; they'd come up to Crestview for the party and were staying in Sullivan's guest room.

The oxygen bar had been great fun. The string quartet Audrey had hired was perfect. As both Sullivan and I had joked, they "classed up the joint." The food had been amazing, and, as Audrey had predicted, the chocolate-drizzled fortune cookies had been a hit and had put just the right exclamation point on the evening.

Audrey had finally shed the staid, silver-haired gentleman who seemed to have eyes only for her, and we three hosts were standing by the door, thanking the last of our guests as they departed. Emily and Richard approached, Richard being her "significant other." Earlier in the evening, Emily had pulled me aside to tell me that he had proposed to her last week. She had given him a "maybe," but she had also decided to rent out her home and follow him to the Western slope, where he'd gotten an excellent job offer. He was a diffident man, clearly uncomfortable at our big party, and yet he'd lasted for two hours now at Emily's side, for which I gave him enormous credit. He gave me an affable smile and said, "Looks like we're the last to leave. It was a great party. Thanks for inviting us."

"Thanks for coming, Richard. Take good care of my mom."

"I will, I will," he said with a chuckle. He gave Emily's shoulders a squeeze. "Both of our fortunes said how we would reap great benefits from our journeys."

Emily was beaming at me. "Happy travels, Mom," I said. Calling her my mother was starting to feel more natural to me; I was certain that my adoptive mother would have approved.

"Thank you, Erin." She and Richard hugged each of us. Emily gave Sullivan and me a beatific smile and said, "You'll have to come visit us. Both of you. Soon."

I merely smiled at her, but as she pushed out the door, I leaned toward Sullivan and said teasingly, "I think my mother must have gotten the wrong impression about us."

He grinned at me. "Maybe she meant as Sullivan and Gilbert Designs. Their new home will only be some five hours away."

"That's not what she meant," Audrey interjected. "Emily and I discussed the matter, and we both feel it's high time you two rethink your relationship. As a matter of fact, the two of us took an opinion poll of your guests tonight, and nine out of every ten agreed that you two should hook up."

"If I were less tipsy, I'd be mortified to hear that you did such a thing, Audrey," I replied. "As it is, I can simply point out to you that nine out of every ten partiers were under the influence of alcohol tonight. They'd have voted for *everybody* to be paired up! But we're doing just fine as business partners, thank you very much."

"That's right, we are," Sullivan interjected. "Besides, what if I did something really stupid and made her mad?" He waggled his thumb at me and said in a joking stage whisper, "You should see what the woman can do to a bad guy in a fight!"

I chuckled, which sounded alarmingly like a giggle. I'd obviously consumed too much plum wine. Audrey laughed as well, but then narrowed her eyes at Sullivan. "You're not still seeing that dreadful Rebecca Berringer, are you?"

"We were never really seeing each other in the first place," Sullivan replied.

"Silly me. I meant to ask if the two of you were continuing to *not* really see each other. All the while as you shared the same table in fancy restaurants."

"Audrey, I assure you. Rebecca and I are not an item. Nor are we ever going to become business partners. Couldn't possibly work out for any of us."

"True. Considering the woman's evil," I grumbled.

"She had nothing to do with Taylor's or Shannon's deaths, Erin," Sullivan snapped.

"We'll never know for sure how much she led Michael on. She might have convinced him that his marriage was the only thing keeping them apart. Furthermore, she merely told the police that he'd said Shannon was 'as good as dead to me,' but that he'd 'clearly not meant that as a threat.' And she didn't even tell them he was stalking her!"

"She hadn't fully grasped how dangerous he was till she came to our office! She went to the police right then!"

"Because you insisted! And it was too late for Shannon by then!"

"Wasn't your friend Linda Delgardio the one who said they'd exonerated her?" His tone was both accusing and triumphant, as if he'd trounced me at the podium during an official debate.

"No, she just said they weren't going to bring charges against her. That's not the same thing."

He glowered at me. "You've got that guilty-until-proven-innocent thing down pat, Gilbert."

I stabbed my finger at him. "Rebecca made the last months of Shannon's life miserable, and she's tried to kick both Audrey and me out of our jobs in our chosen professions. But, yes. She's innocent of murder. I still hate her guts, though. So sue me."

A waiter standing behind me cleared his throat. I very much doubted *he* would say that Sullivan and I should be a couple. He shyly held out a small plate for us, which boasted three fortune cookies. Audrey ushered Sullivan and me closer to the waiter and his tray. "Now that it's settled who hates whom and why, let's have our fortune cookies. Shall we?" She snatched up the cookie that was closest to her. Sullivan and I grudgingly grabbed ours and thanked the man, who silently bowed, then left to help the other caterers with the last of the packing.

Audrey read aloud: " 'You must never carry your anger far. The weight will be heavy and the journey unsatisfying.' She wiggled her eyebrows at us and added, "So there."

Neither of us replied.

She grinned at us. "Well? Go on. Read me *your* fortunes."

I broke open my fortune cookie. Then I chuckled and read aloud: "*When searching for love, do not overlook the one who is already right beside you.*"

Sullivan snorted, but said nothing. He opened his cookie and looked at the slip of paper inside. Judging by the inordinately long period of time that he stared at his tiny slip of paper, he had to have read it multiple times.

"What does it say, Sullivan?"

"Same thing as yours."

"You're kidding me!" I cried, just as Audrey was saying, "Wow! What are the odds?"

Sullivan handed it to me. Indeed his fortune was identical to mine.

"Audrey," I said, trying to read her eyes, "did you plan this?"

"Of course not!" Her face was already too flushed with

alcohol and her actions too animated for me to tell for certain if she was lying, but I would bet good money on that likelihood.

Sullivan sighed, reclaiming his sliver of paper from me. "Jeez, Erin. I think we're stuck."

"Pardon?" I asked, utterly confused.

"We can't simply *ignore* such an obvious sign from the Fates. I have to confess, I *am* finally ready to settle down and find the love of my life. So I guess there's really only one thing to do, Gilbert."

My heart started pounding so hard it felt as if my chest might explode. Sullivan seemed to be totally sincere, staring into my eyes as though mesmerized. He must have had much more to drink than I'd thought! I was just about to suggest as much when he turned, grabbed Audrey's hand, and said, "Audrey? Will you be my first wife?"

Audrey laughed heartily. Then she straightened her shoulders and said, "No, Steve. Sorry. We don't know each other well enough. Tell you what. You go ahead and marry our girl Erin here, and if things don't work out, I'll be your *second* wife."

Steve sighed again and said, "What do you say, Erin?"

"About what? Being your first wife? With Audrey waiting in the wings?"

"Hmm. Doesn't really sound like Sullivan and Gilbert's usual impeccable style, does it?"

"No, it certainly doesn't."

"Then how 'bout we start small? Say... dinner and a movie?"

I couldn't help but smile. After all, the man was wearing a tailored tuxedo. He looked incredible! "When?"

"Tomorrow night."

"Can't. We've got to appraise the lots at that estate sale."

"Oh, right." He frowned a little, grabbed his BlackBerry out of his jacket pocket, and pressed a couple of buttons. "Next week?"

I fetched my Day-Timer from my purse. "We're jam-packed now with all our new prospective clients."

"Right again." He continued to press buttons. "Saturday night's free. After eight-thirty. That sound okay to you?"

I shrugged. "Maybe. We'll see how things go Monday through Friday."

"Does either of you have a tissue?" Audrey asked sniffing. "This is just so romantic, I think I'm going to cry."

We laughed. I quietly stashed the small strip of paper from my fortune cookie into a zippered pocket in my purse for safekeeping. To my amazement, I caught sight of Sullivan carefully slipping his into his inner jacket pocket and giving his pocket a tender pat. He looked up. Our gazes locked.

about the author

LESLIE CAINE was once taken hostage at gunpoint and finds that writing about crimes is infinitely more enjoyable than taking part in them. Leslie is a certified interior decorator and lives in Colorado with her husband, two teenage children, and a cocker spaniel. She is at work on her next Domestic Bliss mystery, *Poisoned by Gilt*.

If you enjoyed Leslie Caine's FATAL FENG SHUI, you won't want to miss any of the wonderful mysteries in the Domestic Bliss series. Look for them at your favorite bookseller.

And read on for an exciting early look at the next Domestic Bliss mystery,

POISONED BY GILT

a domestic bliss mystery

by Leslie Caine

Coming July 2008

POISONED BY GILT

ON SALE JULY 2008

chapter 1

Steve Sullivan's handsome face grew pale as he listened intently on the phone in our posh office. I had no clue who was calling, and Steve seemed to be deliberately avoiding my gaze. As the seconds dragged by, my imagination ran wild. Was the landlord of this building suddenly giving Sullivan and Gilbert Designs the boot? Had a loved one died? Was the IRS going to audit us?

In any case, this phone call was atrocious timing. I'd been just about to tell him something excruciatingly difficult for me to say. Now, based on his reaction to the one-sided conversation, I was bracing myself for bad news.

He raked his hand through his light brown hair—yet another bad sign—and finally said, "Sure, Richard. We'll be here, in our office, for at least the next half an hour. See you then." He hung up and promptly rose from his red-leather office chair. His brow was furrowed, and his jaw was clenched tight. He strode to the palladium window.

"Was that Richard Thayers, calling about the contest?"

"Yeah. Bad news."

"But... I thought his appointment as contest judge wasn't even official until today. Did he *already* decide that Burke's house didn't win?"

"It's worse than that." He stuffed his hands into the pockets of his black jeans. "Richard is withdrawing as judge for 'personal reasons.' He's also citing our client for possible rule violations. They're going to have to launch a full investigation. Might even turn the whole thing over to the police."

"What? That's ridiculous! You and I have been to Burke's house fifty times since we first got the rulebook from Earth Love! We went over everything with him with a fine-toothed comb. His house sailed through all the judging for the previous rounds. How could he *possibly* have cheated?"

Sullivan remained silent and turned his back to me. I couldn't begin to guess what he was thinking, which was unusual. In the past two years, we'd gone from bitter rivals to business partners. Along the way, we'd endured more than our fair share of trauma, which has a way of revealing a person's true nature very quickly. Fortunately, the first six months in the life of our new business had been relatively smooth—not silk, maybe, but top-grade linen. Our personal relationship, on the other hand, was, as always, about as smooth as jagged glass. We were constantly plagued by bad timing and bad luck. Steve's last two phone conversations with his "mentor," Richard Thayers, were the perfect example. I'd yet to as much as meet this man whom Sullivan greatly admired. But last night, Richard had called Sullivan's cell phone and interrupted my hopes for the perfect ending to what, up until then, had finally, *finally* been Steve Sullivan's and my perfect date. Then, Richard's call moments ago had occurred just as I'd worked up the courage to suggest to Sullivan that, tonight, we should pick up where we'd left off the night before.

Sullivan continued to stare out the window as though

fixated with the view of the Rockies. I decided to scrap my memorized-but-heartfelt speech. Time for Plan B, which was to turn brazen hussy—but a cute brazen hussy, maybe?—and simply blurt out: So, Sullivan. My bed or yours tonight?

"So, Sullivan. Are we being investigated too or something?" (Somewhere a chicken was squawking, just for me.)

"Sure hope not," he mumbled in the window's direction.

I struggled in vain to put together the meager shreds of clues that Sullivan had given me to this point. This contest for energy-efficient homes meant much more to Sullivan than it did to me. He was behaving as though this award would be his crowning professional achievement, whereas *I* felt that the contest's lucrative cash prize went to the homeowner, not the interior designer, for good reason. However, the finalist judge, Richard Thayers, had been Steve Sullivan's favorite professor at the Art Institute of Colorado, which he'd attended a dozen years ago. Sullivan had even gone so far as to claim: "Thayers taught me everything I know," and he was at once ecstatic and anxious at the thought of Thayers perhaps choosing *our* design from the three finalists for "Best Green Home in Crestview, Colorado."

Still trying to extract some answers, I asked, "By 'personal reasons' to step down as judge, does Richard mean the fact that he's your mentor? Didn't he tell you earlier that the contest sponsors were fine with that?"

"Look, Gilbert." He turned and glowered at me. "You'll have to grill *him*, all right? I already told you what little I know."

My heart sank. Wasn't it only last night that his dreamy, hazel eyes were staring into mine with loving tenderness? He needed to be reminded to keep things in perspective, not to allow a skirmish at work to turn us into adversaries. But all I said was: "You're obviously only giving me *part* of Richard's message, though. What exactly did he say?"

"I wasn't *recording* him, Gilbert."

"That's a pity, Sullivan," I snapped. "Because if you *had* been using a tape recorder, it would be great of you to hit the rewind button—clear back to our date last night, when you were calling me 'Erin' as if you liked me."

"You're the one who made the rule that we were to stick with 'Gilbert' and 'Sullivan' when we're at work!"

"I'm objecting to your tone of voice! Call me... Princess Dagweeb, for all I care! Last night, when you took my hand and you asked if I minded if we skipped dessert, I thought . . ." Damn! My throat was getting tight with emotion. No way was I going to start crying.

"That *is* what I meant," he said gently. He crossed the room, but stopped short of rounding my desk. "And, believe me, I was sure it was going to be a two-second phone conversation when Richard interrupted us last night, or I'd have let it keep ringing. But he was acting weird. He greeted me with: 'Why the hell didn't you tell me Burke Stratton was your damned client?' Like I'd stabbed him in the back or something."

That caught my attention. "Why would he have a problem with Burke?"

"That's just it." He spread his arms and grumbled, "I still don't know. Richard wouldn't tell me. Just claims the guy wrecked his life... says if I'm smart, I'll stay way the hell away from Burke, before he finds a way to wipe out Sullivan and Gilbert Designs."

I nodded, beginning to understand. The thought of having his life ruined by a business arrangement would have been a painful déjà vu for Sullivan; years ago he'd been conned by a corrupt business partner and had nearly lost everything he owned.

"Having Thayers freak out at me was the very last thing I wanted to happen last night," he continued. "By the time he calmed down and I got off the phone, it was too late for me to call Burke and get the story from him." He scowled at me. "And *you* were acting so crushed that I didn't know—"

"You left the table, Sullivan! One second you're holding my hand, smiling at me, happy because it was your long-lost friend, Richard Thayers, on the phone, the next you're striding out the door!"

"One of the two men I most admire was yelling in my ear, accusing me of betraying him!"

"I didn't know that! All you had to do was whisper to me, 'Something's wrong,' or 'He's upset.' Or you could have explained things a little when you returned to the table. Instead, you were distracted and abrupt, and you gave me the brush off when I asked what Richard had said to spoil your mood."

"Yeah." Sullivan sighed and ran his fingers through his hair a second time. "Guess that wasn't one of my better moments." He added with a charming smile, "Although, again, *you* made the rule about not talking business after hours."

"*Again*, I couldn't read your mind," I explained gently. "All I knew was, you chose to take your phone call over continuing our date, and then you were in a funk. Put yourself in my shoes."

He gave me an exaggerated wince. "I would, but high heels make my calves look too big."

"Don't try to joke your way out of this," I said, though I was already having a hard time keeping a straight face.

"Erin." The man had a gift for saying my name in a way that could instantly make me melt. He rounded my desk and leaned toward me, filling me with relief at the thought that, *for once*, we were going to avert a potentially disastrous argument. "I promise you that—"

The door burst open. In walked a man in smudgy gray pants and a ratty-looking forest green sweater that I'm pretty sure was on backwards. He had a sizable bald spot amidst his wild, unkempt hair, and a large red nose that perhaps signified a drinking problem. But, at that moment, he could have been Santa Claus himself, and I still would have hated him, as well as his each and every reindeer. To make matters much worse, Steve's eyes had lit up as though the man *were* Santa.

"Richard!" Sullivan said, beaming, and striding toward him.

"S.S.!" he returned, giving him a bear hug. "Ridiculous that we live in the same town now," he said in a raspy voice, "yet we hardly ever see each other."

What happened to Sullivan's face-paling angst? I wondered. *To Richard Thayers's your-client-is-going-to-destroy-you doomsaying?*

"No kidding. We should go have a beer once a week or so. Maybe I'll finally manage to teach you how to shoot pool like you mean it."

Oh, goodie. Weekly beer swillings and pool shootings. That *will make the world a much better place.*

"You got here pretty quick." Sullivan wore a boyish grin on his face and rocked on his heels as though half ready to leap with joy.

"I was just around the corner when we hung up, and I found a space right away. Did you get my email about my night-ed class?"

"Tonight at CU, right? Mind if I drop in?"

"That's a great idea! It's in room one-ten of the history building. We can go hit a pub afterwards... grab a sandwich and a brewski."

"Sounds good."

Richard and Sullivan continued to make arrangements, but all I could think was: *So much for our picking up where we left off last night.*

Remembering belatedly that I was still in the room, Steve clapped his mentor on the back and turned toward me. "Richard Thayers, this is Erin Gilbert. Erin, Richard."

I rose for a moment, and we exchanged "Nice to meet yous" and shook hands over my desk. I hoped that his socially required pleasantry was less insincere than mine. It was not as though I'd set the bar especially *high*, after all.

"Have a seat," Sullivan suggested, giving Richard a pat on the back. The three of us moved from our desks to our cozy nook near the window. We always allowed our visitors to sit first, then, if it was available, Sullivan would grab the leather smoking chair and I would grab the yellow slipper chair. Today I strode directly to Sullivan's smoking chair and plopped myself down in advance of our guest. I hated that I was acting so petulant, but it was the best I could do. At least I was keeping my mouth shut. Part of me wanted to ask Thayers: Do you realize you're wrecking my love life?

Sullivan took my usual seat. Once Richard looked settled into place on the sofa, I said, "Steve tells me that you're stepping down as Earth Love's finalist judge."

He nodded grimly. "It was the only responsible thing to do." He sighed. "Too bad. I read the reports from the initial-rounds' judges and saw the photographs. Stratton's interior was by far the best. Not surprisingly." He winked at Sullivan. (Also known as "S.S.," apparently.)

"Thanks," Sullivan said, beaming. "Got to say that I

agree with you. Though I'm partial. But I also have to admit, Darren Campesio's architectural design is interesting and really energy efficient."

"That's the one that's partially built into the hillside, right? So that the place is part cave? À la 'Batman'?"

He was mocking the house, sight unseen. Annoyed, I chimed in. "The design compensates for the windowless portion fairly well. The space makes great use of skylights and mirrors."

Richard looked at me with wide eyes, then blinked a couple of times, as if puzzled. "Ah. Glad to hear it."

"And I've got to say that the interior for the third finalist has a lot to be said for it, too," I added.

"She means Margot Troy's place," Sullivan explained unnecessarily—assuming Richard could subtract two from three. "But Erin's hardly unbiased. She designed Margot's kitchen, a couple years back."

"Did she?" Richard asked, again raising his bushy eyebrows. "Too bad you both didn't just stick to working on Margot's house." He shook his head. "When I agreed to judge, I didn't know Burke Stratton was even in the competition, let alone a finalist."

Sullivan was nodding as though he was following Richard's thread, but I remained on the outskirts. "And you're biased against Burke, so you recused yourself?" I prompted.

Richard nodded and, in a gesture eerily reminiscent of Sullivan's, dragged a hand through his messy, patchy hair. "The two of us have a problematic relationship, and I can't begin to be impartial toward that pompous peacock." Shifting his gaze to Sullivan, he said, "If I were you, I'd disassociate with Stratton A.S.A.P."

"Because you think he cheated somehow?" I asked.

"Oh, he most definitely cheated," Richard said with a snort. "There's no doubt about that."

"How so?"

"Evidence, my dear. Evidence." He chuckled. I battled the urge to grit my teeth or to fire off a sarcastic reply. Before I could ask: *What* evidence? he continued, "Sorry to be so vague. But when word of what Burke is *really* up to gets out, no one will want to have their names associated with him or his residence."

Sullivan and I exchanged glances, although his was something of a glare. Why was Richard paying us a personal visit if he wasn't going to pass along any helpful information? "I'm sorry, Richard, but I'm confused. You didn't know till last night Burke was in the contest. His house passed the numerous inspections for the previous rounds with flying colors. And yet this afternoon, you've found such a major violation that you've suggested it may be a criminal matter. How did you get from point A to point F so quickly?"

Richard stiffened and all but sneered at me while giving me a visual once-over. "As I believe I already told you, Miss Gilbert, I can't go into the details. I'm sorry." He rose, faced Steve, and only then forced a smile. "Well. I've wasted enough of your time." Steve, too, got to his feet as Richard continued, "I just wanted to apologize, face to face, for jumping down your throat last night."

"Hey. That's all right."

"No, it isn't. I leapt to ridiculous conclusions. I'm not always rational when it comes to Burke Stratton. The man is bad news. If you continue to work with him, you'll regret it. But, that's your decision. And this has been a hell of a lousy way to resume our friendship, S.S."

"Yeah. Cruddy circumstances." The men shook hands. "Thanks for coming."

"I *shouldn't* have come, like I said on the phone. But I felt you deserved the heads up. It was the least I could do, really." He gave me a thin smile. "Sorry that I'm forced to be so cryptic, Miss Gilbert."

Not knowing what else to say, I muttered, "Thank you. Drive carefully."

The moment the door closed behind Richard, Sullivan dropped into his desk chair, eyed me, and snapped, "*That* was awkward."

"Yes, it was. And I'm sorry, but, truth be told, my questions seemed completely reasonable to me."

"He'd just got through telling us that he shouldn't even have been talking to us in the first place! That he wasn't at liberty to discuss any details!"

"No, he didn't, Sullivan. He must have told *you* that over the phone. All he said at first in *my* presence was that he was sorry to be so vague."

"It's the same thing!"

"No, it isn't. Apologizing for being vague is not at all the same as being ethically or perhaps legally under a gag order."

He made no comment and returned to his work—rifling through pictures of myriad formal dining room sets in order to whittle down the selection process to the best two or three for our client. His every motion was made with extra zeal and noise. I reclaimed my seat at my desk, which was at a right angle to his, and tried to get to work as well, but gave up within a minute or two.

"Why are you angry at me, Sullivan? Could you please just explain to me what's going on here?"

"I don't know what Richard knows, Gilbert. But I do know he always tells it like it is. *Always*. So we need to listen." He paused, still so edgy that it was wisest not to interrupt. "I wanted you two to like each other. He's a great motivator . . . has such great vision. He believed in me first. When no one else did, including myself. And now, last night was . . . just last night."

My heart leapt to my throat. "What does *that* mean?"

"Nothing."

I stared at him in profile. "*Nothing?*"

He lifted his hands in exasperation. "Damn it, Gilbert! I quit seeing other women because nobody measured up to you. But when I'm with you, I'm not measuring up to *your* standards, and—"

"That's not true," I cried, but he was talking over me—something about how dating *me* was even *worse*.

"I'm always screwing up. It's always wrong! You were right before. We shouldn't date."

At once, his words seemed to hang in the air and yet to drop like an axe. I swiveled in my chair to face my monitor and hide my expression from him. "Oh. I see."

The phone rang.

"I didn't mean 'we shouldn't' as in 'we won't.' Just that . . . you were right about its not working."

"No, that's fine."

"I didn't mean to hurt you, Erin."

"I'll get over it." Just like I could dive face first through the window and probably recover. Eventually. Despite wanting to burst into tears, I picked up the phone.

Sullivan had risen and was now leaning on my desk. He whispered, "I didn't mean that the way it sounded."

I was too upset to listen. I cleared my throat and said, "Sullivan and Gilbert Designs" into the phone.

"I don't want to stop seeing you."

A woman was speaking. I told her: "Can you please hold?" and pressed the button without waiting for her response.

"Who is that?" Sullivan asked.

"I don't know. A soon-to-be-former client, most likely." I sighed and looked up at him. I felt a horrid pang that made it hurt to breathe. If only he weren't so close to being everything I wanted, and yet never within reach. "We can't do this now."

"I don't want to do this at all."

"Oh, Steve." I massaged my temples, willing myself not to lose my composure. "I don't know if you mean 'do this' as in breaking up or as in being together. But *I* just meant that this isn't a good time for us to talk about it."

"No kidding. It's a train wreck. Look. Let me cover our last two appointments this afternoon alone, while you see if you can get us caught up here. Okay? Meet me tonight at Richard's class. Please."

I nodded as I clicked back into the line and said, "This is Erin Gilbert. I'm sorry to keep you waiting." Silence. "Hello?" Nobody was there. Sullivan pushed out the door.

"It *is* a train wreck," I muttered to myself.

The phone rang again, and I answered immediately.

"Erin, it's Burke," he said. "I need your help."

Had he been told about the charges Thayers had made against him? "Why? What's wrong?"

"Some idiot with an axe to grind has put me under investigation for false claims of rule violations. Turns out the finalist judge is this guy named Richard Thayers, who hates my guts. He did some work for me three or four years ago, and it was all such garbage, I refused to pay. So it was probably him who leveled these outrageous charges. But I don't know for sure. Nobody at Earth Love would tell me."

"Should I—"

"At any rate," he interrupted, his words gushing out in a semi-tirade, "I'm telling you, Erin, *promising*, you, even, the claims are totally bogus. But my status as a finalist is now pending. Worst part is, there'll be some sort of trial. It'll be covered in the *Crestview Sentinel*. My name will be dragged through the mud."

"I'm so sorry, Burke. That's terrible."

"I need you and Steve to testify. I'll get Jeremy Greene, my architect, to testify as well. Once I find out what the charges *are*. Earth Love won't tell me *that*, yet, either. They said I'll have to call back tomorrow morning, after they've had a chance to read through the reports."

"I'll do what I can, Burke, but—" I stopped. This wasn't the time to explain about Sullivan's possible conflict of interest. Burke was our client, and we'd been paid to be on his side.

"'But' what?"

"Steve's not here, and we'll need to talk this over. All three of us. Let's aim for sometime tomorrow, after you've learned exactly what you're up against. Or Friday, if that works better."

The other line was flashing with an incoming call. I set a tentative time to meet at our office in the morning, said a hasty goodbye to Burke, and answered. "Erin, this is Margot Troy," a woman's voice huffed. "Did you realize you hung up on me?"

"Was that you on the phone just now?"

"A minute or two ago, yes. You tried to put me on hold."

"I'm really sorry, Margot."

"This is the reason I didn't hire you to spruce up for the open house last Saturday. Today I'd decided I wanted to hire you *again*, for a second small job, but now I won't. In any case, it was nice seeing you at the Earth Love open house, and best of luck to Burke."

"Thank you. That's very kind of you, Margot. And I'm—"

"True," she interrupted, "but it's also just basic manners. You should have thought to wish me well, for old time's sake. But you're obviously too busy to answer my phone call."

"Margot, I am so—"

She hung up. "Sorry," I added to myself.

Margot Troy. My *former* client from hell. I found both her and her home fascinating, though. The woman was filthy rich, yet believed so strongly in recycling that she'd built and furnished her home entirely from secondhand or salvaged materials. I couldn't work for her until the contest was over, in any case, but I needed to repair this new rift. Tomorrow, maybe. If Sullivan and I had any free time.

Thinking about Steve's and my schedules reminded me that I didn't know what time Richard's class was. Had either of them mentioned it? And what on earth was going on between Richard and Burke?

More importantly, were things over between Steve and me? Were these walls thick enough that I could let out a scream without causing anybody to call 911?

I took a calming breath and counted to ten. Okay. I could still breathe. And count. All was not completely lost.

I love my job. I truly do. Just not today.